D1378318

For Heather

on THESE SHORES

A NOVEL

by

STEPHEN R. PASTORE

Cohort Press

First U.S. Edition

ISBN 978-0-9777196-2-4

NEVER
on THESE SHORES

May, 1942

On the anvil of war is the true spirit of man forged.
                                                    Hemonides

San Francisco, California

The rising sun cast long beams of golden light through the clouds over the bay. A heavy mist rose above the water penetrated by the two towers of the Golden Gate Bridge. Waves lapped at the iron abutments and seagulls tipped their wings into the light morning breeze. They scattered quickly as the drone of airplanes echoed across the bay and the sun glinted off the polished aluminum of Japanese Zeros, the dreaded phalanx of the invasion of the United States by the Empire of Japan.

San Francisco Mayor Frank DeRitter waited quietly just in front of the toll booths at the San Francisco side of the Golden Gate Bridge. Next to him was his wife, Nancy, the City Council Chairman, Matt Smith and the new Chief of Police, Tom Blair, whose predecessor, Chief Davis had died at the Battle of Seattle. The newspapers had run a photo of Chief Davis; his body had been hung upside down from the pediment of the Seattle City Court House. Frank DeRitter had convinced the City Council to quietly surrender San Francisco to avoid the atrocities that the Japanese had committed in Seattle and Portland. Most of

3

the elderly men had been summarily executed; young people who had not already been drafted, had joined the army months before and were stationed in Los Angeles. Women had been brutalized and raped. Both cities were nearly burned to the ground.

Mayor DeRitter, a trim man in his late forties in an impeccable blue suit, shifted nervously from side to side and cleared his throat repeatedly as he mentally rehearsed his speech. He was drawn between a simple one-line surrender and a lengthier speech and plea for mercy at the hands of the invaders. A few minor politicians and business leaders who had supported the mayor in his bid for election milled about awkwardly in dress clothes. Some stared vacantly into the calm waters of the bay, not quite comprehending how the United States could have miscalculated as badly as it had. Others looked skyward and watched the V formation of Japanese planes buzz over the bridge and across the water to the city. In the mist, the planes sounded like a beehive.

From the echoes of buzz bombs and the hissing of incendiary devices dropped from strafing Zeroes, the listeners knew that thousands of their fellow citizens were being systematically annihilated by the never-ending onslaught of small planes, stationed only a few miles offshore on the carrier group that had inflicted such surprise devastation on Pearl Harbor only a few months before. Only scattered anti-aircraft fire could be heard from the battlements behind them and along the curving expanse of the Pacific Ocean that hugged the green shoreline of the jeweled City by the Bay.

Within moments, the cloud enveloping the bridge's roadway at its highest point between the two towers was broken by the chrome grill of a green Packard convertible. The highly polished metal of the Packard glistened, reflecting the morning sun, low

4

above the Oakland hills. Only after staring intently could one see the round head of the Japanese general sitting triumphantly in the car. Behind the convertible, several thousand troops in drab brown uniforms flanked tanks and troop carriers. They goose-stepped with iron-edged precision. The army of the Empire of Japan revealed itself over the crest of the Golden Gate as a huge python might slither over a boulder to bask in the noon light and patiently wait to devour any living thing that crossed its path.

As the entourage neared, all American eyes were on General Tamiko Yashita's face. The mayor stopped clearing his throat, noticing that his tongue had turned to cotton. It was the right thing to do, he hoped fervently, to surrender this city he loved so much. Peaceful surrender had to be preferable to destruction and carnage.

The Packard came to a halt twenty feet from where the mayor stood. The Japanese soldiers quickly arrayed themselves into military formations, standing at attention. A small group of soldiers broke rank and scurried toward the American greeting party. They crouched and pointed their bayoneted rifles at the mayor and his small group of observers. Another soldier, bowing low, opened the door of the car and the general slowly stepped to the tarmac. General Yashita was short and portly, with piercing eyes shaded by his helmet. He walked over with his aide-de-camp to where the mayor stood.

Mayor DeRitter made a weak attempt at a salute while all the Americans stood at attention.

"It is with a heavy heart," the mayor said, "that I surrender the city of San Francisco to the Army of Japan." He had opted for the short, one-sentence speech, finding it too difficult to put into words what he knew he should say and the emotions that he wished to express. He had served in the first war and the idea of surrender was alien to him. Yet he hoped that his actions would save hundreds of thousands. In time, he thought, all this would change.

With no warning whatsoever, with a quick jerk of his sword into the air and a quicker downward slash, General Yashita severed the mayor's head from his body. The startled eyes stared blankly at Yashita as blood seeped from the diagonal slit in the mayor's throat. His head momentarily perched on his neck, slid off onto his shoulder and to the ground. The body simply collapsed like a pile of laundry. Blood oozed onto the tarmac in a dark pool as the mayor's wife fainted and dropped to the ground, lying only feet from her husband's body. People near her gasped, fearing to move. A few made the sign of the cross. Frozen in the terror of the moment, no one went to the woman.

The general replaced his bloody sword into its scabbard and stared at the empty space where the mayor had stood seconds ago, as if idly looking at his ghost. Police Chief Blair, as shaken as the rest of the assemblage, walked over to where the mayor had stood. He felt as if his legs would not support him as he walked the few steps. Facing the General, he removed his blue hat. In a faint voice he said, "It is my honor to surrender the City of San Francisco to the Army of the Empire of Japan."

"Better, much better," replied the General. "Now take me to your headquarters."

*

On a normal day, the mayor's office would be an unceasing swirl of activity. Supplicants for this cause or that would sit on the highly polished but nonetheless uncomfortable benches, patiently awaiting their turn to lodge a plea for their special cause with the mayor. Secretaries and clerks would bustle in the marble hallways and wood-paneled offices of the grand edifice on their various missions, stopping at the water fountain to refresh themselves, or to meet fellow workers to exchange the gossip of the day.

But this was not a normal day.

The halls were empty except for Japanese sentries in full combat gear, posted outside each office. Every soldier sported a rifle at the ready. It was eerily silent in the great building except for the faraway clicking of combat boots where a small group of Japanese soldiers marched in perfect formation to an unknown mission.

In the former mayor's office, General Yashita and San Francisco's Chief of Police, Ed Blair, stood on the luxurious carpet, each avoiding the other's eyes. The Japanese man was used to power. He surveyed the office. Standing quietly and obediently by the door, was a young Japanese adjutant.

Yashita broke the silence, seemingly addressing thin air, but his words were obviously meant for the adjutant. "Bring in the casualty reports and notify Admiral Yamamoto of our current status."

"And you." Yashita snapped his finger and pointed at the former police chief. "You. Bring me the maps of the city."

Blair was used to taking orders. The mayor had not been given to mincing words. But the two men had shared a camaraderie that spanned more than a decade. Taking orders from this short, insolent man grated on Blair. Nonetheless, having witnessed his brutality, Blair thought better of resisting, held his emotions in check, and went quickly into a small room adjoining the mayor's office.

The young Japanese adjutant bowed and wheeled, also ready to leave.

"Wait!" General Yashita snapped. He quickly surveyed the office, sweeping his short arms across the former mayor's desk and whisking pictures of the man's family and other memorabilia into a trash bin.

"Here!" He tore down an American flag from its pole, roughly bundling it and handing it to the surprised young adjutant. "This is for your children so that they may be proud of their father."

The surprised man quickly took the flag and cradled it in his arms. He clicked his heels and stood, bowing, looking at the floor.

"Thank you General-san. It is a proud day for our Emperor and our nation to have defeated this enemy."

Yashita grunted.

"This enemy is like an old dragon, the old dragon of legend made up of pieces and parts of other dragons that died of old age and disease. This enemy, this America, is a nation of fools and old women, arguing over every little thing like fishwives in the market. Yamamoto, himself, had some fear of this dragon, that it might have the will to fight after our glorious destruction of its navy at Pearl Harbor."

The young adjutant was surprised at such talk. His eyes fixed steadfastly on his polished boots, he murmured, "With all respect, General Yashita, the Admiral is a great man."

Yashita's small, dark eyes focused on the young officer.

"I need no reminder from you. He simply over-estimated this old dragon. Now, it lies before us in just so many parts, ready to be divided up and carried off."

"Yes, General."

The adjutant clicked his heels again and quickly left just as Blair came back into the office. His arms were full of carefully rolled maps.

Yashita seated himself in the comfortable leather chair. To Blair he said, "You, spread out these maps here and tell me about this city of yours."

Blair placed the rolled maps on one side of the desk. He extricated the largest map, unrolled it and held it in place with the others. He wondered what he could use to hold down the other side. Finding nothing, he simply stood next to the desk and held the map in place with his hand. Yashita had not invited him to sit.

With intense curiosity, the general looked at the map. Again seemingly addressing the air in the room, Yashita grunted and thoughtfully stroked his chin.

"I want a list of all your citizens and especially those who have so kindly registered their weapons with your office."

More out of habit than anything else, Blair responded, "Yes, sir. Anything else?"

"Yes," the general said, pointing to the map. "Show me where your Chinatown is. We have some unfinished business with them. And I will need a list of all the Japanese you transported out of here to your concentration camps."

"We have no concentration camps, sir," Blair responded dully.

Slamming his fist on the table, Yashita exploded. "You are a fool, Baboon! You transported the Japanese only weeks ago and I want to know who and where they are now!"

Blair's resolve faded rapidly.

"Yes, sir," he responded, more meekly than he ever had to his former boss, who had been given to his own famous tirades.

9

Yashita went to a window and stared out over the city, his arms clenched tightly behind his back.

San Antonio, Texas

Around the outskirts of San Antonio, Texas, the dust devils came to life in the hot, dry morning wind, precursors of a blistering summer. The Alamo squatted smugly in the sun, as it had done for over a hundred years and the state flag of Texas fluttered defiantly in the south wind. The thick dust in the air obliterated the frayed edges of the flag and the architectural details of the old stucco fort, a symbol for so many years of courage and freedom. The sandy ground was the same color as the hot sky and the wind.

In an instant, two thousand pounds of dynamite the Germans had wired to the revered monument reduced the hallowed mission to dust, blistering the air with a blinding light; the circling desert birds reeled chaotically as the sound wave launched thundering tremors upward and into the crowds of Texans watching and waiting, disbelieving.

A cheer rang out in the dusty morning air as ten thousand Mexican soldiers threw their hats in the air. Their bright blue and red uniforms were in stark contrast to the drab work clothing of the captured civilians. Behind the Mexicans were three divisions of Nazi SS infantry. At their head was Lieutenant General Erwin Rommel. The Panzers had arrived in Texas three days earlier and already the state was under Nazi control.

The Mexicans began to cheer. "¡Viva Mèjico! ¡Viva

Alemania!" and "¡Muerte a los Estados Unidos!" Their fervor was contagious and fed upon itself.

The violet-colored plume in the helmet of the Mexican general vibrated with his energy as he shouted, "¡Silencio!" The troops ceased their cheering and stood in motionless rows even as their uniforms collected the falling dust from the shattered Alamo.

One of the Americans, a young rancher named Jeb Reynolds, broke away from his family and ran toward the rubble, his clenched teeth in a grimace of deadly determination. He picked up the Texas Lone Star flag from the ground and waved it in the air, defiantly.

"Jeb, no!" his wife cried out. He turned toward her as the first volley of bullets hit him in the chest and face. He was knocked backward from the barrage. When the dust cleared, he lay in a rumpled heap across some of the adobe chunks that had been the Alamo.

A Mexican lieutenant ambled over to Jeb's body, reached down and wrenched the flag from the dead man's hands. He spit on the body and then took the flag in his hand and pretended to wipe his ass with it. "Fock you, Tejas! Y fock you, 'merica!" His insult was greeted with derisive cheers and laughter.

"¡Viva, Mèjico!" responded the troops.

General Erwin Rommel, erect and proud despite his relatively short stature, watched the entire incident disinterestedly, then spoke quietly to his aide. "These are now our allies. A hundred years ago they were eating lizards and cactus in caves. Send a message to General Vasquèz that we are marching on Dallas in the morning. Round up all civilians and diffuse any retaliation attempts. Bring their leaders, if you can find them, to my headquarters."

"Ja, Herr General." The response was quick and assertive.

New York City

The plane had circled New York City for nearly half an hour. Lillian Marshall struggled to maintain a normal demeanor and remain calm. She tried to get her mind on something else while she read her dime novel. After re-reading one page three times and not remembering any of it, she gave up and tossed the book into her bag.

Lillian stared out the window trying to concentrate on something else, something logical, something realistic. She thought of her husband, Dean, but that didn't help. Divorce was in the air and she dreaded the idea of it, the failure it indicated and the guilt. She was 25, trim and shapely, dark. She could find someone else; she already had. But this did not make her feel better. How hard was she supposed to try to save her marriage? And wasn't Dean letting it slip away? Did she have to do it all?

Through the small round window, she could see Coney Island, could make out men in Civil Defense outfits piling up sandbags and wearing their yellow helmets and armbands. American soldiers were scattered about setting up machine guns and small cannons. Barbed wire was coiled and menacing on the beaches. No one would have believed this. The peak of the roller coaster, the same one she rode with her first boyfriend, the one where she had had her first kiss, had a makeshift crow's nest on it now. She could discern the profiles of two men holding binoculars, scanning the sea, rifles sticking up oddly.

Looking out the small round window, Lillian saw the Statue of Liberty glowing orange in the rays of the setting sun. Another watch tower had been erected in Liberty's headdress; howitzers were planted at the statue's base and soldiers scurried from one place to another. Another circling pass and the Empire State Building came into view. Even though its windows were ablaze with reflections of the setting sun, the building seemed lifeless. Long caravans of jeeps and troop carriers drove sluggishly up Fifth Avenue, like snakes migrating. Tanks in convoys moved along Sixth Avenue. No one would have believed this, she thought again, no one.

"We're cleared for landing," the pilot announced.

Thank God, thought Lillian

The plane landed at LaGuardia Airport and Lillian quickly found a Yellow Cab waiting at the departures lane. With little traffic, the cab made its way across the Triborough Bridge onto the East River Drive heading downtown.

Driving west on 57th Street, a Jeep filled with soldiers passed Lillian's car. A soldier who looked no more than sixteen years old eyed her as he passed by.

As her car reached Madison Avenue, Lillian saw two elderly Japanese, a man and a woman, a middle-aged couple and two small children, a boy and a girl, pressed up against a building, their backs to the street. Six armed soldiers surrounded them. Three generations. Their arms were raised and they were being searched by an MP while the other soldiers kept their rifles pointed at the civilians. Their luggage was open on the street and the wind was blowing their belongings haphazardly. The little girl's doll was twisted in a heap at her feet. New Yorkers walked by briskly, eyes down as if looking for dropped coins.

Farther on, three businessmen and a woman were joined

together by handcuffs and were being shoved down a side street by armed guards. Two Brinks trucks were parked in front of a nearby bank as more guards loaded them with bags of money. A hand-lettered sign on the glass door of the bank read, "CLOSED."

On Fifth Avenue, long lines of people stood patiently, waiting to get inside a church. On the marquee above the entry, the sign said, "TODAY'S TOPIC: God Save Us From Our Enemies." All the side streets, as far as Lillian could see, were cordoned off and many shop windows were boarded up. The few shops that were attempting to stay open had prominent signs reading, "No Germans Allowed" and "No Japs" and "Wops Not Welcome Here."

A small supermarket, with fruit and vegetable bins on the sidewalk under the awning displayed a large sign reading, "Live Free or Die." People were jammed at the entrance, fighting over groceries as troops tried to restore order. Grapefruits tumbled out of a bin and rolled onto the sidewalk as if trying to escape. What few apples were left, erupted onto the pavement, only to be quickly picked up and hidden away under shirts or in purses. The synagogue next door was surrounded by armed guards as worshippers entered. Everywhere, pedestrians moved surreptitiously, anxious and concerned, trying not to draw any attention to themselves. The body of a woman was sprawled on the street, her skirt blown up over her face, her arms and legs twisted unnaturally, police tape encircling her position. Two soldiers standing nearby were looking up and pointing to an open window, obviously surmising from where the suicide had jumped. No one inquired about the identity of the dead woman; no one seemed to care.

Sirens screamed their piercing wails as one faded in the distance then another approached close by. The sporadic roar of diesel engines was deafening and their distinctive odor permeated the heavy air. School buses drove by jammed with armed soldiers in helmets, holding rifles between their legs. Someone had repainted the side of the bus to read "School's Out" instead of "School Bus."

Lillian had difficulty swallowing as she observed a world gone mad. This is no nightmare, she thought to herself. This is real. The gray hulk of the museum walls came into view. Police cruisers sped by and the popping echo of gunfire filled the air.

"Here's where you get out, Ma'am."

"Thank you." Lillian nodded at the driver, paid the fare, opened the door and stepped into the street next to the curb. Holding her purse close to her body and trying to keep a businesslike expression on her face, she walked to the entrance of the museum, conscious her knees were trembling slightly.

There were armed guards at the large double doors and banners reading "Closed Until Further Notice" were swagged from the large columns; one banner was half ripped away by the strong spring winds that scampered between the buildings. "Rough winds do shake the darling buds of May," Lillian remembered Shakespeare saying. Shakespeare never imagined New York City with the Nazis on their way.

Miami Beach, Florida

Fred Jamison slapped his weathered hand down hard on the front page of the Miami Herald. His face was contorted in anger as he attempted to disguise his fear.

"My God. The bastards have taken almost all of Texas and northern California." He paused, squinting at the printed words in disbelief, his trembling hands shaking the pages.

"Says here they could strike anywhere any time and our guys think the Italians have landed in Puerto Rico and Cuba! I could'a told 'em those bastards would stab us in the back, first chance they got!" He wiped his brow and waved away a persistent mosquito. The humidity was higher than usual for May.

"Dad, please! Don't talk like that first thing in the morning." Susan Jamison looked pleadingly at her father across the breakfast table then glanced helplessly at her son, Jason.

"I'm sorry, hon. I know it's hard, I know. . ." Fred rolled up the newspaper and slapped his knee with it impatiently. "Just drives me crazy trying to cope with it."

"Mom, Grandpa is right. Jackie Moore told me that…"

"That's enough! Jackie Moore doesn't know anything about anything. He's just another dumb kid. Now, eat your breakfast."

"I'm not hungry." Jason rested his elbows on the tabletop and propped his chin on his clenched fists.

"Don't argue with me. I said 'eat.' We don't know how much longer we'll even be able to get any food. Miller's Market was shut down yesterday."

Fred's eyebrows shot up to his hairline. "You mean old Jake Miller packed it in?"

Susan stared at her clasped hands in her lap and her voice steadied.

"No. The cops closed the store and confiscated all the food for the war effort, they said. Someone said Margaret fainted dead away and Jake thought she had had a heart attack and he couldn't stop crying. It was horrible."

"I'll be damned." Fred pushed his chair back and walked over to the kitchen window, staring at the nodding blossoms on the orange trees he had planted years earlier. "Yes, and we'll all be damned if somebody doesn't do something. Fast."

Tears ran unchecked down Susan's cheeks. "What's going to happen to us? I don't know what to do. . .I don't know what's going to happen. . ." She began to twist her fingers together tightly, as if her strained knuckles could force a solution.

Jason stood up and put his strong young arms around his mother's shoulders. "Don't cry, Mom. Please don't cry. If those wops show up here, we'll kick their asses, won't we, Grandpa?"

"You damn right, sonny! Why. . ."

"Stop it! Stop it, both of you!" Susan's black eyes were flashing sparks of fury. "This is no game. There's going to be actual fighting in the streets! Our streets! Here, Right here! Fighting and killing. My God, this is no game and I don't want you filling Jason's head with impossible. . ."

"Hold on, Mom. Hold on. We can lick those guys...we're Americans! We can lick anybody they got. Grandpa was in the Great War. He kicked ass all over the. . ."

"Stop it, I said! Dad, you've got to talk some sense into him. He's just fourteen and he's talking about fighting armed soldiers. Please tell him war is bad, evil, and there's nothing good or heroic about any of it."

"Listen, Susan. We didn't start this here fracas but we may have to finish it. I know how bad war is. I saw my friends killed, wounded, blown to bits around me. Those trenches weren't like hell, they were hell."

"Mom, Grandpa fought to keep us safe here at home, and to try and keep the whole country safe. . ."

"I know, I know. I'm just so frightened I can't think."

"Don't be scared, Mom. We're going to fight for our country right here, if we have to, me and the. . ."

"That's enough, son. Don't say anymore. . ."

"What? What have you been telling him, Dad? Have you filled his head with. . ."

"Nobody's filled my head with anything, Mom." Jason realized the double entendre of his remark and he and Fred both started to grin. A knock on the front door caused all three to freeze like human statues.

"I'll get it." Jason started to rise, pushing the white wicker chair back from the table.

"No, you won't. Sit down and eat like I told you to do."

"Aw, Mom. . ."

"Mind your mother, son. I'll get the door. Everybody just relax now. Stay calm."

Fred walked slowly from the sunny jalousied Florida room, his eyes traveling the familiar view of the green palm frond print on the wall paper and on the chair cushions, the family photos arranged on the sideboard, the mounted yellowtail jack he had caught two years earlier in the annual fishing competition. He walked into the entry hall and saw the top of a baseball cap on the other side of the leaded glass inserts in the door. The visitor knocked again, impatiently.

"Hold your horses! I'm coming. . ." Fred unlocked the bolt and pulled the heavy mahogany door open. His old friend, Jimmy Montenegro, stood outside, his brow furrowed with anxiety. He pulled open the screen door, walked inside and Fred shook his hand warmly.

"Sorry to bother you, Fred. I need to talk. . ."

"No problem." Fred shut the door and locked it, leading

Jimmy into the living room, out of earshot of Susan and Jason. "What's up?"

"Word has it that a bunch of warships are headed this way…"

"Whose ships? Do they know?"

"Not ours. They're not ours."

"Well, then, whose are they, damn it?"

"I dunno, Fred. I dunno. Probably the Eyetalians. Or maybe the Krauts. I don't know! Maybe both."

"What's being done about it?"

"Police are driving through neighborhoods and usin' megaphones tellin' ever'body to pack up and get the hell out. Fast as possible."

"Get out to where? Where do they expect us to go? Are they nuts?"

"The whole world is nuts, Fred. Just crazy nuts. They're tellin' us to head north. There's a militia or something forming up near Atlanta. Maybe it's part of the National Guard. I'm not sure."

"Shit! And we're just supposed to tuck tail and run?"

"That's what they're sayin'. Roosevelt's gonna be on the radio tonight, they say. But the cops are sayin' we need to leave now. Today."

"Is Jack still in town?" Fred rubbed his forehead with the thumb and middle finger of his right hand.

"Yep. Sure is."

"And Mel and his brother?"

"Yep. And so's Pete. And Pete's wife. Everyone thought she was gone for good."

"Shut up a minute and listen. Get your butt over to everyone's house as fast as you can and tell them to meet me at the Marina at nine tonight, on the dot. And not to tell a soul, nobody. If any of 'em want to leave instead, fuck 'em. That's what I say and you can tell 'em I said so. You got all that?"

"You bet, Fred, I got it. I'll tell 'em."

"And you'll be there, too, right?"

"Fuckin' A! You think I'd leave and miss all the fun? No way, Josè!"

Jason rounded the corner from the entry hall, smiling at his grandfather's close friend. "Hi, Mr. Montenegro."

"Hi, Jason. How come you're not in school today, boy?"

"Geez, sir. It's Saturday. Gimme a break!"

"Sorry, Jay. I forgot. Gotta run, Fred. Things to do. Say hi to Susan for me. Loose as a goose, Jason."

"You bet."

"Don't forget, Jimmy. Nine sharp." Fred's expression was grim.

Jimmy nodded in the affirmative, touched the brim of his cap with his fingers and disappeared, closing the front door firmly.

"What's up, Grandpa?"

"Never mind for now, Jason. I want you to listen to your mom and not get her riled up, you hear?"

"And make sure you don't leave home the rest of the day. I mean it."

"Aw, c'mon, Grandpa. . ."

"I'm serious as a heart attack. I mean the rest of the day and tonight as well."

"What?"

"You heard me!"

"Yessir." Jason pretended to salute his grandfather and tried to hide his disapproving grimace as he shuffled off toward his room.

Fred walked back into the breakfast room, sat down and

started reading the newspaper again, scowled, stood up and threw the paper into the waste basket. He leaned against the cupboard, his arms folded across his chest.

"Hon, we gotta talk."

Susan, her hands busy with sudsy water in the sink full of dirty dishes, looked at her father-in-law with grave concern.

"Yes, I know."

from The Complete History of World War II by D. L. Zimmer, London, 2012

Adolf Hitler called a council of his general staff. Der Führer had successfully negotiated a treaty with Josef Stalin of the Soviet Union who gladly joined Hitler in dividing up hapless Poland. Great Britain has been bombed into near oblivion. Now, Hitler thought, was the time to take Soviet Russia and teach that Bolshevik barbarian a lesson. Hermann Goering, as ever the dutiful Luftwaffe lapdog, had assured Hitler that England would fall and with it, the British Empire. Hitler's hatred of Stalin and Bolshevism and Goering's promises overcame Der Führer's qualms about opening a "second front." General Irwin Rommel counseled otherwise. He warned Hitler about draining forces to fight Stalin, with England still capable of defending itself. The real prize, he said, was not the frozen lands of the Soviet, but the industrial giant in the west, the United States. Stalin could wait, Rommel suggested. Defeat Britain and the Americans would have no place to land in Europe. The Axis allies in the east, the Japanese, would sever the right arm of the United States by destroying the Pacific Fleet in Hawaii. With a full blown invasion of England, the Atlantic Fleet would attempt to support the English. When they launched from the United States, the U-Boats would strike and, thus, the left arm of the giant would be severed. On this day, Der Führer succumbed to the higher reason of Rommel.

Within four months, Rommel's plan played out as if he had had a crystal ball. With both fleets either destroyed or heavily damaged and two million American soldiers stranded in Southeast Asia, Sweden and Scotland without lines of supply, the United States was helpless. A centuries old theory that no foreign power could successfully land on American shores was still true. Anti-war advocates in the United States had emphasized that fact for decades, so much so that there was no production of war armaments undertaken; the American fleets were decades old and the air force consisted mainly of preserved WWI planes, hopelessly outdated. Even American rifles had not been improved upon since 1918. What had not been foreseen was a foreign power landing on the soft underbelly of North America: Mexico and Cuba.

So it came to pass that one million German troops landed in Mexico along with four thousand Panzers after a negotiated treaty that left the weak Mexican government in no position to argue. Another seven hundred fifty thousand Japanese landed in western Canada and five hundred thousand Italians landed in Cuba. With the collapse of Great Britain and France, Canada signed a treaty of surrender with the Axis and became known as

Vichy Canada. Lightning quick strikes against American aircraft and armament manufacturers from bases in Vichy Canada aided by pro-Nazi underground forces within the United States irrevocably destroyed the American capability to build sufficient war materials, tanks, troop carriers, ships and planes. The United States of America, the giant, helpless and fat, dormant and isolationist since the Great War, floated aimlessly on the twin oceans whose protection no longer existed. The sharks circled for the feast.

Washington, D. C.

"Goddamn it! Those sonsabitches have gone and done it. They really have. Krauts in Texas, Nips in California and Wops in Florida. All we need are some Martians in Iowa. Who the hell do they think is in charge here?" Senator Rooster Reilly slammed his fist on his desk and two Congressional aides leaped to catch the coffee cups that edged toward the floor.

"Get Jackson Delacorte in here, goddamn it. Now!"

The two aides scurried like rabbits in front of a coyote.

It's about time they invaded, Senator Reilly thought. This country needs a breath of fresh air.

United States senators were elected even-numbered years to serve six-year terms. One of these prestigious gentleman was named Phillip Taylor Reilly, a Democrat from Illinois, sixty-eight years of age and as wily and duplicitous a man as ever served in Congress. He had many loyal supporters, all mesmerized by his adopted southern charm and mannerisms and his ability to deliver a brain-numbing filibuster whenever his committees needed to have concessions made. He reminded his enemies, and there were many, of an arrogant and pretentious fighting cock; they referred to him privately as "Rooster." And they hated his guts.

Rooster Reilly was notoriously difficult to work for. Nothing seemed to be good enough to warrant even a nod or approval. His steely-blue eyes and his ramrod-straight posture intimidated even the Speaker of the House and his counterpart in the Senate, the Vice President of the United States. Rooster shouted and yelled and scowled and shook his silver-tipped cane at every intern he had ever trained and never once allowed a single one to think of him as a friend. But they learned reams if they were smart enough to put their egos in the bottom drawer and observe Rooster's maneuvers carefully. His influential power was legendary and his constituents loved his brassy bravado, his assertive confidence, and his unflappable demeanor under any kind of stressful objections from anybody, even members of his own party.

Rooster was a consummate showman. He was performing from the time he finished his breakfast of imported Turkish coffee topped with thick English cream, crumpets toasted golden brown, fresh creamery butter and orange marmalade from Spain, and a steaming bowl of oatmeal with brown sugar, cinnamon and raisins, until he returned to his Silver Spring apartment after another long day prancing in front of his colleagues and fingering the ever-present white carnation in his lapel. Not even his housekeeper knew what the "real" Rooster Reilly was like. On many a night when his driver would stop in front of his sedately conforming residence, Rooster would smile to himself. None of his acquaintances would believe the truth, even if it slapped them in the face.

Phillip Taylor Reilly had attended prep school in England at the insistence of his father and his uncle. Irish immigrants who had settled in Texas and managed to buy a few hundred acres of poor grazing lands, his father and uncle had saved to buy more lands and heads of cattle whenever the opportunity arose. In old Irish tradition, they controlled the family fortune and dominated Phillip and his siblings. By the time he had made his political debut, Rooster's family inheritance was nearly ten thousand acres of oil-soaked land near Beaumont. Rooster didn't have to work for a living but he was compelled to, for reasons other than greed.

When Phillip was in his last year at Eton, where he roomed with Detlef von Erlsberger, he had opted to accept the oft-extended invitation to visit his roommate's family in the countryside outside Munich. That summer he had fallen in love with his friend's family and had also fallen in love with the social elite of the German community. It was the Kaiser's Germany in 1888, and he, with his acquired English accent, was a likeable oddity among the Germans who often invited him to their homes as an interesting foreigner. He would relate tales of the Old West and would detail the exploits of cowboys out on the open range fending off rustlers, thunderstorms, stampedes and red Indians. The closest Phillip had ever been to any of these was on a trip to a cigar store in the rain.

Detlef was an interesting person, to say the least, Phillip recalled. Fascinating, actually. He was what Americans called a dandy. Tall, trim and immaculately groomed with a pencil thin mustache and silk garments of every type. He had a young couple working as household help, a handsome pair with two children, a boy nine or ten and a little girl of four or five. One day, Phillip had walked into Detlef's private study on the third floor of their sprawling mansion to discover Detlef nude on the sofa fondling the little boy. Phillip, unflappable, simply said "Pardon," and left the room. Nothing was said between them. Hell, Phillip thought, what he does for fun is up to him. A few weeks later he heard the boy's father's raised voice and Detlef calmly responding. The words were indistinct, but clearly "Detty" had been found out. Two days later, there was a flurry of activity at the front door; the police had arrived. Phillip thought they had come to arrest Detlef. He was wrong. It seems the father had run into some toughs in town while running an errand and had been killed in the course of a robbery. The boy's mother was distraught, but Detlef soothed her with soft words and a few deutschemarks. With a letter of reference, she found employment at a neighboring hotel. Detlef generously let the children stay in his manor house. Another maid and butler were hired, also with a child, another little boy. Yes, Detty was a "card."

His father had bought young Phillip's way into Yale and insisted that the young boy adhere to his command. The family had all the money they would ever need, but Phillip Taylor Reilly was expected to add something to the immigrant Texan-Irish: respectability. And that type of respectability could only be bought with a degree from a prestigious institution like Yale or Harvard. Young Reilly performed dismally, going through the motions of attending classes, pretending to study, and flaunting and spending his Texan allowance. He was popular with his classmates, but he never knew whether it was his money or his developing personality as a showman and orator that accounted for his invitations to the most elite parties and campus societies.

After the less-than-spectacular standing in his graduating

class that allowed him only barely to graduate, Reilly was ordered by his father to learn the cattle business in the family's offices, virtually in the stockyards in Chicago. While he had a natural flair for turning a profit, his real talent was salesmanship; "bullshit among the bulls" he called it. Often, he left cattle buyers or sellers speechless when he launched into one of his famous discourses or raunchy jokes. Then, when his aging father announced that oil had been discovered on their lands, and an opportunity to seek the local Congressional seat in Chicago arose simultaneously, Phillip Taylor Reilly knew where his future lay. His new bride, Eveline, and her family, distant relatives of the powerful Chicago O'Connor family, supported him in the effort. He sought the seat and won handily. The year was 1914.

"Where the hell is Delacorte? Isn't that boy ever here when you need him?"

"You sent him over to the House to see to that amendment Ways and Means is going to debate tomorrow," said his personal secretary, Emily Fairleigh. In her fifties with a neatly tied bun holding her graying hair in place with a silver burette, she had been with Rooster for more than a decade. She was used to his idiosyncrasies but no longer intimidated by the venerable politician, no matter what he said or how loudly.

"Right, Em. Guess we won't see that boy today any more." He knew that calling him "boy" was inappropriate, but it was his way of continually being superior to the young "upstart."

Reilly looked at his expensive Patek-Philipe watch. The golden hands showed nearly five o'clock.

"Why don't you close up and go home, too."

Emily was the only person other than Phillip Reilly's wife who ever saw a more benign side of the old man. Her discretion and silence had bought her that privilege on more than one occasion.

She tidied up her desk in the quiet and empty front office, securing everything in locked cabinets. Sweeping the room with her pale, blue eyes, there was no sign of the official work of government that was conducted in these walls every day. Her eyes came to rest and lingered lovingly for a second on the silver-framed picture of a young man in uniform. Her nephew, just twenty years old, had been killed in action in Europe only days after the President had mobilized troops to England just hours after Pearl Harbor. He and her sister were the only family she had.

As she wrapped a light green coat around herself, she was startled by the intrusion of the front door being thrust open. A tall, well-built man in full military dress regalia strode into the office. Three stars gleamed on the man's shoulders.

"Emily! The old boy keeping you late?" said General Waldo Dellinger jovially.

"No, General, as a matter of fact, I was just leaving. Can I get you anything?"

"No thanks. He's in?" Dellinger pointed to the senator's private office.

"Yes, sir, go right on in. Good night."

Emily Fairleigh grabbed her massive brown purse, slung it over her left shoulder, nodded to Dellinger and exited through the open front door. She shut it gently behind her, and the general heard the echoing click of her diminishing steps as she made her way down the marble hallway toward the bank of elevators.

The general entered Rooster's private office without knocking. He briefly paid homage to the all-too-familiar pictures on the walls that fed Rooster's ego and confirmed to the world that he was a man who moved in the proper circles. There was, of course, center stage, a picture of the senator with Franklin Delano Roosevelt. It was signed over an inscription extolling Phillip Taylor Reilly's service to the Administration and to his country. In a smaller frame, there were pictures with him and FDR and Churchill at Placentia Bay. There were others featuring present and past Vice Presidents and Speakers of the House and Congressional colleagues for whom he had helped to pass bills or whose handshakes were important for future purposes. Cordell Hull, the Secretary of State, might come in handy. So might Henry Morgenthau, Secretary of the Treasury. On the right wall was a small gallery of men in uniform. General Omar Bradley, Dwight Eisenhower still wearing his light colonel's insignia, that madman, George Patton, Doug MacArthur and, of course, General Waldo Dellinger graced this corner of the wall.

"Waldo, have a seat. You're early," Rooster Reilly said, holding open a fine box of Cuban cigars. "Smoke?"

"Don't mind if I do," said Dellinger, pulling a nicely wrapped H. Upmann Montecristo from the box, examining the distinctive red and yellow label with its six crossed swords. He carefully lit the cigar, and rolled it between his thumb and forefinger while holding the match steady. When the cigar held a constant glow, the general puffed luxuriously and watched the senator with amused attention. A thick cloud of grey-blue smoke glided to the ceiling.

"What's up, Phillip?"

"We got a sitch-ee-ation here, Waldo," said Rooster. He liked to revert to his Texas drawl when talking to military men, especially this military man. Waldo Dellinger hailed Corpus Christi as home and, unlike Rooster, was seriously as proud of the fact that he was a Texan. Reilly could not care less. At this point in his life, being senior Senator from Illinois was infinitely more advantageous, especially with "that cripple" in the White House.

"I think I'm aware of that, Phillip," said Dellinger, watching another perfect circle of smoke winging its way to the ceiling.

"I know you are. And I think you're pretty pissed off about Eisenhower out- maneuvering you for the command position. Should have been yours. So I repeat, are you ready?"

"Ready for what, exactly?"

"Listen, cut the crap, Waldo, and stop playing games!" Reilly thundered.

"I don't play games," retorted General Dellinger calmly.

"Have it your own way, Waldo, but I won't ask again!"

"Relax, Phillip. Of course I am. No luck with the old man?"

"On the compromise? No way! Fucking Roosevelt is hunkered in for the long haul in a battle he can't win. This country is going down the drain unless we do something about it."

"Well, he's the Pres ..."

"I don't give a shit if he's the goddamned Pope. He thinks this is some goddamned 'political situation' just like he thought it was a 'situation' when he read the Navy intercept of the purple code wire from the Nips. He knew that the Jap fleet was headed for Pearl Harbor, but he did nothin'. I'd rather make a deal with Rommel any day than with that cripple in a wheelchair."

"Careful, good buddy, that almost sounds like treason." chuckled Dellinger.

Reilly ignored the general's remark.

"Have you contacted Gibbs and Porterfield?"

"Yes, they're both in. That gives us a little air power and lots of manpower, including most of the DC defenses. Have they developed a strategy?

"They couldn't develop a plan for angel food cake, and you know it. But they know how to listen and what's best for them." Dellinger roared with laughter as he crushed out the last of the Upmann.

"So, if the President and Vice President were to meet with Nazi sabotage or some unfortunate accident, we won't have a competent leader," reiterated Reilly.

"Precisely. Look, Rooster, we don't have to pussyfoot around any more. Should that tragic scenario come to pass, I am ready to assume the reins of government. It's only appropriate, with the enemy at the gate, that a military man should lead us out of this difficulty. Then, when order is restored, that man will turn the government back over to its elected civilian representatives. Just like George fucking Washington."

"Look, this is what I need you to do. Meet with the German attaché traveling with Rommel. Here's the contact and code information." Reilly handed the general a small sheet of paper.

"Tell them we will let them get as far as the western Virginia-Tennessee border with little or no resistance. They are not to advance beyond that point and they are not to unduly disturb the industrial cities that I would prefer they bypass altogether. They can round up any Jews they can find—I don't give a rat's ass.

"At the appropriate time, you will take over as Commander-in-Chief of the American forces and as acting protectorate of the civil government.

"You will declare martial law, of course, although I think that goddamned gimp in the White House will do that for us shortly, anyway. Gibbs and Porterfield will take charge of the forces in and around Washington and do nothing to encourage a battle with Rommel."

"It will appear as a standoff," said Dellinger, emphatically nodding his head up and down.

"That's correct. We will negotiate a treaty that I have already drafted and which has been approved by Berlin as we speak." Phillip Taylor Reilly earned his nickname, preening like a rooster and letting the import of his words sink in upon the general with unabashed pride.

"You do work fast, Senator."

"Someone has to. Here's the gist of the treaty. We will cede to the Axis all territories west of the Mississippi. They can sort out by themselves how to divvy up the west coast and what the nips already occupy. California is nothing but a bunch of crackpots, Jews and fags anyway. Fuck 'em, the Godless bastards."

"And keep the industrial areas of the north intact. Almost along Civil War lines," interjected Dellinger. "And then you declare yourself President?"

"Something along those lines," said Reilly. If Dellinger knew more about psychology he would have noted the studied nonchalance in Reilly's words.

"What makes you think that Herr Hitler, or for that matter, the Italians and Japanese, are going to honor an agreement with you? After all, you are not the President of anything," General Dellinger argued more for the sake of arguing than from conviction. As far as he was concerned, Reilly was the perfect candidate to pull off a coup of this magnitude.

"Leave that to me!" said Reilly testily. "Let's just say that we've got several millions of men in uniform ready to fuck them up, even if ultimately they could fuck all of us up! If they fuck with me, we'll burn this whole country to the ground. It'll make China look like dreamland by comparison and those nips have fucked up that country so bad you can't find a chop and a suey together in one place."

"So, in short, they get a cooperative leader in DC, half the American continent or more, and ..."

"Every Jew they can lay their hands on."

"And they get the rest of the friggin' world?"

"Listen, Herr General. They're going to ease up and head back under the rocks from which they have so successfully crawled. I know those Germans! When they relax and feel that they can do business as usual, we'll push them right back to the fucking ocean. Only this time we'll be prepared. History will not repeat itself."

"And us, Phillip?"

"We get the richest country in the world. We force a fucking new treaty down their throats and we will have a new world order, as Hitler shouts so loudly. But it won't be his; it'll be ours."

"And if your plan fails?"

"We'll all be fucked, anyway."

"All thought out, eh, Mister President?"

"To the last detail," said Phillip Taylor Reilly, senior senator from the great state of Illinois and ranking member of five of the most important committees of the Senate.

"Reminds me of a story I heard a preacher back home tell us from the New Testament. Something about dipping both hands in the brine at the same time. Something about the Last Supper, I think."

"Can't recall I ever heard that one, Waldo. You'll have to tell me sometime."

"Yes, sir. You know where to find me."

Dellinger saluted in earnest, turned snappily on his heels and left the senator's office, leaving the older man to stare thoughtfully across the capitol of a country of which he had once been proud but which he now stood ready to betray.

Things had changed in America, though. He was already forty years old when the first war broke out in Europe, too old and too proud to enlist, eager to please his father in turning the new black gold into more Reilly properties, cattle and oil wells. He also wanted to devote himself to making his new bride, Eveline, proud of him, and happy to be his wife. Before the end of the war he had given his wife two daughters on whom they both doted. And, unbeknownst to anyone, including his wife and family, he had stayed in surreptitious contact with Detlef von Erlsberger through a trusted mutual friend in Germany.

After the Great War was over and the Allies had exacted their Versailles treaty upon a defeated and demoralized Germany the two men had joined up for a visit, discussing the shape of the new world, the fact that the old world would never be the same, and the opportunities petroleum offered. The old aristocracy in Europe could live in the illusion of its faded dreams; the new powerbrokers from ancient families would have to explore the new areas of politics and business that promised the continuity of mankind.

"And America, my dear friend, America will play a major part of this century, make no mistake about it. Germany and America must unite, shed this burden of Versailles, and avoid the results of what the rabble brought about in Russia. Our Kaiser may be gone, but the spirit of the German people will not be crushed the way the Russians are. It will just take a new voice to reawaken them.

"You, my friend, should look to your own country and help steer its course. Together, then, we can forge the trans-Atlantic bonds and cooperation that will be necessary to make the future safe against any calamity like the war again," his German friend had told him. That visit, more than anything, had convinced Phillip Taylor Reilly to commit his life to politics.

By the time he assumed his Senate seat, Reilly had made a habit of taking regular trips to the new, more vibrant Germany that was emerging under leadership of the dark-haired, intense man from Austria. He assisted in trade missions and helped arrange quiet loans through the top echelons of America's financial establishment. Detlef von Erlsberger did the same in Zurich and Geneva.

Phillip spent the three summers of the mid-thirties in Munich, accepting Detlef's invitations to Essen and Stuttgart and, most importantly, to Berchtesgarten, Hitler's compound. He was wined and dined along with a number of wealthy Americans and British, all of whom saw in Der Führer a model of Twentieth Century leadership. The old order was dead and Hitler's brand of "Real Politik" was clearly the wave of the future. And this group of the elite of Western society wanted in.

Phillip had noticed how incapable Hitler was of relaxing, that he often looked sideways in the mirror and was never offhanded about anything. He was humorless, but polite, intelligent, but guarded. Phillip could not tell if Hitler was simply insecure or diabolical. He knew now.

Reilly was especially impressed with the new crop of the youths of Germany. The area around Munich in Bavaria was throbbing with barely disguised agendas and enthusiastic, motivated and, most importantly, disciplined young men and women. The Hitler Youth numbered over 30,000 and Detlef made no secret about their scorn of American military training and the superior abilities of members of the Hitler Youth. While Americans had their Boy Scouts making fire by rubbing sticks together, the Youth were learning how to toss grenades.

"You must use your power in the American Senate to build the same spirit among your young people. We went through a much longer depression, defeated, shamed. Your 'Great Depression' is nothing by comparison. And look, Hitler is doing in Germany what your Roosevelt is doing in the United States – using his power to force through what he wants! To solve the same, and greater problems. To use the power of the State to move those forward who rightfully deserve it, and to weed out those who would fall by the wayside no matter what." Von Erlsberger, an aristocrat by ancestry and upbringing, understandably had no use for the communists, but he fervently supported his country's new Führer, even if he was clearly insane. Reilly had always longed to be accepted by the people he viewed as aristocrats. Now, in the company of his long-time friend, he was.

Phillip was enthralled with the concept of superiority over those who did not "measure up." He rapidly fell into the Aryan belief system and the innate superiority of the Master Race. While the German aristocracy despised Hitler, they saw him as a tool for effectuating change and they firmly believed that when his usefulness had expired, he would simply be removed from office by an election.

The Reilly family was Irish to the core and had a deep-seated hatred of the English. So did the Germans, for different reasons. As Rooster had learned early on, the enemy of my enemy is my friend. The American ambassador to Great Britain, Joseph Kennedy, admired the Germans as much for the financial recovery under Hitler as for their disdain of the English. There was no question but that Rooster Reilly would be a valuable asset for the Third Reich, and the Reich would help propel him to his rightful place in history: to become President, and to unite his country and Germany to look forward to a new world order.

Rooster Reilly looked out the window of his office at the city of Washington. There were pigeons casually flocking on the rooftop of an adjacent building and Rooster watched them strut and meander around each other as the setting sun cast long purple shadows on the deserted streets He pondered how the buildings and monuments built by the government over the years all resembled or duplicated the architecture of ancient Rome and the Roman Empire.. He could make out the pointed roof of the Lincoln Memorial. Now, that was a building he thought. It was a replica of the Temple of Jupiter on the Palatine Hill in Rome. There was Honest Abe sitting in a god's throne. He must be spinning in his grave, Rooster thought, spinning; old Pinwheel Abe, they should call him now. But there was something to be said for the grandness of it all. Someday, he imagined, there would be a Rooster Reilly Memorial. Only he wouldn't mind the throne, the arcade of columns and the throngs of worshipful visitors. He would see to it that the building would not be a memorial after death, but one constructed while he was alive, as a tribute to saving his country and to making it the greatest power on earth.

He had started scribbling down little notes in his journal about how things would change. The Nazis would have eliminated most of the blacks and the Jews; he didn't want to get rid of all of them, just the troublesome ones. People who did not have jobs would work on public projects in exchange for room and board. People who could not get at least a B in high school would have to serve in the army for five years. These two things alone would eliminate unemployment. And criminals, they would be dealt with more harshly. Shoplifters would be branded on their cheeks with a large "T" for thief. That would stop them.

Child molesters would be boiled from the knees down. Repeat offenders from litterers to murderers would be publicly executed. Punishment would be more than a deterrent; it would be a warning. This was only a beginning. There was so much to do, so much to accomplish once he held the seat of power. He would have Congress suspend the Constitution and the Bill of Rights as an emergency procedure for national security. Then he would suspend meetings of Congress. He would hold power until he could decide on a successor. He was the only one that could see the big picture. It was obvious. The Supreme Court would be abolished and small "Executive Courts" would be established to enforce his rulings.

I'm going to push those greedy sonsabitches right off the continent. I'll be the savior of this country and people will see it and know they owe their lives to me, he thought. After he kicked their asses out of North America, he would let the Germans and Italians keep Europe; they earned it and who would be better suited to keep a lid on it? Hitler and Mussolini were definitely organized. The Japs could have China and Southeast Asia. Same story. They were organized and industrious. That little two by nothing island, he mused, had created the best navy on the planet. Who'd a thought it? He wanted North and South America. Canada? Too few people for such a huge place and they couldn't figure out how to shoot a bear in the woods. Every province that bordered the U.S. would be incorporated as a protectorate and then, a state. Mexico? Those slimy bastards. Turned our back on them and they joined with the enemy. That was a bunch that needed a lesson. Labor camps for them and enforced work on roads, bridges, dams. Work and the lash, that's what they needed. So much to do, he thought. But everything must begin at the beginning and the beginning was ridding the country of Roosevelt. Nothing personal FDR, nothing personal. But you've gotten us into this mess and I'm going to get us out of it. If you can't even figure out how to fucking walk, how are you going to lead this country to its rightful place in the world? I'm the right man to step up to the plate, only I'm going to take the plate and the whole goddamned ballpark.

Now was his time to act, and to act decisively. He had not colored the truth when he had told Dellinger that his proposed treaty with Germany had been approved by Berlin. Detlef had the direct attention of Der Führer, and Phillip's plan to give Germany control over much of the country appealed to Hitler's sense of conquest.

Phillip Taylor Reilly ceased his musings, collected his hat and cane, phoned for his car and driver and threw an expensive cashmere coat over his shoulders. It looked like rain.

San Francisco, California

Dodge Madison ran outside his bar just off Columbus Street to see planes flying overhead. The Japanese Zeros were only a few hundred feet above him as he stood, dumfounded, watching as an explosion ripped off the top of Coit Tower on Telegraph Hill blocks away. The tower had been one of San Francisco's landmarks ever since he could remember, standing in silent vigil overlooking the city's harbor. The flying invaders were hitting North Beach on their way to the docks and dropping the odd bomb here and there on his neighborhood. Apparently the air raid sirens had failed to operate. Civil Defense wardens, distinguished from fleeing civilians only by small armbands, tried to shepherd the jumble of people crowding the street into some semblance of order. Only a few posters tacked on windows and doors indicated basements that could, in an emergency, give shelter from the rain of lead that poured from the skies. Buses jammed the street.

"Damn!" Dodge exhaled rapidly, knowing that the long-anticipated and feared invasion of San Francisco had begun in earnest. Where the hell were the American troops, he thought viciously. He and everyone he knew had speculated about this eventuality for weeks, ever since Portland had fallen. Like so many Americans, Dodge could not imagine an invasion of his adopted homeland, yet it was happening. So many of his friends had headed south to LA.

Seconds later, he heard a whistling sound and, as he looked from his doorway at people running down his street, an explosion shattered storefront windows just a few doors down from his. A young girl on an old bicycle who had been trying to make a left turn across the confusion now lay motionless on the ground like a rag doll carelessly left where a child would have dropped it. But these were not dolls, Dodge thought in his confused daze as he saw more bodies strewn in the rubble. They were people. He looked up into the morning sky visible between the buildings. More planes, larger ones, were flying overhead in formation, heading east.

"Well, then, this is it."

Dodge flew back through his open door, past the old, familiar polished wooden bar and its ten worn stools, and rushed into his office. He grabbed the phone, dialing frantically. A man's voice answered.

"Yeah?"

It was Carlton. Dodge did not bother with formalities. His friends knew his voice instantly, the raspy Irish accent unmistakable.

"They're here."

"They're early." Carlton's voice was aloof, even over the scratchy telephone connection.

"Meet you in an hour. Think you can make it from Berkeley?

"Fuckin' A."

That instant, the concussive wind of a detonated bomb shook the walls, enough to make the stools dance across the floor.

"Holy shit, did you hear that? Carlton? Carlton?"

The line went dead. Dodge shook the instrument as if to revive it, then listened again. Disgustedly, he slammed the receiver into its cradle. He heard the sound of muffled screams and general mayhem from outside. Dodge heaved a heavy sigh and then headed back out into the street, locking the front door behind him. His bar-front window was still intact, he noticed with relief. Heading down the adjacent alley, he jumped into his old Ford roadster and started the engine. There were fewer people now, and the explosions were farther away to the east.

Clouds of black smoke rose from the direction of the docks. A piercing cry behind him down the alley caused his head to jerk. He looked over his left shoulder, but saw nothing. He revved the engine, released the parking brake, and pulled away. He raced down the alley dodging debris from blown out windows and shattered roofs. Pieces of his city were everywhere. For the first time he realized what the quake of '06 must have been like. He had to reach the levy just below the Bay Bridge before the Japanese cordoned off the area.

*

In a different part of town, near the intersection where Sixteenth Street met Castro and Market Street, Carmine Puzzo watched the Japanese fighter planes as they flew northeast toward the city's financial district, North Beach and the piers. A street car in the middle of the intersection had been crumpled into waste metal, its passengers a tangled mélange of dead and wounded bodies. Carmine briefly saw one young man trying in vain to squeeze through a shattered window, shredding his clothing and skin in panic. He turned quickly away.

At less than five hundred feet above the housetops, the high-pitched scream of the Zeros was deafening. As he watched in terrified amazement, he saw and heard the explosions of the attack, as one plane after another dropped its deadly load on strategically picked targets in the city. A lone Zero dove in over Twin Peaks and barreled down the center of Market Street causing Carmine to duck and skirt an open manhole. A wrecked streetcar had backed up all traffic on the rail line on Market Street, and people were scrambling from the cars to reach some modicum of safety in the buildings lining each side of the road. Puzzo ran to a nearby phone booth, dropped a nickel in the slot and dialed, hoping that the phone would work. He was in luck. The phone on the other end started to ring.

"C'mon, c'mon. Pick up, dammit!"

After waiting through a dozen rings Carmine slammed the phone down. He started sprinting down Market Street in the direction the planes were heading, towards the Ferry Building. The street was virtually deserted. Those who had shelter did not venture out; an occasional face could be seen in a second or third story window. Those who had been caught in the Japanese attack and survived had quickly ducked into any door that would open. Those who had been caught in the hail of bullets and bombs lay in grotesque positions wherever they had fallen. He ran past two small girls still holding their mother's hands; all three were crumpled in a line on the pavement like paper dolls smeared with blood.

*

The main quad of San Francisco's Presidio military head-quarters was abuzz with Japanese activity. It, along with the ship-yards and the city's port, had been spared the attack because the occupiers needed them. The immediate surrender of the city had made life easier for the invading forces, giving them clear access to its key military installations. The Presidio's defeat would disrupt much of the area's military communications. With San Francisco in its control, the Japanese forces would have a clear road to Los Angeles, the ultimate target for securing and holding the west coast of the United States.

Scores of vehicles circled the stately adobe headquarters of the Presidio, much like Indians surrounding a wagon train in a John Wayne western. Japanese troops disgorged from their vehicles with guns drawn, some crouching, some standing, their guns at the ready. American military clerks and petty officers came out with their hands up, waving white handkerchiefs. There were quite a few women in uniform. The American commander of the Presidio, a retired three-star general, and his staff stood slightly to one side with his staff, listening silently as a Japanese officer besieged him with questions, gun drawn. Another Japanese officer approached one of the taller American men in civilian clothes holding his young son's hand. The soldier addressed him in Japanese, oblivious of the American's lack of understanding.

"Coward! Pathetic coward!"

The American did not understand the words, but knew their implication. He had seen enough anti-Japanese propaganda, never thinking the war would actually come to him. Frightened, he shook his head pulling his child closer to him. A soldier rushed over to the American and yanked the child away. The boy started screaming. Almost simultaneously, the Japanese officer pistol-whipped the tall man to the ground. An American woman in civilian clothes screamed, ran forward and knelt to the wounded man's aid.

"Save my son, someone, help me." The officer pulled out his pistol and shot him through the head. The child was hauled off to a basement room.

The Japanese officer yelled at his compatriots. "Get her up."

The woman screamed in protest as she was yanked up by the soldiers.

"You can't do this! You can't do this!"

The woman, though frightened herself, pulled herself together, confident in her knowledge of war-time laws in confrontation with an enemy. At first, the Japanese ignored her, but she persisted.

The Japanese officer matter-of-factly relayed an order, and a soldier leapt forward and thrust his bayonet into the woman's belly. She grabbed the hilt of the blade reflexively and her fingers dropped to the ground like small sausages. She fell to the ground in agony, but before she could scream, the soldier stabbed her in the throat with another thrust. The air in her lungs bubbled out through the bloody hole in her neck as she lay there on the sidewalk staring icily into the pale blue San

Francisco sky

Inside the Presidio headquarters building, civilian clerk Jack Maxwell helplessly spied the murder safely through the curtains of a nearby first-floor window. He knew that he could not surrender as his fellow workers had, despite instructions to do so. He had different imperatives. He heard the Japanese officer bark instructions at subordinates who began to head for the building entrance. Jack bolted down a hall and out an unguarded side door, running into the nearby forested area to the south of the main building hoping no one could hear his labored breathing.

*

Jimmy Aoki's bedroom was pitch black. He was a second generation Japanese-American. The once-opulent but now shabby velvet drapes of his flat were drawn tightly closed, shutting out any sign of the daylight outside his third story mansard window in North Beach. A loud muffled banging at the door in another room intruded into Aoki's befuddled brain. The banging made him unconsciously bury his head under a pillow. As it continued, a fat arm popped out from under the covers and a ring-studded hand waved away the intruding noise. The banging continued. Defeated, Jimmy blinked, then cautiously rose up in his bed, his eyes closed, presenting a decidedly pouty face to the world. He heaved a big sigh and stumbled out of bed, wearing nothing but a sheet that he dragged with him. The banging continued unabated.

Aoki stepped over the remains of last night's big party in his living room. He vaguely recalled the increasingly obvious source of his hung-over disposition. As he reached the front door there was one last excruciatingly loud set of bangs.

"All right already."

He opened the door to the very perturbed look of his neighbor and friend, Lindy Montoya. She was in her early twenties, a good-looking Latino woman, whose lesbian-chic wardrobe enhanced the tough-as-nails disposition written all over her. She laughed briefly as she saw Jimmy. The makeup that he had been wearing the night before was still smeared across his face. Quickly, though, her passing mirth changed.

"I knew it. I fucking knew it."

She pushed past him into the apartment, knocking away debris aggressively with her feet as she disappeared into his bedroom.

"Knew what?" Jimmy managed to squeeze out as he stared uncomprehendingly at Lindy. Within seconds, she reappeared with a pair of his pants and a shirt.

"Get dressed."

"Look, whatever it is, you need to stop, honey. I got a major fucking hangover and..."

"Didn't you hear it? You must've."

"Hear what?"

"For Chrissakes, Jimmy, the Japs have been bombing the city all morning! No insult intended, honey, but your third cousins are fucking up this town big time."

Jimmy, still groggy with his rumpled clothes in his arms, draped in his sheet and sporting raccoon eyes from his smeared mascara, looked perplexed.

"I don't hear nothing."

"You drag queens live on another planet. Get dressed, dumpling, and fast!"

"O.K., all right"

He looked at his choices of wardrobe with disdain.

"What's a girl to wear?" he sighed.

New York City

Lillian entered "the Met" after walking by several security stations, at each of which she showed her special permit and ID badge. She noticed paintings stacked against walls, some in crates and some just strewn about leaning against the walls or in piles. A large number of well-dressed people milled about carrying objects, paintings, paperwork. A huge marble statue of a Greek goddess was being moved by several men and women using a dolly and a system of cables and pulleys. The figure of the goddess seemed to hover over the tumultuous disarray below her like a giant above a disturbed ant hill. Lillian noticed dark rectangles on the walls where paintings had been removed; some held smaller paintings in their place. The government of the United States was shipping the irreplaceable treasures out of the city, hiding them in caches known only to a few trusted agents. Soldiers stood casually about, disinterested in the whole process, most not understanding what all the fuss about "pichers" was about. Several clergy tenderly carried religious artifacts in their hands as they hurried to leave. An Egyptian sarcophagus, shimmering with ancient gold leaf emblazoned on the lid, was precariously balanced on two grocery carts and was being wheeled through the halls. An ornate gold frame was hung peculiarly around an electric 'Exit' sign. Ladders and scaffoldings were everywhere. An elderly woman was seated behind a desk, which had a sign on it reading "Admission Free, Donations Accepted."

She was gathering up papers in a neat stack and weeping quietly. A man wearing a navy blue suit was pointing out which paintings were to go and which were to stay. Crumpled debris scrunched underfoot and a janitor worked slowly with a push broom moving as if in a trance.

"Ma'am? What is your business here?" The guard had appeared from behind Lillian, startling her out of her shock.

"I'm – I'm – working at the museum. I'm a volunteer."

"Nice to hear that, ma'am, but I'll need to see some identification."

Lillian opened her purse and showed him the I.D. in her wallet.

"You look prettier in person." The guard's eyes roamed over Lillian's body, brazenly appraising. "Looks in order. Move along."

Lillian shivered and moved through the chaos toward the office of the museum director, Lucien West. His door was open and she tapped lightly to announce her presence. She edged inside, noticing there were a number of people sitting around the large desk, reviewing photographs of artworks. Lucien glanced up and nodded slightly in her direction, acknowledging he knew she was there.

"The concept, ladies and gents, has already been approved by the governor and General De Witt." Lucien looked around the table at the earnest expressions listening to his every word. "Our volunteer and staff copyists will copy the paintings the Germans expect us to have; it should fool them for a little time. The originals will, of course, be put back into the storage area and be prepared for shipment."

One of the men cleared his throat. "How much time do we have?"

"No way of knowing at this point. I gotta hope it's at least two or three months. Certainly no less than that."

"If it's less, no one will give a damn anyway. We'll all be dead or under arrest." The sophisticated-looking matron spoke with an attempt at bravado.

Lucien scowled in her direction. "I don't want to hear that kind of talk. We'll make it fine and we'll get this material into safe hands. Prepare for the worst, hope for the best. And I want all of you to think that way. Positively. This work is preventative. No one thinks the Germans will actually make it this far."

Another younger man spoke up. "I think we can get some of the less important works out of storage quickly and install those."

"Good idea, Bill." Lucien was relieved to hear cooperative optimism. "You take care of that. And if you need help organizing and choosing, let me know."

"Will do."

Lucien stood up, indicating the conclusion to the meeting. "I think we all know what we need to know. Let's do it."

Everyone nodded, gathered up their notes and left the room. Carrie Olsen, 25, short, blue eyed and blond remained, writing rapidly in a small red spiral notebook. Carrie was one of those women who never seemed to stand out despite all the trappings. Her husband had been one of the first to join and sent to the European front and one of the first to be killed. It had been a little over a year since his death and there was still the trace of a shadow on Carrie's face. She never spoke of him but people who knew her said she looked different, not quite knowing how, since she had gotten the telegram from the Army. She had no family that she ever mentioned and seemed friendly and kind so long as her personal life was not discussed.

"Lucien, is there anything you need me to do for you right

now?" Lillian's tone of voice was conciliatory and empathetic.

"Good morning, Lillian." Carrie deliberately pre-empted any answer Lucien might have made. She winked at Lillian and smiled like a conspirator.

Lillian barely nodded in her direction. "Hi, Carrie. Looks like I might have missed something."

"Not really. Same plan, different day."

Lucien seemed genuinely glad to see Lillian. "I need you to be in the Impressionists wing for the rest of this week. Did you get hold of that girl. . .?"

"Mariel Gelder. Yes, I did. She should be here by now. . ."

"Good. You'll definitely need her help. We need to be done with that section by the end of the week, if at all possible."

"I'll do what I can."

"Good. I'll be gone for a few days. If you have any questions about anything, ask Roberts." Lucien was stuffing papers in a briefcase. "He's fully aware of my plans regarding the entire operation. Good man, Roberts."

At the mention of Lucien West's name, Lillian's adrenaline lunged up against her eardrums and her heartbeat accelerated ten-fold. She couldn't wait to see Lucien again; her body craved him, morning and night, even lying in bed next to her husband.

A tall, lanky teenager walked into the room carrying a tray of overfilled coffee cups. "Good morning. Would any of you like a cup of coffee?"

Both Carrie and Lillian shook their heads negatively but Lucien answered immediately.

"Yes and I'll take it black, thank you. Listen all, I've got to leave for a meeting in five minutes...and Lillian, I know I'm plac- ing a heavy load on your lovely shoulders. . ."

"Here's you go, sir. Anything else?" The young man sat the

coffee cup down on the tabletop.

"Another hundred volunteers would be helpful – but no, that's it." Lucien sipped his coffee and stared at Lillian over the rim of his cup. "As I was saying, I'll be back in a few days. So get with it, kid. And remember, talk to Roberts if you need any help at all, with anything."

Lillian smiled and nodded. "Will do."

*

Later on that same day, during a slump in the feverish activity, the larger storeroom emptied of people and everything grew suddenly quiet. Lucien West motioned for Lillian to enter an anteroom he was using for an office and she felt herself flush as she walked inside and he shut and locked the door. His black hair and blue eyes ignited Lillian the first time they met. The angle of his jaw and the small scar on his chin, the full lower lip, just screamed passion to her. His confident take-charge air and the way he seemed to walk so deliberately while others scurried, made him seem a safe haven in a sea of troubles.

He said nothing but reached out for her and she rushed into his embrace, hungry for his touch and his smell. He began kissing her face, her ears, her neck and his hands moved constantly from her breasts to her belly to her buttocks.

"Oh, God, I want you so badly." She whispered, afraid someone might overhear her. She was being pressed up against his desk and was almost laying back on it.

"Not as much as I want you, Lillian, my adorable Lillian." His fingers were sliding her dress upward and she had thrown her head backward, her eyes closed in abandon.

The telephone on the desk shrieked its ring. "Shit," she said catching her breath. Lillian had turned to ice and had side-stepped away from Lucien, her eyes wide and unblinking. She straightened her clothing as he answered.

"Lucien West, here. . .Oh, hello. . .Yes, very busy, and I'm sorry, I really can't talk right now. . .Yes, of course. . .No, I can't get home tonight; I have to work late. . .I told you how much there is to do around here and I am in charge of most of it. . .Fine. Don't hold dinner. I'll see you in a while. . . Don't wait up...No, don't worry. Everything will be fine." He hung up and turned to Lillian. "Sorry about that."

Lillian edged toward the door, her head bowed, avoiding eye contact with the man she loved. "I gotta get going."

"Tonight then? At the Madison, as usual?"

"O.K." Lillian glanced up briefly, unlocked the door and hurried out to lose herself the rest of the afternoon in cataloging and filing reports. She cleared off her work table and checked out at five, anxious to get home and prepare for her dinner and night with Lucien. Her head was swimming with excited antici-pation, so much so that she hardly noticed the strained expres-sions on the worried faces of everyone on the subway.

She got off at the subway station nearest her apartment and hurried to the door, planning her lies for her husband. But when she walked in and saw Dean standing there in the living room, in full dress uniform with his packed duffel on the floor, she became flustered, then angry, then guilty.

"Well. This is a surprise." She put her purse and hat on the entry table.

"I had a chance to come home for an hour or so and want-ed to see you."

"You look. . .you look good."

"So do you, Lil. How about some dinner? I'm starved."

Lillian looked from side to side, as if for a solution to her problem. "Sure. . .sure. I'm. . .I'm supposed to meet another volunteer for dinner and then more work at the Met and I just got into town myself. I can open a can of soup."

"O.K. That sounds pretty good." His mouth smiled but his eyes remained darkly serious. "My leave is cancelled. I'm shipping out in the morning, I thought we might spend the night together. Do you have to go?"

"Can you tell me where you're heading?" Lillian hurried into the kitchen, heating up the soup and acting as if she hadn't heard him.

Dean looked at her, shaking his head 'no.' She served the soup unceremoniously with a few saltine crackers and managed to keep busy at the sink while he ate.

"I understand. I'll be O.K."

"I know. I need you to do something for me. . ."

"Sure. What is it?"

"Keep an eye on Susan. . ." Susan Jamison was Dean's married sister. They had always been close and when she met an Air Force Lieutenant stationed in Florida, he was happy for her.

"Is she coming up here from Miami?"

"Probably. They're evacuating Florida, as far as I know. She has no place else to go." Dean cleared his throat, and was decidedly uncomfortable.

"I'll do what I can, you should know that. I'm very fond of her."

"I'm. . .I'm sorry."

"Me, too. Me, too." She reached over and took his hand.

"We loved each other once, didn't we?" His eyes suddenly softened as he put his arm around her shoulders.

"Yes, of course we did." She pulled back from his affectionate gesture and stiffened. "I need to be getting ready to leave now."

"O.K." He leaned forward and kissed her on the forehead. "Take care of yourself. I'll miss you."

Lillian said nothing as her husband gathered his things and left the apartment. After she was certain he was gone, perhaps for a long, long time, she got up slowly, and stumbled into the bathroom, drawing a tub of hot water and sinking down into the gentle, healing warmth. She couldn't wait to meet Lucien at the hotel.

San Antonio, Texas

On his way back to the Presidio of San Antonio de Bexar which the German general had turned into his own command post, Rommel mused about how he had engineered the entire American campaign and how it was going as planned. No, it was better than that. Operation Sleeping Giant. While the American Atlantic fleet was ineffectively attempting to help Britain, Rommel and Admiral Doenitz had landed over 800,000 troops in Mexico along with all the armaments they would need to establish and maintain a permanent presence in North America. Another 200,000 Italians were landed in Cuba. Americans had always assumed a landing would be attempted on American soil where it could be readily rebuffed and controlled; no one figured coercion with Reichmarks and the threat of force would convince the Mexicans it was better to aid than resist. A friendly government in a country that shared a two thousand mile border with America. A strategist's dream. The Mexican government was toppled and a puppet regime put in place supported by the Fatherland and a huge number of Mexicans that had long harbored resentment against the "Yànquis" and much of their own leadership. Montezuma would have his revenge and it wouldn't be diarrhea.

By the time American intelligence discovered the Rommel Plan, half the Atlantic fleet had already been sunk. The rest of the ships were holed up in neutral Iceland awaiting orders from a beleaguered President Roosevelt. Britain had fallen and Moscow had sent words of congratulations to Hitler. Rommel had persuaded the Führer to forego the invasion of Soviet Russia; their time would come. One front at a time, my Führer, one front at a time, he had argued. Yes, he thought to himself, the plan had worked very well. The soft underbelly of America, the swaggering, self-important Texas, had opened like a rotten melon. Cowboys against the Panzers. It was a mockery of an honorable battle. It was just a matter of cleaning up the debris and moving northward to cut the sleeping giant in half.

"Herr General?"

"Ja?"

"We have received confirmation an hour ago that General De Vito and the Third and Fourth Italian divisions have secured Cuba and the amphibious attack on the Florida coast is under-way."

"Ah. That is better than I had hoped. The Führer will be very pleased."

*

In his commandeered offices of the San Antonio Presidio,

Rommel conferred with his field commanders, and with Dietrich Himmel, his counterpart in charge of the SS troops. The plan to subjugate Texas was much easier than his campaigns had been in Africa. He pointed at a large part of a map of the state.

"Gentlemen, our objective is in two parts. Today, at 1600, we will reach, circle and hold Austin, the Texan's capital. It is only about 130 kilometers. We do not expect a prolonged battle, and we will leave sufficient troops to hold the city. Then, at 600 tomorrow morning, we will push further north to reach Dallas, roughly another 325 kilometers from Austin.

"Our intelligence advises us that there appears very little organized resistance on both legs of the operations. Most of the enemy will consist of the remnants of their "National Guard" units. These will be most concentrated around the cities of Austin and Dallas. The majority of their uniformed men are already in Europe, where we are defeating them soundly, or in the Pacific arenas, where the Japanese are quietly eroding their remaining strength. The terrain is easy. There are no major mountains or rivers between us and our targets. And in most cases, the Americans have built excellent roads to speed us on our way. They do love their motorcars.

"After Dallas is ours, we anticipate the Americans will eventually counter, probably here, from Oklahoma. We will wait. Any questions?"

There were none. Rommel surveyed his team. Building loyalty had been one of his strengths; taking control and leading his men had been another. His instructions had always been precise, leaving no doubt in the minds of his people.

"Good, Then we will leave the Mexicans in charge of San Antonio and Port Arthur until I return. Guten Tag. Heil Hitler!"

The group rose to its feet as a unit, returned the Heil Hitler salute. Rommel went into his private quarters.

New York City

Mariel Gelder was a classic beauty. She was five feet nine inches tall, dark- haired with blue eyes, and she carried herself proudly not seeming to know she caused heads to turn and eyes to stare at her striking presence. She was her father's pride and joy. The current flow of events caused Papa Gelder to warn her about attracting too much attention to herself. She had heard disturbing stories off and on that made her wary and watchful, more than she wanted to be.

The Gelders lived on the lower East Side of Manhattan, in a predominantly Jewish neighborhood, in a fifth-floor walk-up. Mariel walked with long, athletic strides along the sidewalks, heading home, her head bowed, her thoughts miles away. As she started to climb the front steps of her the tenement brownstone that held her family's apartment, an old man appeared suddenly out of the shadows and grabbed the sleeve of her dress, jerking her to a stop.

"Juden!" He hissed the word through his yellow, broken teeth.

"What? What did you say?" Mariel was shocked and a little frightened.

"Juden!" The man repeated the word and spat on the sidewalk, close to Mariel's feet.

Mariel yanked her arm free, ran up the steps and hurried through the door, slamming it behind her. The cooking odors filling the entryway were comforting and familiar. She quickly climbed the stairs passing groups of small children playing games. But Mariel never slowed down as she usually did to say hello and watch their antics. Some neighbors silently descended as she climbed past.

"Good evening, Mrs. Cohen," said Mariel, recognizing one of the ladies. There was no response.

Mariel reached the fifth floor and walked down the hall to the door of her family's apartment. She took out her key, entering the narrow, dark hallway, then closed the door quietly. The delicious aroma of her mother's cooking comforted her.

"Mariel? Is that you?" Jacob Gelder was always anxious about his daughter's whereabouts.

"Yes, Papa. Is Jonathan home yet?"

"No, not yet. He's late and so were you." Monica Gelder, Mariel's mother, was slightly angry but was more thankful her daughter was home safe, even if she was late. "Where have you been?"

"At the museum, Mama."

"Again at the museum? Aren't they finished there yet?" Papa was indignant.

"There's so much to do there, Papa. So much."

"There's a lot to do here, too. You should know better. It's time you stopped. Are they paying you anything?" Mama was building up her anger again.

"No, there's no pay. You know that. What was I supposed to do when I got laid off at Bloomingdale's? I had to do something."

"You could help at the synagogue. With the children. That's what you could do. Then at least we would know where you are. Now that David is gone, God knows where. And Susan? Married to a Catholic boy and living in Miami?" Papa was almost babbling with frustration.

"Mama, please tell Papa to stop. Susan loves us so much, you know she does, she. . ."

"Papa's right. You could help with the small children. What's the good of all that old art? It doesn't belong to us. It's not our business. Just like David, going off to war, changing his name… How does a David Gelder turn into a Dean Marshall? And marry a schiksa? How our friends talk."

"Mama, Lillian is a wonderful girl. David, I mean Dean, is lucky to have her. David has his life, I have mine. I'm trying to keep busy and the art is very important. If the Nazis get here and. . . ."

"If the Nazis get here you won't be worrying about a bunch of silly old pictures. You'll be looking for a place to hide. You think your friends at that fancy schmancy museum are going to hide you and your Mama and Papa and baby brother? They'll turn us all in, we'll all be turned in and taken to the ovens. . ."

"Jacob!" Mama began to shout. "Stop that talk this instant! Don't talk like that. Shame on you."

"Shame? Shame on me? What do you think will happen? You think we'll be just fine and go on with our lives like the goyem? You forget the stories we've heard from back in the old country."

"Enough! I said enough! Those stories are impossible. They are made up to frighten us, that's all. No such things could happen, not anywhere, not here!" Mama stamped her foot and wiped her hands fiercely on her stained apron.

"They did happen and they will happen again, here." Papa's voice dropped to a rumbling baritone.

Mariel started to cry. "Please stop. I can't stand it, I can't take this anymore. Papa, I was actually holding a Van Gogh in my hands today, these very hands! Van Gogh, an artist touched by God Himself. A priceless treasure. I was holding it when it slipped from my hands and fell into a pile of tools some workman had left on the ground. Oh my God, Papa, it tore. The painting tore! It was cut. The Van Gogh was cut." She sobbed, her hands covering her face. "And it was my fault…"

"My brother, your Uncle Samuel, held his wife, dear Aunt Tovah in his arms. The Nazis had just cut her throat. She bled to death in his arms. Don't weep for a painting, Mariel, weep for her and for the others left behind." Papa's eyes were dry but his expression was one of deepest grief.

"Oh, Papa, Papa. Forgive me." Mariel ran to her father and put her arms around him.

The front door opened and Jonathan walked in. Papa pushed Mariel away and glared at his son.

"Where have you been? What did we tell you about the curfew? You're late!"

"I'm sorry, Papa. I was coming home from the Abraham's house, just like you told me to do and I saw soldiers breaking into a house on Mott Street, right next door, almost. I stopped and watched. . ."

"You stopped and watched? Are you crazy?" Mama asked incredulously.

"I stopped and watched the soldiers. They arrested a bunch of men and women, pulled them out into the street handcuffed to each other. One of the ladies said something and a solder hit her, hit her in the face and one of the men jumped on the soldier and the other soldiers hit him with their rifle stocks."

"Oh, my God." Mariel said softly, trembling all over.

"And then they all got thrown into a black truck. One of the men that got arrested looked right at me and yelled 'Juden!' and

NEVER ON THESE SHORES

spat on the ground. Then they pushed him hard and slammed the door on him and the others. What's a 'Juden', Papa?"

No one answered right away.   Finally, Mariel spoke gently to her younger brother. "'Juden' is German for 'Jew', Jonathan."

"What will become of us?" Mama started to cry, softly, wiping her eyes with a lace-edged handkerchief she had pulled from her sleeve.

"The soldiers were arresting them, Mama, they were arresting them. They must have been Germans." Papa's head was bobbing up and down, up and down. "They will be punished. Maybe they are in the Bund. They are crazy, crazy."

"But they looked like everybody else, Papa. How can you tell?" Jonathan was confused and began to pace the floor.

"Because I can tell. Meanwhile, let's stop this talk. And promise me you won't make your mother sick with worry anymore and you'll be home on time. Let me hear you say it."

"I won't be late anymore."

"And don't wear your yarmulke anymore outside the house."

"Oh, dear God." Mama cried even harder.

"No more outside the house. Do you understand?"

"But the Rabbi says. . ."

"I don't care what the Rabbi says. I am your father and I say not to wear the yarmulke outside the house!"

"Yes, Papa."

Mariel broke the tension. "Come, Mama, I'll help you with dinner."

"There's not so much tonight. We've got to cut back."

"I know, Mama, I know. I heard on the radio about the rations. Don't worry, don't worry. We'll be all right." Mariel hugged her mother who seemed to shrink in stature by about two inches.

"Make sure Jonathan locked both locks on the door." Papa nodded at Mariel who hurried to double-check the front door and returned to stand at the table.

"Papa? Can we light the candle tonight? Can I light it? Please!" Jonathan wanted the world to remain like it had always been.

"Of course you can light the candle." Mama had wiped her tears and was trying to be as cheerful as possible. "Right now, let's go ahead and light the candle and sing a song. Let us also say a prayer for David, that he will be kept safe. So dinner can wait. A few more minutes, what's the harm?"

Jonathan opened the sideboard and lifted out a white candle in a brass candlestick with a Star of David on it. He placed it carefully on the table.

"Wait," Papa said. He got up and pulled the shades closed.

Mama wrung her hands in her twisted apron. They all looked at each other across the table. The candle was lit in the darkened room. The four faces stared solemnly at the flickering tongue of flame as if waiting for something inevitable and unstoppable.

*

The next day, Mariel walked to work, more anxious than ever. Her shoulders were bowed under the guilt of having been less than meticulously careful with a Van Gogh and she was heartsick about the damage. She wasn't aware of the atmosphere of despair permeating the city.

She arrived at the museum without incident, walking more quickly than usual as a cold but light rain turned the city drab and wet.

By 11 o'clock, she got to the Impressionists' wing and saw Lucien West directing removals and firmly controlling the frenzy of activity.

"Mister West?" She was shaking like a leaf.

"Yes? What is it?" he asked abruptly.

"I'm sorry, but I'm the one that is responsible for the damage to the Van Gogh. It was an accident and I'm sick about it."

"Well, it's certainly obvious you wouldn't do something like that on purpose. But I've checked it out and even though we simply do not have time now to get it done, the repair will be a simple matter. It could have been worse, young lady. What is your name?"

"Mariel. Mariel Gelder."

"Ah. I appreciate your concern. But you needn't beat yourself up. Now please get to work."

Mariel left the director's office and resumed helping in the storage areas, mainly removing outlines of paintings that were no longer there, obliterating the trail of their evacuation. Priorities had certainly shifted. She was subconsciously puzzled by West's apparent indifference to the damaged painting.

At her lunch break, she looked around for Lillian. She needed companionship, but she couldn't find her anywhere. She worked steadily sorting and filing throughout the day. Her volunteer work at the museum was keeping fear at bay and she knew that if she worked hard enough, she would be safe from its insidious effects.

Mayfield County, Texas

Travis Beecher sat on the living room sofa in his ramshackle farmhouse less than twenty minutes' drive from the outskirts of Dallas. With his feet tucked under him, a dirty blue shirt half-tucked, he was listening to an old Atwater-Kent radio. The dark wood instrument was highly polished and it was obvious that, despite its age, it had been lovingly cared for. The broadcast was the only local station still operating, reporting a minute-by-minute account of the battle. Only moments ago, the announcer, in a hushed, quiet voice had given Texans the unadorned facts.

"Ladies and gentlemen, it is now official. German troops under the command of Lieutenant General Erwin Rommel, have captured the city of Dallas after a battle lasting only about an hour and a half. This follows on the heels of the surrender of Austin, the state capitol, last night and places Texas officially under German rule. We have no word from the federal government in Washington. We will remain on the air as long as possible and will provide you additional details whenever they become available. In the interim, please stay tuned. God bless America, and God bless our listeners."

The radio crackled briefly, then launched into Copeland's ballet music from "Billy the Kid."

"Another one of your Jew composers, when we're losing our ass," said Jonas Kincaid. The young man had been sitting on the floor in khaki shorts and a white undershirt, also listening to the radio broadcast.

"What an idiotic thing to say, Jonas," Travis retorted. He was dark-haired and slight in build, compared to Jonas' short-cropped blond hair and nearly two hundred pounds of football-player physique. Thankfully, he was much more mouth than action, Travis thought. Just a good ole' Texas boy, and, in a strange way, his friend.

"Look, music is music, no matter who wrote it. I happen to like Copeland. He's pretty innovative," Travis insisted. "And what could be more American than Billy the Kid?"

"That's fag music. O.K, you've always been daydreamin' with your music. How'd you ever make it in high school? Can't tell me those Germans don't have the right idea about Jews and niggers, though." Jonas was adamant.

"I got beat up a lot," Travis confessed. He had been a classic teacher's pet. His homework had always been done neatly and correctly. He had always been dressed properly. His mother and his sister, Hannah-Lee, had seen to it without fail. His father had been too busy with their fifty acres of sharecropped land. No one had time for listening to music. Few people in his community listened to anything more taxing than John Philip Sousa at the Labor Day picnic played by the high school band. What they wanted was Hank Owens and Gene fuckin' Autry. Fewer still enjoyed some Strauss waltzes at a fancy dinner at the Adolphus Hotel, if they could afford it. Almost no one ever listened to more difficult classical music. That's why Travis was glad that his favorite station had stayed on the air,

"Tell you this, Hitler's got the right idea about keeping white folks white. And for keeping fags in their place, even if they're white. Just ain't natural! Can you imagine bein' butt-fucked?"

"Watch your mouth, Jonas. Mom could be back any second!" Travis began to redden imperceptibly.

Jonas kept silent for a second.

"Where'd your mom go, anyway?"

65

"To Arnie's Grocery. She wanted to stock up on some things before the Germans got here," Travis said, looking at his watch. "Gee, she's sure been gone a long time."

Travis stood up and marched out the front door. It was a perfect spring evening. The sun sat low on the western horizon and the heat was beginning to moderate. His mother's neatly kept flower patch with its late jonquil blooms was abuzz with bees, gathering their last nectar before nightfall. Standing on the screened porch, he could just see the skyline of Dallas to the south. A few black clouds of smoke rose from the city, but otherwise there was no visible evidence that anything out of the ordinary had happened. Travis guessed that the Germans would eventually come up their way, but he neither saw nor heard any signs of Panzers or trucks or troops. The American troops were still near Oklahoma City, some two hundred miles to the north. He hoped that the two forces would not meet nearby and devastate the farm. It was hard enough for him and his sister to keep the place up. Being a sharecropping cotton farmer was bad enough after his father had left more than a year ago to join the Army.

Maybe his mother had run into a friend and gossiped at Arnie's. He certainly did not see her brightly painted blue bicycle on the dirt road leading to the general store some three miles down the road. Maybe he would ask Jonas for a ride in his jalopy later on to find his family.

He walked back into the house, and found Jonas fiddling with the radio dial.

"How many times did I tell you not to play with the radio?" Travis was peeved.

"Heck, I just wanted to see if I could find anything other than that sissy Jew music."

"Turn it back. I told you there are no other stations."

Jonas sullenly spun the dial and set it back on the Dallas station that had remained on the air.

"If that fuckin' Hitler was runnin' things, we wouldn't have to listen to this shit," Jonas said ferociously. "He'll know what's best for everyone to listen to. By the way, I'm goin' to see Doc Peterson tomorrow night. Wanna come?"

Travis knew Doc Peterson, one of the neighboring farmers, to be the local head of the Ku Klux Klan. He was a big, bullying red-faced man in his late fifties with a bald head. Travis's dad hated to deal with him. He was fairly wealthy by farm standards and ran the co-operative, so just about everybody had to deal with him to sell their cotton crop each season.

"Naw, I don't think so. Don't much like Peterson or the group he hangs around with."

"Listen, if you wanna get through this war in one piece after the Germans win, you'd better be on the wining side. And Doc and his group are gonna be. Heck, they share the same goals. They just wanna keep white people for white. America for Americans. That's all the Klan ever wanted. Is that so wrong?"

Travis remained silent. It was no use arguing with Jonas when he was on his hobbyhorse. Travis was by no means a friend of the Blacks. They were all right doing what they were doing. He did not wish them any ill, nor would he go out of his way to help them. He did not know exactly why he felt the way he did. No Blacks had ever done him or his sister any harm.

"Look, Jonas, I'm an American. So are you. I don't like what they're doing in Washington. I just don't want to upset the apple cart. If they're going to win, I don't know what I'm going to do. I just want to live. But I'll tell you this: I know them Nazis are a bunch of assholes and this is our country and they shoulda stayed in fuckin' krautland."

"Well, you just come along with me tomorrow night, and see what Doc Peterson has to say. Heck, there's a lot of folk who'll be there. And I've got it from Doc directly that he's on the ins with a group of SS guys. Thanks to some folks from the German-American Bund. You know, that bunch that's supported Hitler since before the war. They never liked that Jew, Roosevelt, and neither does my Pa. Nor me, neither."

Travis had heard of the Bund. They were the folks who had opposed the establishment of the detention camps at Crystal City and in Kennedy, Texas, when it became known that Germans, along with Japanese and Italians, would be interned there. It was one thing to put Japs behind barbed wire, Travis thought, but Germans were good people, by and large, he figured. Many of his neighbors were German. They were good people; they were white.

"I'll think about it, Jonas. Right now, I'm more worried where Mom and Hannah-Lee are and what's taking them so long. It's almost supper time."

"Like you said, your mom's probably gossiping with a neighbor. As for Hannah-Lee, why, she's probably lookin' to give a good time to a German soldier in Dallas."

"Go fuck yourself, Jonas. Don't ever talk about her like that. Get out."

"Just kiddin'. Just kiddin'." Jonas smirked a lascivious grin, winked at Travis, and left.

Travis went to his bedroom at the end of the hall. The bunk beds, as always, reminded him of his older brother Garret and the terrible argument they had had about two years back. Garret had run off and joined the army. Travis couldn't understand how they would enlist a queer.

Miami Beach, Florida

Miami Beach was a white, pristine strip of sand that ran for over twenty miles north and south, snuggled up against the green waters of the Atlantic Ocean. The 1920s and 30s had discovered and claimed the natural beauty of this place and with the proliferation of the automobile and the interstate highway system, resort hotels sprang up like dandelions in the spring in America's version of paradise. Stucco in Easter egg shades of pink, sea green, blue, and lavender covered new buildings that were embellished with aluminum and stainless steel. The art deco of the northeast, which had worshipped the machine age, had become soft and mellow in Florida. Thin, nude female figures cast in bronze clung to the rooftops or floated above the awnings of the hotels – the Beaumont, the Cardozo, the Tides. Exotic and bejeweled, Miami Beach was a land of endearing silliness, a place for flappers and philosophers, a place where Scott Fitzgerald could fuck Zelda three times in one night, even in his forties. Miami Beach was a city made of dreams and for dreams. But, a nightmare was looming on the horizon.

On a specific night designated by Fred Jamison to his friends and fishing buddies, nine p.m. seemed to arrive sooner than usual. The emerald-green Atlantic turned a steel gray-blue under the soft glow of a crescent moon. There was no heavy surf, only the gentle lapping against the sand by the sleepy ocean. Hermit crabs skittered nervously and small bubbles popped up randomly on the damp sand as if someone were buried alive there and the last breath of air before death had been released from his lungs.

Fred hurried toward the old boathouse, a place he and his buddies affectionately called "the Marina." It sat on the end of a short pier on the intercoastal waterway. The boathouse was nothing more than an old-fashioned weathered-board shack sitting on half-rotten timbers. The soft night air was the usual tranquil Miami spring night, a gentle breeze stroking the tops of the dunes and rustling dried palmetto fronds into whispered warnings. Waves lapped gently against the pilings and weak rays of light from a swaying lantern streamed from the cracks between the boards of the shack.

Fred looked back the way he had come out of cautious habit, and recognized Jimmy, turning into the street alongside the piers jutting out into the water. He stepped into the shadow of an overhang and watched as he opened the door to the shack releasing a momentarily bright scythe of light slashing the shadowy pier. Darkness returned when the door shut with a clack. Fred wanted to arrive last on purpose and after waiting a couple of beats, entered the shack himself.

The men's voices grew silent as Fred entered. Three men, Pete Kozac, Mel Levi and Harry Ryan were seated at the table and Jimmy stood off to one side. The ceiling lantern, an antique from no one knew where, hung low above the table. In the shadows along the walls, nautical memorabilia were reminders of happier times and long-ago people: photos, netting, an old spear gun, a mounted marlin, dried conchs and starfish, everything immobilized in frozen time.

"Hey." Jimmy smiled at Fred.

Fred smiled back and they sat down with the other men, their chairs scraping roughly loud against the wooden plank floor. The steady beat of the tide against the pilings lulled no one.

"I really appreciate you guys showing up." Fred nodded at each one in turn.

"What'd you expect? You thought we'd leave?" Pete's eyes twinkled, even though his lips were folded tightly in a thin line of tension.

"Yeah. It's bass season. You geezers should be out there fishin'."

There were a few chuckles as they settled more comfortably in their seats, awaiting Fred's plan.

"No, I didn't think any one of you would leave. But I wouldn't blame you if you did. Even now."

"What do you think is gonna happen, Fred? I'm scared shitless. My sister called from Detroit and said everything is shutting down except for car factories that're turnin' out tanks. And she can't get nothin' to eat. They's waitin' in line at the post office for food ration books." Mel's voice rose at the end, but he managed to calm himself.

"No shit?" Jimmy looked incredulous.

"I'm dead serious. Anybody who ain't workin' for General Motors or Chrysler or Ford is in deep shit."

Harry nodded in agreement. "I heard that, too. My brother's in Chicago. He used to be a CPA. Now they got him in a slaughterhouse canning meats. He was too old to draft but they got this new Civil Draft and he got caught in that. Anybody that can walk and talk and has both arms workin' is in the war effort, that's for damn sure!"

"That's not happenin' here." Fred was speaking very slowly, as if measuring out his words carefully.

"How come?" Mel leaned forward.

"I think they're pullin' everyone outta here, that's what I think."

"But why?" Mel looked at each of his friends.

"'Cause Florida's too fuckin' big and spread out to defend. Too much coast. Shit, we got more miles of beach here than in all of Europe put together. How you gonna defend that?"

Harry stood up, almost at attention. "Get us the guns. We'll defend it ourselves."

"Shit, Harry! You crazy? I haven't held a gun since the Ardennes." Mel's face was the color of chalk. "Not one of us has held a gun for twenty-five years! Fishin' poles, yeah, but guns? No fuckin' way."

"Shut up, Mel, and sit the fuck down." Harry's fists were clenched. "You're forgetting...."

"Look. I've been listening to you guys long enough." Pete shifted nervously in his chair. "You think we're gonna hold off an invasion here in Miami Beach? You must be out of your skulls. There's awreddy scuttlebutt that Italian warships are due here any day now."

"I fought for my country in the Great War against them Krauts and I'm sure not gonna run from them when they're at my fuckin' door!" Fred's shoulders seemed to rise an inch or two.

"I still say you're crazy. All you got down here is some fishin' boats, a few pleasure yachts and an old Navy warehouse full of who knows what that has been stored for over twenty years! That shit probably wouldn't blow up if it was set on fire"

"Look, Pete. We fought for this place, our country, overseas." Fred was trying to be conciliatory. "You gonna bolt?"

"Fuck no. I'm not runnin'. I'm listenin' to what the government is telling us. They want us to head up to Atlanta and defend the mainland from there."

"Listen, Pete. This is where we live! What the hell are we supposed to do in Atlanta? You puttin' the wife and kids in a fuckin' barracks?" Jimmy joined in, waving a clenched fist. "I'm not seein' Rosie in a tent with curlers in her hair."

"Look. This is all bullshit." Fred stood up wiping his sweaty palms on the front of his t-shirt. "We need to figure out a way to fuck up whoever is landing here. I don't give a shit if it's the Pope. If all hell breaks loose, we can run later. I'm no asshole and neither are you guys. I didn't die in the Ardennes fightin' those fuckin' Krauts and I don't plan on dyin' here, either. Besides I gotta make one more payment on the Ford and it'll be mine."

The sudden silence was palpable, then the room exploded in laughter.

"You are some dumb shit, Fred!" Pete was still chuckling. "That fuckin' Ford is a piece of crap."

"Yeah, but it's my crap and Adolf fucking Hitler ain't never goin' for a ride in it. Under it, maybe, but not in it. Now listen up, let's cut the crap and get down to business."

Mel reached over and thumped Fred on the shoulder affectionately. "Friend, you are something else."

"We're all going to be something else. Killing machines, nothin' less. Pete, remember your mother-in-law. When those fuckers hit the beach, we're gonna be waitin' for them with everything we've got."

"What does my mother-in-law have to do with it?"

"I want you to imagine every kraut, wop or whoever the fuck lands on that beach is your hatchet-faced mother-in-law. Get it?"

"Where's my rifle?" Pete grinned.

They all laughed again and then hunkered down around the table as Fred laid out his plan.

The gentle waves still lapped at the pilings underneath the shack and no one heard Jason as he shifted his crouched position under the window, outside on the pier, listening to every word said inside the old boathouse.

New York City

New York's skyscrapers stood as an enduring symbol of man's reach for the heavens. Now, in the New York of 1942, the grey and drab spires were like the skeletal remains of huge beasts, larger even than the dinosaurs, that had come to this place to die eons ago. People were as ants scurrying between the bones, oblivious to what had happened and narrowly focused, eyes down, on each minute as it came and went. The future was too daunting to think about, too terrifying. The usual spring bulbs and blossoms in Central Park and the warm southerly breezes reminded no one of the rebirth of spring. This was to be a year of eternal winter.

Cabs were only half as numerous as usual and the drivers were charging double and triple their standard fares; traffic lights were erratic and there were no policemen in sight, walking their beats or on horseback. Papers and debris floated through the concrete canyons on the spasmodic currents of random winds and out on Liberty Island, near the base of the famous statue, the flowering Kwanzan cherry trees framing a picturesque view of Manhattan were dropping their bubblegum pink blossoms weeks too early. There were no tourists walking around the 12-acre island, enjoying the spring weather, photographing each other in all corners of the memorial honoring immigrants seeking a safe future. The dearth of happy crowds presented a strange emptiness that had never had a precedent. The silence was loud and pervasive. Nothing was as it had always been.

To celebrate the opening of the Metropolitan Museum of Art in the late 1800s, an annual gala attended by every important donor and potential donor was a highly publicized event. The museum was a major force in the art world. Mariel Gelder had been accepted as a volunteer cataloguer brought on board because of her success in art courses in college and, oddly, for her meticulous handwriting, which was almost as perfect as professional calligraphy and easily read in ledgers and on file folders. When the world began to disintegrate, the director of the museum, Lucien West, recognized the need for a thorough indexing of everything irreplaceable. The staff of the museum began to transfer as many important pieces as possible to an underground vault in Upstate New York.

This was an involved undertaking requiring the organizational ability of Lucien West's brilliant mind. He was on top of every situation encountered by the workers and ahead of every difficulty before it surfaced. Mariel had watched him work from afar, intimidated by the way he could manipulate everyone around him, even Lillian Marshall, the young woman who had inveigled Mariel to apply for work at the museum, working with her under Lucien's direction. She had learned a tremendous amount just observing and listening and when the invasion started, she was happy to work overtime whenever she was needed, just for the experience of learning about art and artists, but mainly to focus on something other than fear.

"Ah...Mariel. Come in here for a moment, would you

please?" Lucien's question was more of a command. "There's someone here I want you to meet..."

"Of course, Mr. West." Mariel put her fabric-covered ledger down on the table next to a stack of twenty identical ledgers, closed her fountain pen and walked into Lucien's office.

Seated in a mahogany library armchair on the far side of Lucien's desk, was a ruddy-faced smiling man with beady porcine eyes, seeming much too small for the size of the jowls that wobbled on each side of his neck. He was smoking, using an elaborate mother-of-pearl cigarette holder and he periodically tapped his cigarette on the edge of a lead crystal ashtray. He made no pretense of being respectful or decorous in staring at Mariel's nubile figure, all but licking his lips in appreciation. He sat with his knees resting slightly apart because of his thick thighs in his snug black trousers. He wore the black waistcoat favored by many in the ministerial profession.

"This is the famous Earl Holloway, Mariel, the Reverend Earl Holloway. I'm sure you've heard of him? He's a leader in the community, an eminent spokesperson for the God-fearing public. He is helping many of us to stay focused and to remember our faith is our strength." Lucien smiled gratuitously at the reverend and nodded in Mariel's direction.

"And what is our Mariel's full name?" The minister never took his eyes off Mariel's face. "She looks. . .looks quite exotic, like one of those Gypsy paintings you've got here!" The Reverend's tobacco-stained teeth flashed.

"Mmm. . .my name is Gelder, sir, Mariel Gelder."

Lucien and the Reverend exchanged glances. "That does not surprise me, my dear."

"Excuse me?"

"Never mind. Let's get back to our discussion, Lucien. I've

76

got places to go and, if you'll pardon the expression, rats to kill!"
He stood up and put his cigarette out in the ashtray, pocketing
his cigarette holder and bowing slightly toward Mariel. "Good-
bye, my dear, and perhaps we'll meet again soon and better yet,
perhaps you will come to one of my sermons. At the Second
Baptist Church a few blocks away, on Fiftieth Street. You are
always welcome!"

With a flourish, the rotund man swept from the room as if he
expected curtsies from ladies-in-waiting and sweeping bows
from obeisant men doffing feathered caps. Lucien cleared his
throat impatiently.

"Thanks, Mariel." Lucien stood up and turned away from
the girl, then turned back, abruptly. "Oh, by the way. . .if you
ever feel like you might need help, I want you to know you can
. . .you can depend on me. I'd be happy to help you in any way
I can. We're all in this together, you know."

"Thank you, Mr. West, thank you." Mariel kept her eyes
down and left the room, walking as fast as she could. She could
not shake the discomfort the pudgy minister had made her feel.
She was glad it was close to quitting time and she could hurry
home and take a long hot bath.

*

The lower East Side had been, at one time, the world's
largest Jewish community. Mariel loved walking home down
Orchard Street, where the bargains in the garment industry
were born and where the greatest pastrami sandwiches and
bagels were available. On payday, she often stopped at the
famous Katz's Delicatessen for blintzes and cheesecake to take
her parents but lately, most stores were closed and she felt lucky

to be able to purchase anything to eat, let alone something as frivolous as cheesecake. Her savings were dwindling. She hurried past a group of men on the corner without acknowledging them.

Ed and Ellie Jacobs, Sam and Rhoda Rabinowitz, Gil and Gladys Pasternak, all were lifelong friends of the Gelders and all lived near the deli in the lower East Side. They were sitting on the stoop of one of the tenement buildings. Their conversation was hushed.

"Yah. Dot's vot I say. This man, this so-called man of God, is blaming us Jews, can you believe? He is standing up in front of a Christian public saying we are to blame for this whole mess."

"You are right, Sam." Gil's hands were trembling. "It's frightening. Rumor has it that he's also trying to get support for shipping all the American Jews to Germany to Hitler, in exchange for preferential treatment, if you can believe that. He wants to sacrifice us. And he also has started repeating that lie about Jewish bankers financing both sides of this nightmare, both the German and the American. This has to be stopped!"

"Absolutely, but how can ve stop dis man?" Ed put his arm protectively around Ellie's shoulders. "We've had doz young delinquents, doz 'Blue Shirts' they call themselves, push us out of the way on the sidewalk and one time, one of the sons-of-bitches tried to jerk Ellie's purse off her shoulder and my little dumpling kicked him in the shins so hard he ran away limping like a cripple. She should'a kicked him in the balls!" He beamed at Ellie then grew serious again. "Dis is getting to the point where we are either going to have to fight back or end up in a ghetto. Or worser."

Mariel listened carefully and wasn't surprised to hear the name of Earl Holloway. He was a very busy trouble-maker, working overtime to stir up hatred against the Jews, rather than against the invading hoards. He was accomplishing as much or more than the Nazis themselves could, turning American against American. Hitler had shown that old prejudices never died, they just slept under a veneer of civility.

Mariel listened to her good friends for a little longer, then excused herself to hurry home, silently confused on the connection between West and Holloway.

The next morning, Mariel got dressed quickly and left the apartment for work at the museum. The morning dragged, not because the work wasn't interesting but because she wanted to get the to Second Baptist Church to hear Reverend Holloway speak. There were services everyday at noon, every day since the Axis powers began their assault on the American mainland.

She scurried through the streets the twenty odd blocks to the church. It was a magnificent building, more a cathedral than a church. A light rain darkened the sandstone spires which reached almost to the dun clouds that hung like dirty cotton in the sky. Everything was glazed with the falling mist and traffic moved slowly. Brakelights reflected in the glassy surface of Fifth Avenue. The metal marquis outside the church said "Every Day in Our Time of Need, I shall be there for Thee, Earl Holloway, DD."

The church was packed with people and the scent of wet clothing and sweaty human beings filled the air. The pews were filled, but Mariel made her way boldly up the center aisle and two men gladly made room for her to sit down. She had taken her scarf off her head as she entered.

"Deary, deary?" a woman's voice from behind said.

Mariel turned. "Yes?"

"You must cover your head in here. It's the Lord's house."

"Oh, I'm so sorry. I forgot. My scarf was soaked."

"Haven't ever seen you in here before," the woman continued. Mariel stared at her thick lips packed with lipstick. "Are you sure you're in the right place?"

"Oh, yes. I'm a personal friend of Reverend Holloway and…"

"Forgive me, dear. Praise the Lord."

Mariel turned, put her scarf back on her head and waited for Holloway to arrive. A number of people overheard the conversation and whispered to each other surreptitiously pointing at Mariel.

Mariel looked around the room and noticed that the walls were lined with men wearing the same navy blue colored shirts, buttoned tightly to the neck. They all had short, neatly cropped hair and stood at attention as if in the military. These were the Blue Shirts that Mr. Pasternak had told Papa about. Her first thought was to get up and leave.   She grabbed her purse and just as she began to get up, two Blue Shirts stepped to the podium in front of the altar. One looked around suspiciously and the other spoke into the microphone, "God Bless Reverend Holloway and God Bless the United States of America." They stood aside.

Everyone got to their feet as Earl Holloway entered the room dressed in a tie and what appeared to be a black graduation gown.

"Please be seated," he said. Five hundred people including Mariel Gelder sat in unison.

"My words will be short today for I am on my way to Washington to speak to members of Congress." He looked around the room and nodded approvingly to one of the Blue Shirts who saluted, Army-style, in response.

"Dearly Faithful, we are gathered here in this House of God to seek his help in this time of most dire need. Our country is beset by an enemy whose purpose only God knows. We are drowning in fear of what will become of us; of our parents, our children our friends. The Lord is our shepherd, we shall not want. You know this I am sure. Yea, though we walk in the valley of the shadow of death, we shall fear no evil. The psalm does not say what that evil is. Is it an evil from without? I think not. I believe it is an evil from within.

"Yet we know that fear is but a reaction to the unknown. We are afraid of the dark, until a candle is lit. We are afraid of what might lurk in the shadows, only to be relieved when we discover it is a friend. Do we know what the Germans want? Do we know that the Japanese who now march in the streets of San Francisco are not our brethren? Is the nation of DaVinci, Michelangelo and, yes, even Columbus, a nation we should dread? The fear is from within because we do not know what lurks in our neighbors' hearts. And we have but the shadow of things to guess what the true shape of those things might be. Was not France a faithful and religious country and did it not fall? And was not England a country of the devout? Indeed, was it not the very basis of our own? And did England also fall in the face of the Germans?

"If the shadow we see tells us that the Germans and their allies are victorious over all, should we believe that God who is in all things and creates all things and knows all things is mistaken? Does He not bless the Germans with victory and crown their heads with the laurel wreath of the victorious?

"We must never fear the unknown. God has given us a sign that to defy the Germans may be to defy Him. Are we so proud that we, as Americans, know better than God? Have we not strayed from the path of righteousness and suffered the dreadful consequences? Can we forget our own Civil War, slavery and the Great Depression which still ravages much of our beloved nation? Six hundred thousand men died in that great conflict to free the Negro. And how does the Negro repay us? With rape, robbery and murder. That is how.

"And did we not welcome the Jew to our shores? And how do they repay us? With high rent, high interest, high prices for food, shelter, clothing. Indeed, they control the very basics of our lives. And do they not harbor a hatred and a disdain of our Lord, Jesus Christ. It was He they crucified with their own hands.

"It is time we leave our pride on the doorstep and enter a new world, a world where God's will prevails. What, you may ask, is God's will? I must answer and say, 'Look around you.' God has given the Earth to the Germans and their allies. Might we not consider, as God-fearing people, that it is His will that we yield to the Germans and embrace them as the symbol of God's presence on Earth. All of us, united, not under a twisted cross, but the Cross of our Savior and Lord who died for our sins. We must sin no more and I say unto you all: Consider what we have seen in the past 3 years and ask, 'Do we dare defy God Almighty?' Let us pray."

The entire congregation knelt and clasped their hands in prayer. Mariel, almost in a daze, stood up, alone. Immediately, Holloway saw her, recognized her, and nodded. His eyes shifted to the young officer of the Blue Shirts, but Mariel didn't notice. She hurriedly walked down the aisle and back out into the street. The rain had increased and by the time she got back to the museum, she was soaked to the bone.

San Francisco, California

Jack Maxwell burned rubber as he flew down Market Street, braked and made a hard right onto Castro Street. He barely missed the demolished streetcar in the center of the intersection as his jalopy swayed dangerously and strained the springs. He viewed the scenes around him with shock and disbelief. With the actual air raid attack well past, people were scurrying around streets trying to stockpile. A few slovenly teens were looting a liquor store. "They would need it," he thought Some women cried hysterically, while others yet, apparently recounting the morning's events, pointed up at the sky. Jack hung another precarious right into his parents' neighborhood, not too far from Buena Vista Park. He pulled up outside their adobe house with a squeal of the brakes and rushed inside, flinging open the front door in a panic.

"Mom! Pop!"

He charged deeper into the house and out into the kitchen. Finding no one, he darted back out to the front room and up the stairs.

"Mom?"

As he reached the top of the stairs, his parents came out of their bedroom. His mother stretched her hands forward in tearful joy to hug his head.

"Jesus, Mary and Joseph, Jack. Oh, thank the Lord. Thank the Lord you're O.K.."

Jack's Scotch-Irish father, a stout farmer in his earlier days, smiled with pride and reached toward his son to pat him on the back. Jack half-responded to his mother's embrace and whimpering. On the other hand, he had immediate business with his father.

"It's O.K., Mom. Everything's gonna be O.K.. Pop, is everything still in the basement?"

"It's all there."

"C'mon."

Jack broke from his mother's embrace and she reluctantly let go. His father put his arm around her while Jack bolted down the stairs to the basement.

"Megan, pull yourself together, darling. You've got to be strong."

His father headed down the stairs after Jack. Jack's mother folded her arms together, and put a hand over her mouth as more sobs erupted.

A light flicked on as Jack and his father quickly climbed down the stairs. Jack headed toward a large bookcase filled with books. He immediately tried to push, but the heavy case did not budge.

"You said make it hard to find."

Jack's eyes widened with a smirk that said "You aren't kidding".

"C'mon, give me a hand."

The two men heaved the book case two feet to one side to reveal a locked wooden cabinet.

"Here, I have the key."

Jack waited impatiently while his father extricated a huge key ring from his trouser pocket. Searching through the selection, the elder man held one key up, smiling broadly. Jack snatched it away and slid it into the padlock. He unlocked the cabinet and pulled open the doors to reveal a cache of military items including field radios, gas masks, pistols, rifles, and military rations. Jack grabbed a pistol and some boxes of bullets.

"I'm gonna need these."

Jack started to load bullets into the chamber.

"God in heaven. I never thought it'd come to this. Truly, I didn't."

Jack snapped the chamber into place.

"Well, Pop, it has!"

Jack's mother came down the stairs just as the men started up. She noticed the gun and it visibly upset her.

"Sweet Jesus!"

"They've killed the mayor, son. Killed him dead. Did you know?"

Jack's head and shoulders drooped in anger and dismay. He shook his head.

"Pop, keep the short-wave operating as long as you can. Use only the three frequencies we agreed on, got it?"

"Yeah, Jack. No problem. The yellow bastards have shut down the radio stations, too."

"God, Jack, please, can't you stay just a bit. Please?"

"Mom, I gotta go. It's gonna be dark in a few hours. I don't know how long before they get down this way. Just sit tight, keep an eye out and take cover at the first sign of..."

Jack looked at his mother's worried face then his dad's bold, determined, brave look.

"Just lay low. Hide in the basement. I wish you had both left when I told you to."

His mother started crying again. Jack touched her cheek and she grabbed his hand, not wanting to let go. Jack's father put his arm around her and turned her away as Jack, with one last look, headed out the door.

＊

Not too far from where Jack Maxwell had briefly met his family and stocked up on weapons and a few military supplies, Angie Puzzo, Carmine's younger sister, stared unbelievingly out the storefront window of the Safeway where she worked. She was a beautiful Italian girl in her early twenties, buxom, with long black tresses tied at the back with a yellow bow. They had been working in the closed store hiding food in the basement. She, along with several other store employees, most of them women, stared at the masses of Japanese troops marching by. Angie's best friend Harriet Millgate, a short, demure and sweet girl also in her early twenties and, judging by her accent, a recent transplant from Alabama, broke the hushed silence.

"How many of them do you think there are?"

"I dunno, babe. I dunno."

Glad that the earlier silence was broken, a young pimple-faced checker piped up. "Geez, I thought we just got rid of the Japs in this town!"

Another joined in. "Looks like they're back...with tanks."

At the same moment a tank rumbled by outside, its cleats eating up the pavement. Angie quickly made the sign of the cross.

"Holy Mary, mother of God. This stinks!" Harriet looked unbelievingly at her friend, and asked, "How can this be happening, Angie? Where are our boys?"

The young checker said, "I'll tell you where they are. They're all deployed. Philippines, Europe, Africa. Anyone who wasn't ancient or 4-F or a faggot was shipped out six months ago. Now all that's left to defend us is the geezers, the crips and the queers."

"Geez, would you just shut up?" Angie's fear translated into anger at the thoughtless remarks. The young checker, equally scared, retorted, "You shut up, you wop! What the hell's it matter where they are? They ain't here."

The second young checker joined in again. "Yup, we're screwed."

Harriet looked at Angie for reassurance. At her age, everything she had been taught by her parents about the country's invincibility was destroyed. She had come to the city to leave the small-town world of her parent's farm in Nakon, Alabama, a town of about 400 people. She was not prepared to be in the middle of a war. Angie's anxious face only made Harriet feel worse.

The store manager, Paul Renfro, a thin wiry, man with a pince-nez on his nose, furtively stole up to the women peeking out the windows.

"For God's sake, girls, get the hell away from the window. Don't let them see us. Get to the back of the store! Now, I say!"

He was the only authority figure around so the girls obediently pulled themselves away from the storefront spectacle and started to walk down a grocery aisle with the manager. Harriet took a furtive look back. Angie pulled her back around and shepherded her down the aisle. The checkers were close behind.

"I wonder if school will be out," one said.

"You dumbass. School? You better start learnin' fuckin' Japanese," the other said.

"Both of you, shut up," said Mr. Renfro.

"Gee, Angie, I don't like this. I don't like it one bit."

"I hear ya, kid. I don't like it one bit, myself."

Suddenly, the front entrance burst open. Carmine, Angie's

older brother, was doubled over by the cash register, out of breath. Angie, alerted by the noise, looked up to see him. She ran back up to the front of the store.

"Carmine? Christ, Carmine, are you O.K.?"

Carmine regained his breath momentarily as he met Angie at the start of the aisle.

"You've got to get out of here! All of you," he gasped between big gulps of air.

Paul, the manager, rushed back to the front of the store. He wanted to see what had caused the commotion. He was not at all happy about these young "kids" making all this noise. He was afraid they would draw attention to his store.

"Now, see here...!"

Before he could get another word out, Carmine threateningly looked at the older man.

"No, sir. You see here. You've got to get these girls outta here. Now!"

"And what, pray tell, do you suggest we do? Just stroll out, hop on the trolley and head uptown? Do you see what's going on out there?"

"Of course I see."

"Then you come banging in here and cause all this commotion. How do you know a dozen Japs didn't see you come in here just now?"

"Look, we don't have time for this. We've got to get outta here."

At that moment, the front door opened slowly. Three Japanese soldiers stood in the entrance, their faces stoic, their rifles held at the ready. Carmine and Paul stood frozen, while Harriet hurried forward to be with Angie. Upon reaching her, she clutched the young Italian girl tightly. Paul, barely audible, cleared his throat.

"Do what I say. Don't stare at them. Raise your hands above your head and when they approach you, bow your head."

The Japanese barked at them loudly in their own language, frightening Harriet enough to let her force out a short shriek. Angie whispered anxiously,

"Harriet, be quiet!"

Harriet's eyes went wide. Angie lifted her hands up. The men followed suit. Harriet, watching the others, raised hers, trembling.

Three more soldiers came into the store and began perusing the shelves, taking boxes of crackers and produce and snacking as they strolled around the front of the store. They kept their eyes peeled on the silent, surrendering Americans.

Carmine struggled to keep his temper in check. He wanted to clench his fists but thought better of it, with his hands raised in the air. He hoped the Japanese would not understand the narrowing of his eyes into what would have been a telltale sign on the streets that said unmistakably to anyone crossing his path

"Don't mess with me, paisan!"

The look was especially menacing whenever anyone confronted his sister. People in the neighborhood knew Carmine's protective manner when it came to Angie.

Harriet virtually shook with fear, so much so that it drew attention to her. One Japanese soldier came closer to her, commenting to his friends in Japanese and laughing.

"Look at this one. A little mouse. Cute though."

The Americans did not understand the soldier's words, but the Japanese's looks and mocking voice conveyed the message well enough. Harriet was in mortal fear. The Japanese soldier darted his eyes at his comrades.

"This one."

The Japanese pointed at Harriet. He then looked up and down at Angie, who stood at eye level with him.

"And her."

Something crashed toward the back of the store and the soldier's head jerked around briefly. He then returned his focus to the foursome in front. He motioned to his comrades to go check out the noise. Carmine wanted to call out and warn the people in the back. Paul anticipated Carmine's intentions and whispered through clenched teeth,

"Not a sound, goddamn you!"

Carmine, teeth clenched, whispered back, "We can't just stand here and ..."

The Japanese soldier yelled at them to be silent. Though they did not understand the words, they understood the menacing tone and his gestures.

The two other Japanese soldiers quickly ushered the two female checkers, a stock boy and the butcher whom they had found in back to the front of the store. As they saw the others with raised hands, they too raised their hands. The butcher was a very fat man, with prematurely thinning hair, a greasy apron tied around his waist. The stock boy was very skinny, his thin arms sticking out of a green, short-sleeved shirt hanging over faded khaki pants.

With the exception of Carmine, none of the American men seemed to represent any type of threat, the Japanese soldier mused as he continued to eye the women. These were the feared enemy, he thought, amused by the lot of them. If these were the geijin his commanders had often preached about, this would be an easy war.

The soldier escorting the two checkers grabbed the cheeks of one of them as he called out to his comrades.

"Look at the make-up on this one. Thinks she's a geisha!"

The girl was not as afraid as Harriet.

"Hey, getcha hands off me, jerk!"

The Japanese, equally unable to understand his captives' language, snapped insultingly at the girl,

"American whore!"

In a split second, he stepped forward and backhanded her. She reeled and blood began to trickle from her nose; a huge welt blossomed on her cheek. Harriet started to cry while Angie hugged her.

"Come on, Harriet, stop. Stop crying."

Carmine's temper welled up. Despite his raised hands, the look on his face showed anyone who was astute enough to know that he was only seconds away from rushing the soldiers.

Paul had met Carmine shortly after he hired his sister and had begun to read the Italian's body language. He whispered again, this time more a supplication than a threat, trying to keep Carmine relatively calm.

"If you try it, they'll kill all of us and take the women.

The Japanese soldier, hearing the whispered words, drew his pistol and fired point blank into Paul's head, splattering blood onto Angie and Harriet. Harriet screamed and buried her head into Angie's bosom in hysterics.

The soldier who had fired the shot replaced his pistol; he waved to his cohorts and said, "Take the women and let's go."

The Japanese started pushing the women toward the door and they, immobilized by fear, tearfully complied. Angie looked back at Carmine in anguish. She shook her head in a stern gesture of "no" at him.

As he saw his sister and the other girls being herded to the front door, tears streamed down Carmine's face. The tears were a combination of fear for his beloved sister's safety and his internal rage. Everything inside him wanted to beat the Japanese to a bloody pulp with his bare fists. In that instant, he hated the army for not letting him enlist.

Calmly, the Japanese soldier withdrew his pistol again, this time planting it squarely against Carmine's temple. Carmine's face was beet-red and sweat poured out. He tightly closed his eyes. As Angie was being pushed towards the door, she turned around once more to see her brother about to be executed. In an agonizing cry, she screamed "No!"

The Japanese soldier pulled the trigger. There was just a click. The soldier cocked his head with a smirk. In English, he said flatly, "Bang!"

He laughed and strolled out behind his comrades and the four women. Harriet was pleading in tears to the soldiers as the door swung shut. The last sound heard by the petrified men in the store was the sound of the front door shutting with a bang.

Carmine fell to the body of the store manager, hunched over and cried. He knew the man was dead and there was nothing he could do. He sat quietly, never feeling so helpless as he did this minute. He rose up in fury ready to charge out after the Japanese. The butcher and box-boy restrained him.

"Don't do it son. They'll just mow you down and it won't save nobody," said the butcher.

"That's my sister, goddamn it!" Carmine said tearfully.

"C'mon son. We got to try to get outta here. Through the back. Hurry!"

Carmine was paralyzed with utter frustration and anger. Shame overwhelmed him.

"Angie! God!"

"Son, if you want to live, you better pull yourself together. We can make it if we hurry. Maybe you can find her and save her. I don't know. But you'll have to do it later, not now."

The three men dejectedly staggered towards the back of the store, leaving Paul, the manager, in a widening puddle of blood.

Miami Beach, Florida

The army and navy had been stockpiling munitions ever since the Great War in all parts of the country, but particularly and wisely at the seaports.

Most of the old, experienced veterans knew about the munitions stored in the navy warehouses and they knew which ones were where. Many of these old war horses, especially the ones that had settled in the area, knew exactly what was stored and what it could do. Fred Jamison was one of these. His patriotism wasn't just the flag-waving kind. He believed in America as the "last great hope of the world."

He had retired to Miami Beach mainly for the fishing, and for a while, sold Chris-Craft boats for a living. He loved deep-sea fishing and his noble demeanor was all most customers needed to be talked into buying into Fred's dreams. For a long time, he managed to make a very good living on the trust he built up from his customers.

The one thing he had never told anyone, no one at all, was the source of his occasional terrible nightmare. The recurrent dream never failed to waken him in a cold sweat. The dream always started with him in the trench, rain pouring down and mud ankle deep. Then the whistle shrieked as the call to go "over the top" and face the barbed wire and the hail of German bullets and the dreaded cloud of yellow mustard gas. This time, when he heard the whistle, he would not go. He simply froze in place and listened to the rat-tat-tat of the machine guns and the incessant screams of his fellow soldiers. Then all would fall silent and the shuffling of dragging feet filled the stifling air of the trench. In poured his comrades, riddled with bullets, limbs and heads blown off. All dead, all climbing as if alive into the trench. "Fred," they would murmur. "Were you out there?" He could not answer. "Were you out there?" They closed around him, the smell of blood and guts like a vapor heavy in the air. "Leave me alone!" he would shout. "Leave me alone!" and he would wake in a sweat.

A buzz bomb, a two ton mass of explosives that the Germans would launch from behind their lines with just the right amount of fuel to make it into the American and British entrenchments, made a terrible sizzling sound and then went silent just before it fell and exploded. Fred was on watch and heard one of the infernal things heading toward the trenches. He cranked the alarm siren, as he had done a hundred times before, at least. Most of the men had fallen into a deep sleep, a trench torpor that settled in after a few weeks of incessant bombardment, attack and counter-attack.

The siren wailed, but the men were just too tired. Fred had a bad feeling about this particular buzzer. He started shouting as he ran through the trench slamming his fist against the makeshift wooden doors of the subterranean barracks. No one stirred. And then the silence. Then the blinding flash. Then the penetrating thud of the blast.

Fred awoke about ten yards from the trench, his legs

wrapped in barbed wire. Where the platoon had been sleeping was a massive crater. Pieces of his comrades covered the muddy, pocked field. He was the sole survivor.

When he was transferred to the 4th Brigade, he thought he heard the men whisper or mumble as he walked by. He had been on watch and ran for cover, they were saying, he thought. He didn't warn them. He was looking out for number one. Fred began to believe it. He became reckless and would lead charges. But he survived to Armistice Day and came back only to live and re-live his guilt over and over in his sleep.

His friends in Florida listened to Fred with respectful attention, aware of his knowledge of the subject – weaponry, torpedoes to be exact. Fred was the owner of a Chris-Craft fishing boat, a 32-foot Custom Sportsman cabin cruiser with a small stateroom. It ran smoothly and dependably. This is what was essential for the execution of his plan.

The Navy warehouses were all near the coast and as far as anyone knew, most of the ordnance and weaponry inside was obsolete, but Fred knew this was not true. And he knew which warehouse held the weaponry he needed for the task, the new torpedoes developed to combat those damned German U-Boats..

One of the last steam-driven torpedoes developed was the Mark 15. It was equipped with a conventional contact exploder and carried a larger payload than its predecessors. It was slightly longer, heavier and more deadly. It could be launched from destroyers against surface ships. The explosive inside was called "Torpex", more powerful than TNT, and the casing was designed to shatter and fragment.

The Navy had stockpiled 452 of these lethal Mark 15s, right in Miami Beach, in a warehouse near the waterfront.

Weeds grew solidly in undulating patches four feet tall around the storage areas which, at night, were lit by one outside hooded fixture over the bay doors which emitted a large circle of yellow light. Moths and mayflies buzzed around the lamp madly in the damp, still Miami night.

Fred stripped his beloved boat to the bare bone so that it sat high in the water and, with the weight of the torpedoes, would sit just right. She could easily maneuver accurately with one of the huge torpedoes strapped to each side of the prow.

Access to the warehouses was also an easy task. Most personnel had been evacuated and everyone wanted to do something to resist; the looming silhouette of the Italian battleship, Marco Polo, which had floated into view only hours before, had triggered a clenched-teeth reaction in any red-blooded American who took the time to look seaward. It's hulking mass sat like a pregnant Leviathan in the dark waters of the Atlantic, waiting to disgorge the invaders.

Fred and his fishing buddies were organized into teams of two men each, with 4-hour watches scheduled with their binoculars and night glasses aimed at the decks of the Marco Polo. The Americans knew they had to act fast in order to have the element of surprise on their side.

Jason had convinced his grandfather that he needed to be a part of this operation and actually Fred was glad to have his help; he was strong for his age, and Fred was beginning to lose endurance. The fishing buddies, transported two of the 21-foot long torpedoes from the warehouse on Fred's boat trailer and pulled it with his pick-up to his garage in the middle of the night.

Using a motor winch, they carefully mounted and lashed the two lethal torpedoes to the sides of the fishing boat, their detonating tips two feet beyond the front of the boat. Then, the boat was slipped into the water.

Fred was to drive the boat directly at the Italian ship, tie the wheel in place and jump free of the boat about a hundred yards from impact. The trusty Chris Craft would do the rest. Subconsciously, he couldn't think of a better way to strike out at the enemy and avenge his old platoon. But he would sure miss that boat.

When Jason asked to accompany Fred, Fred told him, "Are you crazy son? Your mother will have my hide. You've done all you can. Now stay here and watch the fireworks. Then get home as fast as you can. I'll be there shortly. Promise you'll listen!" Jason reluctantly agreed and went into the boathouse to watch out the window.

It was 4 AM and Fred was ready. The moon had dropped beyond the horizon and only a few weak lights from the Marco Polo penetrated the inky darkness over the water. The twin engines started without hesitation, which didn't surprise Fred, since he had maintained his beloved fishing boat like it was new for years. As it pulled away from shore, chugging through high reeds like an overweight alligator, Fred's buddies stood on the edges of the launch ramp and were weak with dread for their close friend. They had two small speedboats at the ready to pull Fred from the water as soon as he jumped off his own boat.

At two hundred yards, Fred cut the engines and let his boat drift, as he had predicted it to do, toward the waiting hull of the Marco Polo. As he drew closer, he could make out indistinct silhouettes on board the Italian ship. Obviously, sentries were lazily walking around the three decks. The ominous shape of the ship's gigantic cannons stuck out beyond its railings. One volley from one of those 10-inch monsters and he'd be blown to kingdom come. "Fuck 'em," Fred said under his breath. "Fuck 'em to hell."

Closer and closer the drifting fishing boat with its porcupine torpedo quills made its way to the Italian ship. Suddenly, like a lightning bolt, a search beam hurled out across the water and lit Fred's face like the noon sun.

"Shit," Fred shouted. A volley of machine gun fire hit Fred full in the legs and he crumpled to the deck. As he fell, he instinctively grabbed for something to break his fall. It was the wheel. The boat veered sharply away from its target and started drifting out to sea.

More shots hit Fred's boat and the beautiful wooden deck shot splinters and ricochets in every direct.

"Shit. Goddamn, shit," Fred wheezed as he lay helpless on the deck, bleeding from the wounds in his legs.

One of the speedboats started up with Pete and Harry on board and raced out into the dark water, churning a blue-white wake that was like a sign post for the waiting Italians.

One of the canons lazily lowered itself as it took aim and a thundering blast shook the earth as a ten-inch shell obliterated the speed boat and its two hapless rescuers. Bits of the flesh and bone dropped from the sky like chum the fisherman would scatter when fishing for sharks and tuna. Fred had heard the speedboat and the blast and looked up at the dark sky and cursed God for letting this happen.

It was the sound of his engines starting that brought him back to life.

"What the…" was all he could think. How had the engines started?

It was Jason. He had stowed away below decks.

"Goddamn it, boy, what the hell are you doing?"

"My duty, Grandpa."

Jason grabbed the wheel of the fishing boat and directed it at the Marco Polo.

"Down, Grandpa, down! Keep your head down!"

Fred looked at Jason with a questioning stare; he had not been able to hear Jason's words. Every machine gun on board the ship was firing at them and one bullet caught Fred right in the middle of his forehead. He collapsed in a heap, half his skull blown away.

"Grandpa! No!"

Jason lunged for his grandfather, grabbing at his callused hand, trying to tell him to hang on and that he loved him, and then Jason saw his grandfather's dead stare and knew he was gone. A machine-gun static of bullets whizzed nearby and one stray shot got Jason in the left wrist, just as his hand stretched to hold his grandfather close. He fell backward. Bullets peppered Fred's corpse, making it twitch as if resisting even in death.

The engines of the Chris-Craft droned silently on. More and more bullets hit it, shredding it into pieces, but still it moved forward as if Fred had been at the tiller.

A siren sounded on the Marco Polo and shouts rang out into the night.

From the shore, a bright orange blast tore a hole in the Italian ship; it illuminated the sea in every direction. The sound of the erupting torpedoes drifted across the water like Thor's thunder bolts..

It took less than an hour for the Marco Polo to sink. By the time it had nestled into the murky depths of the Atlantic, twenty Axis ships floated nearby, six of them battleships that leveled their guns at the bright and cheerful hotels that lined Miami Beach.

New York City

Lillian glanced at her watch, noting it was after six and curfew in New York was at seven. She stared out the huge windows of the Madison Hotel, watching for Lucien, longing for him to arrive, longing for him not to, wishing she weren't so obsessed with him, thankful she was, and her heartbeat thrummed in her ears as she admitted to herself she loved him with all her heart and soul. She took a deep breath and turned to sit down, hoping he could get to the hotel before curfew. Her mind danced over their earliest dates, their first kisses, their first sense of intimacy. She cherished all the details and was maddened and enthralled by his refusal to have sex with her. No matter how close they came, he held back, insisting that they wait until they were "free" of their other obligations.

She remembered meeting him many months earlier at the museum and their attraction had been instantaneous. Dinner at the neighborhood Italian bistro, the red and white checked cloths on the tables, the veal scaloppini and a superb Chianti. Lucien had asked her about her husband, Dean, and her unhappy marriage. She remembered telling him Dean was always dreaming of doing something meaningful, like becoming a pilot or a ship builder, but his dreams didn't pay the rent. She had told Lucien her father had warned her Dean was like Peter Pan, because he was someone who would never grow up. And she also remembered thinking she could change him with what Lucien called "the love of a good woman." It didn't work; it probably never did.

Dean's father had invited him to Seattle for a visit home and she had encouraged him to go just to get him out of the house so she could have time. Even now, she shuddered with guilt. He was more into sports than anything she was interested in. He had joined the reserves and was gone weeks on end without a word. When he was home, he made love quickly and predictably. She had lost all respect for him when he had lost his job and refused to look for another. He became secretive about his reservist duty. Finally, she just didn't care.

Lucien had insisted she was not to blame. No, she had insisted to Lucien, she was not sleeping with Dean; he was sleeping with her, and it was just an accommodation. It disgusted her totally, and was always brutal and passionless. Lillian closed her eyes momentarily. It was nothing like what we have, Lucien darling, nothing. Not even close. But, she admitted to herself, her family still blamed her for not trying harder to make the marriage work. Lucien assured her they didn't understand. They weren't in bed with him and so could not have her full and total point of view like he did. She remembered asking Lucien if he was going to get a divorce and he said yes, that he had told her yes, many times. But he needed more time because of the world situation and the frightening jeopardy they were all living in. He agreed they were meant for each other but he couldn't comply quite yet, and they continued to meet with increasing intensity.

As she stepped away from the plate glass windows, she looked up and there he was, smiling at her from just inside the side entrance. The space between them closed rapidly and neither one was aware of anyone else in the lobby. He pulled her close, holding the back of her head with a strong hand, pressing her back closer, closer, with the other. She nuzzled his neck for a moment, but neither spoke right away. No one in the busy lobby even gave them a second glance.

"I love your breath on my neck." He spoke softly, just for her to hear. "You smell like roses. . ."

She leaned back and smiled up at him. "Let's go upstairs. I've already checked us in." She waggled two room keys under his nose.

Without saying another word, they walked arm-in-arm to the elevator, crowding inside and getting off at the eighth floor. After the elevator doors clanged shut and grinding cables lifted the car up to their floor, they walked to their room as if it was the last walk they'd ever take together. Each seemed to treasure the moment. Lucien took one of the keys from Lillian's delicate fingers and ceremoniously bowed as he opened the door.

"Aha! Our little home away from home." Lillian tossed her purse on the entry console, patted down her hair as she glanced in the gilt-framed mirror and whirled in a giddy dance across the sitting room, flopping on the rose damask sofa in front of the fireplace. She kicked off her black patent pumps and propped her stocking feet on the inlay-design of the ornate coffee table. She watched Lucien as he walked into the adjacent bedroom and came back toward her, a broad smile on his handsome face. "You look like Joseph Cotten, my love. Only better."

Lucien leaned over the back of the sofa and kissed the top of her head. "And you, fair lady, look like Gene Tierney. Only better." He tipped her face backward and kissed her deeply, his tongue probing her mouth, declaring his ownership. "Mmm. You are delicious. He took off his suit coat and sat down beside her on the down cushion.

He reached over and began to unbutton the bodice of her lavender silk shirtwaist.

"Wait!" She grabbed his wrist. "Let's make this last …." She

102

leaned over and kissed his nose.

Lillian looked at him through her long black eyelashes as he snuggled close and wrapped her in his arms.

"You remind me spring is here in spite of everything."

"Hush. You talk too much and remember, we agreed no scary talk. . ."

"Right. C'm here, girl."

They began to kiss each other in earnest and in minutes were stretched out on the sofa, curled together contentedly, whispering and touching as only lovers can.

"I can't stand it anymore. Get your clothes off, woman."

Lillian stood up and slowly began to remove her dress, then her pale pink slip, and when she leaned over to unhook her garter belt to peel off her stockings, Lucien sighed audibly. "I would love to have a painting of you like that." He had kicked off his shoes, pulled off his black silk socks, loosened his suspenders and removed his trousers, hanging them neatly over the back of the sofa, aligning the cuffs first. As he unbuttoned his white shirt, he watched her backside as she walked provocatively into the bedroom, dropping her slip to the floor. He hurried into the bedroom, reaching out to unhook her bra and then placing his thumbs under the elastic waist of her panties, slipped them down over her knees and watched as she stepped out of them and left them on the floor. She was totally nude and lifting her long hair up from her neck, turned around to face him, her nipples erect. He couldn't stop staring at her breasts, her thick dark pubic hair, her smooth belly, the curve of her thighs. His erection was an immediate response, demanding to be satisfied. He threw his shirt on the floor, tore off his undershirt and slipped his boxers off in one smooth maneuver, then sitting on the edge of the bed, drew her close and began to suckle her nipples, caressing her soft breasts as he closed his eyes.

"Oh, God. I can't. . .I can't stand up anymore, Lucien, I can't. . ." Lillian's knees gave way as she tumbled over onto the bed, her hands exploring his muscular body with familiar tenderness.

"You are so wet, so ready for me."

"But we mustn't, you said. Remember, we agreed. . ."

"We're married, you know. . ."

"Yes, we are. To other people,"

They kissed and continued stroking each other's bodies, as familiarly as long-married couples did, as intimately as all lovers have done forever. She held his erection in her hand, rolling over on top of him, reaching down between her legs to insert his penis into her.

"Stop, my dearest. We mustn't do that. Not tonight. Not until we are married for real."

"But I want to. It'll be all right, I promise." She leaned back, looking into his eyes.

"No, you won't. Neither would I. We need to save this; believe me, I know."

"And our feelings? Our hearts? " She began placing small kisses up and down his neck. "What about the possibility time will run out on us?"

"No. . .let's just save it. I want it to be special, precious and pure, when it happens. . ."

"I do love you so. You know that, don't you?"

"God, yes. I have no reason to doubt you. And I love you as well and as much. More, actually."

They lost themselves again in loving caresses, rolling together from one side of the bed to the other.

"This night will be like a dream, Lil. In dreams, when you

think you are making love, you aren't, actually. It's just in your mind. In your subconscious."

"But this isn't a dream. This is real and I'm here in your arms."

"I want it to be a dream, though. I don't want there to be any regrets, ever. I love you too much to risk starting out with a regret. And we can never regret a lovely dream."

Lillian sighed and ran her fingers through his hair. "Lucien, my Lucien, the Lucien of my dream world. No regrets, no sorrow, only our love to remember."

Neither one noticed the increased wailings of ambulances and police sirens nor did they see the searchlights that flashed and stabbed into the low-lying clouds of the spring night. They would not have cared; at least she wouldn't have.

The lovers' soft murmurs finally subsided and they slept, curled together like a pair of nesting spoons, Lillian on her side with her back against Lucien's chest. Long after they had fallen asleep, Lillian's eyes fluttered open and she realized she had heard the click of a door closing. She reached over for Lucien and her hand found emptiness. She called his name softly, several times, but there was no answer. He was gone.

She sat up abruptly and stared at the bedside clock, which read 3:14. She got up and dressed quickly, grabbed her purse, the remaining room key and ran out into the hall. At the elevator bank, she looked up at the indicator and saw the needle trembling at the lobby level. She pressed the button and the adjacent elevator responded in seconds. She exited into the empty and darkened lobby, running through the revolving door into the pre-dawn street. A doorman was leaning against the supporting strut of the awning and she rushed up to him, her fear and concern obvious.

"Excuse me, but did you see the man that just left the hotel?"

"Why, yes, ma'am, I did. Just now?"

"Yes, yes. Which way did he go"

The doorman pointed to the right, east, down the almost vacant street. Beyond four pools of light from the corner street lamps, she could make out the silhouette of a male figure, hurrying along in the darkness. It was he, she was sure of it.

Almost sprinting, she raced along the walkway, moving closer to buildings when she saw him pause as if to look around and then proceed. It did not occur to her to be afraid for herself and this was careless of her. Military and police patrols cruised the street and she managed to stand in shadows until they passed by. She spotted Lucien again, and this time he entered a door that turned out to be the entrance of a small dingy neighborhood bar, apparently one that was open all night. She carefully peered inside, looking underneath the posted "CLOSED" sign. She saw Lucien speaking to a man she recognized as the Reverend Earl Holloway and another man she didn't know. After watching the three talk earnestly for a few minutes, Lillian decided she'd better return to the hotel and pretend as if she had never left.

Lucien returned, undressed without a sound and slipped back into bed, careful not to awaken her. In moments, his regular breathing indicated he had fallen asleep. Lillian stared at the ceiling, watching the ominous patterns made by passing lights of vehicles on the street below and then the fingers of pale early sunlight inched in through the gaps in the curtains and another day was making a tenuous entrance.

"Ah, my love is awake!" Lucien kissed her gently and stroked her hair. "I'm afraid I have some bad news, my sweet. . ."

"What in the world?"

NEVER ON THESE SHORES

"Things are getting very well organized at the museum, as you know. . . and I'm afraid I have to leave the city tomorrow."

"Where are you going? Another museum?"

"You know I can't say."

"Oh, no! I don't think I can stand it here, without you, my darling man."

"Believe me, you have to. And we'll meet again, that you can count on, I promise."

"Yes, I know. You're an important man; that I can tell. And one that I love very, very much. I'm so proud of you, Lucien." She began to cry. "I'm going to miss you every single day." She wiped at her eyes with the back of one hand. "Don't forget me, Mister West. I want to make real love to you one of these days."

"You will, Lillian. You will." He kissed her several times, then patted her on the cheek. When she woke at 8 a.m., he was gone..

Dallas, Texas

The battle of Dallas, Texas had lasted less than four hours. By late afternoon, the city was in German control. The green recruits at Camp Mabry and, an hour north of the city, the slightly larger encampment next to Kileen were no match for Rommel's Afrika Korps. Both U.S. Army installations were severely understaffed, especially lacking combat-seasoned troops. Neither was a match for the highly mechanized German divisions. While much of the civilian population had fled north toward the advancing American lines in Oklahoma, many others remained at home, on their farms or in small towns, their roots and many of their sympathies with Germany. Though Rommel did not count on it, he knew that German immigrants had settled much of the central area of Texas. Though they now might be Americans, in some areas the German tongue was frequently heard on the streets and German customs were upheld faithfully.

Rommel's forces had found virtually no military resistance when they had reached Dallas on his timetable. The prosperous, but militarily neglected city, had put up even less resistance and capitulated in short order. The general estimated that fewer than a thousand American lives had been lost. His casualty count was less than two hundred men for two days fighting.

Rommel allowed himself the luxury of being driven through the prosperous town in an open jeep, its Nazi and General's standards flapping on their petards. He was especially drawn to what appeared to be the tallest building in the small city. He reached across to Himmel.

"Do we know what that building is?" he asked.

"Yes, Herr General. It is the headquarters of a large oil company. Dallas is very famous for its oil, of course. This is what makes it an important asset for the Fatherland. And for their banks. It does not produce much of its own, except cotton. It is the largest inland cotton center of this country. Only a few years ago, it was nothing but a stop in the road. Less than fifty years ago, this city only had about ten thousand people. Now, our intelligence estimates that there are more than three hundred thousand. It's all because of the oil, my general."

Rommel pursed his lips and shook his head. "Yes, yes, I see. An important asset, this oil."

A few blocks later, the jeep and its following entourage came to a smooth stop in the shade of the tall building as huddled men and women stood in silence along the sidewalks. It was not an Empire State Building by any means. But at nearly thirty stories, it was the tallest building in Texas. A large, red statue of a flying horse stood proudly on its pedestal before the entrance to the building. As he craned his head, Rommel could see two even larger versions of the flying horse mounted atop the building, rotating slowly in the bright Texas sky.

Suddenly a single voice started to sing the Star-Spangled Banner. The troops gathered around Rommel instantly became watchful, their eyes searching the crowd. They did not have to look far. A lone American corporal, standing at attention and saluting, sang in a high, reedy voice. Rommel watched in fascination.

Before Rommel realized it, Himmel, followed by half a dozen of his men, sprinted the short distance across Commerce Street, attacked the American soldier, tackling him to the ground and viciously choked him. Brushing himself off, Himmel calmly took his Luger from its holster, aimed and fired three shots into the prostrate man's face making three gaping wounds that splattered blood for a yard in every direction. He left the body lying grotesquely in the middle of the street as he returned to the vehicles.

Rommel stood silently, transfixed by Himmel's viciousness. Rommel was a soldier, but he had never believed in personal brutality. He respected any soldier, his own or the enemy's. If a single soldier stood in his way to an objective, he had no qualms about killing him in military action. But this American, in his opinion, had not been a threat. He shook his head as he heard Himmel call to several of his men.

"Drape the Führer's flag around that statue. Then, as quickly as possible, make certain that the statue, and those symbols on the building, are removed. It is our oil now. It belongs to the Fatherland!"

Rommel and Himmel climbed back into the jeep as four German soldiers unfurled the swastika flag's black, red and white. The men draped the large flag, almost hiding in its entirety the fiery red symbol of Magnolia Oil. The two military men sat in silence as the vista of the defeated town unveiled itself. Rommel sat erect, his eyes now shielded by his legendary Panzer goggles. Himmel, a small, paunchy man, had his hands folded in his lap as the dark visor of his SS cap shaded his eyes.

There had been little visible evidence of a battle in the central business section of Dallas. Here and there, German and a few Mexican troops rounded up local police and other officials, herding them into waiting trucks.

"Where are they taking them," Rommel asked Himmel, breaking the uncomfortable silence between the two men.

"To the Texas Centennial Stadium, Herr General. It will be suitable for our purposes," Himmel replied.

"And what purpose is that, Himmel?" Rommel's tone was matter-of-fact.

"We are combing the city for those who are undesirable, sir. Untermenschen, Jews, and so forth. And, for the time being, we are also rounding up those in authority, government officials, the police. Oh, yes, we will give the police and those officials who wish to cooperate the chance to join with us."

Rommel drew silent again. He had had a growing concern that the Führer's policy of rounding up and killing Jews would eventually be detrimental to the German Reich. Himmel suspected the general's feeling but knew that he was impotent against the man's popularity. More importantly, Rommel had the ear of Adolf Hitler himself.

As they moved to the outskirts of town, though, the evidence of war became more widespread. Those who had resisted the German onslaught had paid with their lives and now lay prone or prostrate in the makeshift battlements that had been hastily erected. A few men wore uniforms. More, it seemed, were dressed in civilian gear, carrying simple rifles used on other days for hunting deer or squirrel or dove.

The task of burying the German and Mexican dead fell to a special attachment of Mexican soldiers who had been assigned to accompany Rommel's campaign to the north of Texas. They attacked the hateful task with the same sullen demeanor they would have shown in any other job that a higher authority assigned to them. They certainly held no more love for his people than they did for the Americans. In their nature, they lacked the fervor that his enemies in the desert had often shown, Rommel thought. He frankly doubted the Mexicans' ability to fight, at least not on the front lines of any skirmish. They were useful in numbers, though. These people could best be assigned to do the tasks for which regular German soldiers were too valuable. Occasionally, he saw one of the Mexicans look up, resentment and weariness both etched into the heavy, brown faces. The Mexicans made a pretext of saluting Rommel as he passed, but he sensed something amiss in their sullenness. This was what had become of the great Aztec empire, he thought, a rabble of short, ignorant half-breeds whose only pleasure was in sleeping in the middle of the day. War and necessity had made strange bedfellows for the Aryan nation.

San Francisco, California

Later that afternoon, Jimmy Aoki and Lindy Montoya walked furtively down a quiet North Beach Street, it's gaily painted houses seeming as welcoming and cheerful as ever. On any other day, the sun dipping in and out of white, puffy clouds rolling by would signify a happy spring day in San Francisco. The pair knew, though, that this was no happy day. Where bombs had exploded, scattered bricks, glass and beams of wood were strewn everywhere. A cat prowled close to the walls, seeking the right place to sit in the sun. On hearing the pair, it stretched, extending its claws as it arched its back.

Jimmy was still dressed in the mismatched slacks and shirts Lindy had picked out earlier for him. On his feet he wore a set of black pumps. He held his hand over his eyes to block the sun. His hangover was still in full tilt and he wanted to stop and lay down right where he was. He knew, though, that a nap would not be in the offing until much later.

"They bombed the shit out of everything didn't they?"

Lindy just looked at him in mock disdain.

"Why'd they have to go and wreck everything? I mean, it's like stealing a car. Would you wreck it to pieces, then steal it? No."

"Jimmy, you jerk-off, this is not stealing a fucking car. This is war. This is what they do. They bomb the shit outta everything and scare the shit outta everybody."

"Well, it's stupid. Look at this mess." Jimmy petulantly screwed up his eyes while daintily stepping over some debris lying in the street. He was only halfway paying attention to Lindy's rambling.

"Oh, shit!" said Lindy, startling Jimmy into attention.

There on the sidewalk just in front of them lay a woman, moving and groaning on the sidewalk. Lindy raced over to the woman, laying her carefully on her side. When she turned her over, Lindy saw that it was an Asian woman, very pregnant and bleeding from the head. She seemed unconscious. Jimmy came over and looked down in repugnance.

"Oh shit is right."

Lindy darted him a hostile look. The woman was only semi-conscious, moaning slightly. Lindy looked as if expecting an answer from Jimmy.

"What are we gonna do? I...I don't know what I should do."

"You can't help her, Lindy. We gotta leave her. We got to get to Madison's."

"I can't leave her here. She'll die."

"We can't take her."

"Why? Why can't we take her?"

"We can't."

In his own fashion, Jimmy was just trying to be a realist. After all, this was war! With a big, huge "W." In that moment Lindy only saw him as selfish. The sound of a jeep engine and Japanese yelling down the street helped resolve the temporary impasse.

"Oh, shit! Lindy, honey, we gotta go. We gotta go now!" Jimmy yelled.

"We can't just leave her here!"

"Yes, Lindy, we can. Soldiers are coming. Jap soldiers."

For an instant, Lindy hesitated. Then she sprang up and tried to hide the woman with anything lying around she could find to camouflage her. She found some loose boards and newspapers and tried to cover her. It seemed a vain effort. Jimmy pulled on her arm.

"Lindy, c'mon! Move your ass!"

Jimmy was about to let go and run for it himself when Lindy gave up her attempt to cover the pregnant woman. The pair took off around the corner, Jimmy's big bulk ambling precariously on his pumps. He was not used to running anywhere, even under the best of circumstances. Dancing, perhaps, even strutting, but not running. Under stress, he was inclined to give up easily. He often imagined himself in a tight nineteenth century corset, out of wind and heading for the nearest "fainting sofa." Actually, he was a tough-as-bone drag queen who had so many street fights growing up, he had one partially cauliflowered ear.

"Those mother-fucking Jap bastards," he muttered.

As Jimmy and Lindy rounded the corner they just missed being seen by the Japanese patrol. The Japanese soldiers easily spotted the pregnant, injured woman, climbed out of their jeep and stood over her.

Lindy stopped the grateful Jimmy after they rounded the corner. The short sprint down the hill had winded him. She had to see for herself and she stealthily peeked around the corner. The Japanese spoke matter-of-factly as they gathered around the injured woman, devoid of compassion.

After a moment, one took his rifle and carefully sliced open her belly with his bayonet. He then prodded her womb and plucked the fetus out, skewered on the bayonet. He flung it across the street and the other soldiers laughed and muttered a guttural curse. Lindy gasped. Fortunately, the Japanese did not hear her as she sharply drew in her breath. Jimmy stared at the soldiers with a hatred he did not know he was capable of.

"She was a Jap or Chinese. I can't tell the difference. She doesn't matter. C'mon now. Let's go, let's go!" He tried to seem stoic and petulant at the same time, but it didn't work. They ran down the street and around the corner out of sight.

*

Jack Maxwell slowly drove his car up a winding road to Twin Peaks. Wisps of fog settled close to the ground. It was nearly nightfall and he decided to turn on his headlights. A moment later, he turned them off again to avoid detection. It made the steep ascent very tenuous. He struggled to see the road in front of him. After a few turns he veered toward the steep cliff on his right side, running his axle onto a small boulder that was placed at the side of the road to stop cars from going over the edge. It worked, but his car was stuck. He killed the engine, climbed out in disgust and frustration..

"Fuck it!" He kicked the car in anger, grabbed a duffel bag out of the back of the back seat and hoofed it the rest of the way up the hill.

*

Distraught and exhausted, Carmine Puzzo finally reached Madison's bar in North Beach. Despite his relative youth and muscular body, it had been an exhausting trip, walking from Castro and Market to Columbus Street, occasionally ducking into alleys to avoid the increasing Japanese street patrols and dodging around bomb debris. His face was sweaty and tear-stained. He went up to the door of Dodge's bar and reached into his pocket for a set of keys. Finding the right one, he unlocked the door and went inside. He locked the door behind him and shuffled around in the semi-darkness while his eyes adjusted.

Thin light from an outside streetlamp flickered occasionally. The irregular rhythm of the flickering indicated a potential power outage. He went behind the small stage where jazz and drag shows had played in happier days and made his way to a store room where boxes of liquor were stacked up.

"Dodge? Anybody here?" he yelled into the darkness.

Receiving no response, Carmine tore open a box of vodka and pulled out a bottle. He hastily unscrewed the top and guzzled down a few hits straight. The impact of the liquor caused him to wince, lose his breath and shake his head. He leaned back on a makeshift seat of boxes and occasionally threw back a swig. The physical and emotional trauma of the day left him drained and the booze did not have the immediate desired effect.

As his eyes became accustomed to the dimness of the storeroom, Carmine noticed some white bar aprons hanging on a hook to one side. An idea sprang into his mind. He removed an apron and dipped the apron string into the bottle of vodka then pulled it out. He pulled a Zippo lighter from his pocket and lit it under the string as he held it up. It ignited quickly with a slimy blue flame. For the first time, Carmine smiled grimly. He would get those Jap bastards, one way or another.

What he hadn't seen, was the small trap door in the floor. It looked like the entrance to a storm cellar. Beneath its dusty, scuffed wood and rusted hinges lay two hundred pounds of construction grade dynamite.

*

Waiting until early nightfall before making his way to the rendezvous with Carlton on Treasure Island, Dodge rowed slow-

ly and steadily in a small dinghy across the short expanse he had
to traverse to reach the man-made island which had been built
for the 1939 World's Fair. His dark, bushy hair and beard were
soaked both with perspiration from the effort and from the spray
which whipped across the Bay with increasing intensity. With a
final pull of the oars, he reached the shoreline. He secured the
boat and tramped up the steep embankment. Dodge followed a
stone path leading up the hill to a cave.

The small cave was pitch black inside and virtually invisible,
its entrance covered with vines. Making sure that he was secure-
ly inside, Dodge took out a butane lighter and lit it.

"Carlton?" he whispered loudly into the gloom, holding the
lighter up like a torch.

A bright beam from a flashlight shone right into Dodge's
face, blinding him momentarily. The man holding the light
shined it momentarily on himself. It was Dodge's friend, Carlton
Savory. He stepped out of the shadows training the light back on
Dodge. In the instant that the flashlight had revealed Savory,
Dodge had seen his friend holding a gadget with wiring and batteries and a small clock attached to it.

"Dammit! Jerk. What'd you do that for?" Dodge exploded.
The strain and tension were getting even to his normally stead-
fast demeanor.

"Oh, nice to see you, too. Lucky for you I didn't get tortured
by the Japs; I would've told them everything," Carlton replied,
placing the lit flashlight on an outcropping of rock so that both
men could see each other in the dim light among the shadows.
The walls of the small cave were lined with shelves containing
various sorts of military hardware, equipment and provisions.

"Been busy I see," Dodge pointed to the device in Carlton's
hand.

"Well, I had to do something to pass the time. By the way, I thought you said an hour?"

Nearly five hours had elapsed since Dodge had made the phone call to Berkeley. "There's a war going on, in case you hadn't noticed? How'd you get here so fast?"

Carlton replied nonchalantly, "I'm Superman, remember?"

"Super Queen, maybe. Seriously." Dodge's tone showed his increasing impatience.

"I drove."

"You what?" the Irishman said incredulously.

Carlton continued his banter. "Well, I rode actually. Caught a ride on the back of some truck headed this way from Berkeley. Dropped off at Yerba Buena. Wouldn't you know, a traffic jam into the city! Really, they've got to do something about that bridge!"

"Dammit, Carlton, could you be any more oblivious?"

"I'm not oblivious. Just struck by the insanity of it all."

In the dim light, Dodge began to pull artillery, ammo and other supplies off the shelves and load them into empty duffel bags stacked neatly to one side of the room. Dodge was rather exhausted and miffed by his friend's cavalier attitude.

Carlton continued, indifferent to his friend's discomfort. "I mean here I am, an absolute electrical genius, of significant value, I think, to the war effort and whadaya know, 4-F'd for being a fag. Ironic, don't you think?"

"Yeah, you're amazing…and quite queer, dearie."

The tall, lanky almost white-blond man railed on.

"So, our right-thinking government ships all our young, able-bodied, red-blooded American boys to fronts all over the world and here we are, duty bound by default to protect the homeland."

"Look, you can run for Congress some day. Are you gonna help or what? We haven't got all night!" Dodge was totally exasperated now. He had heard enough of Carlton Savory III's tirades too often. Even though he might agree with the man's general philosophy, he had more important goals to accomplish than to argue about the government's position against homosexuals.

Carlton, noticing his friend's edgy voice but ignoring it, quipped and made a suggestive gesture with his pants. "Easy tiger. You'll snap a garter."

Dodge had had enough. Quickly, he pushed Carlton up against a shelf hard enough to make the equipment behind him rattle. His face was intimately close to Carlton. Dodge's breathing was labored and his speech shaky. Nonetheless, the Irish temper so few of Dodge's friends ever saw in the bar was reflected in his bright, blue, eyes.

"Look, Carlton. It's been kind of a long day, so if you don't mind saving your Oscar acceptance speech 'til later, I'd appreciate it."

Carlton gently reached up and took Dodge's hands away from their firm grasp on his coat lapels.

"Relax, relax. Point taken. I'm sorry." The effete younger man knew when to back off, even though he might not always be aware of his friend's subtleties.

Dodge let the younger, taller man go and looked down, still angry but calming.

"Let's just get this stuff and get the hell outta here, 'kay?"

Carlton straightened out his jacket in an insouciant gesture as if he had just been a prince assaulted by a peasant. He showed no anger. Instead, he gave Dodge a lusty glance.

"Yes, sir," Carlton said, almost mockingly.

Dodge heaved the first heavily loaded duffel bag over his shoulder and headed for the entrance to the cave. From the dark, he looked back at Carlton in the dim light with a smirk. In a second, Carlton loaded a bag over his well-developed shoulders and followed, grabbing the torch.

"That's more like it," said Dodge under his breath.

*

Jack Maxwell finally finished climbing the rest of the way up Twin Peaks. He was winded as he unlocked the door to a barely visible shack behind some shrubs at the base of a radio tower. He looked around to make sure no one else was in sight and took an appreciative look at the cityscape unfolding beneath him. The city he knew and loved so much was less lit-up with lights than usual. Some fires still burned in pockets here and there and the stench of acrid smoke hung invisibly in the air. What sounded like distant 4th of July fireworks sporadically echoed across the bay and he imagined correctly that the Japanese were going house to house rounding up anyone they thought capable of resisting and peremptorily executing them. His mouth clenched in anger as he entered the shack.

The small wooden plank building was a clandestine cache of military supplies. He pulled rations, guns and ammunition off the shelves, stuffing them into empty duffels. As he passed one shelf, Jack noticed several walkie-talkies. He took one in his hand and turned it on. The instrument emitted only static, but the batteries worked. He pushed the talk button and spoke softly.

"Lauren Bacall to Humphrey Bogart. Lauren Bacall to Humphrey Bogart. Do you read?"

Jack listened to the static but there was no reply.

He repeated the message. "Lauren Bacall to Humphrey Bogart. Bogie, come back."

Again, he listened for a response. There was a short interruption in the static and a click. Suddenly, a voice came through the scratchy instrument, "Yeah, I can read, but I prefer the movies."

"Bogie?"

"Hump's on the horn. Is that you, girlfriend?" It was Walt Chambers.

Jack smiled in amusement. He pushed to talk again.

"None other, sweetcakes. Listen, you busy tonight?"

"I always got time for my wild Irish rose." The carefully rehearsed code worked.

"O.K., O.K.. Listen. Jack's here with his pail of water but fell down and broke his crown.

"Ohhhhh...kay."

"Look, just get...here. You know where. Here, right?" Jack's voice was a little anxious.

"That'd be Toilet Paper Junction, right?"

Jack was relieved again. "Right!"

"Be there in two shakes," Walt came back.

"Be careful."

"Now what fun would that be?"

Only a few short minutes later, Jack, loaded with two duffel bags slung over his shoulder and almost dragging a third, headed back down the steep road. Upon reaching his disabled car, he stood by the old jalopy pensively. He scratched his head, wondering how he and Walt would dislodge the vehicle from the boulder. He hoped that the frame had not been bent. As he scrutinized carefully the only road coming up on this side of Twin Peaks, he saw a single headlight winding up the road. The sound of a motorcycle engine revving as it took the steep corners seemed reassuring to Jack.

As the noisy motorcycle engine preceded its appearance around the last curve, Jack's nerves were frayed. In seconds, Walt Chambers rode up on his motorcycle with a sidecar. He wore goggles and a flamboyant white scarf slung twice around his neck. Between the headlight and noisy engine, Jack was practically beside himself with anxiety.

"For Christ's sake, Walt!" he yelled, certain that every Japanese in San Francisco had heard and seen the noisy contraption.

"Nice evening for a ride." Walt retorted.

"Shit, could you, perhaps, be any more obvious?"

"All the Japs are downtown. We're way up here. Nothing to fear." Chambers, in his early thirties, enjoyed acting the part of his favorite film heroes, especially flyers. Even in his brown leather motorcycle jacket, he looked every inch the aristocrat fly-boy. He turned off the noisy engine and doused the headlight.

"Nothing to fear? They killed the mayor y'know!"

Walt grimaced. "No shit. Damn. I kinda liked him. Radio went out. Haven't heard any news since this morning except what people told me."

Jack was indignant. "They fucking decapitated him. Right on the Golden goddamned Gate."

Walt was shamed briefly into respectful silence. Then, climbing off the motorcycle, he turned his attention to Jack's car. He bent down, shone a small flashlight under the chassis and whistled softly.

"Well, what do we have here?"

"I was driving without headlights."

"Ah! Good detection avoidance strategy."

"I have a rope," Jack offered, trying to be helpful.

"What? No dinner and a movie first?"

"Come on. Would you shut up and give me a hand?"

Jack opened the back of his car's trunk and extricated a length of tangled rope. He took the opportunity to toss the three duffle bags into the trunk. With a bang, he shut it. He moved to the front of the vehicle, hunched on the ground near the front wheel that was lodged on the boulder and laboriously tied the rope under the rear axle.

"O.K., let's see if we can move it now."

Walt started up his motorcycle again and pulled it into position behind the car. Jack tied the loose end of the rope to the cycle's frame.

Jack yelled, "Try it."

Walt gunned his engine in reverse. The machine spun gravel and dirt, but the car failed to budge. He paused for a second and looked at Jack overseeing the progress. As the bike's engine idled, Jack yelled "Could you not rev that thing so fuckin' loud?"

Unperturbed, Walt good-naturedly shot back. "Right. Maybe we'll just push it off the rock."

Walt revved the cycle up again and, with the engine straining hard, the car finally began to move and roll back. Jack quickly hopped in on the driver's side while the car nearly rolled into Walt. Jack popped in the clutch, started the car and put it into gear. He leaned out of the door, shouting back to Walt.

"Follow me!" he yelled.

The two vehicles headed the half-mile up the hill and park. Walt turned off his loud motorcycle engine at the same time that Jack shut down the jalopy. They walked through the darkness in silence to the shack. As they approached the door, Walt, virtually whispering, said, "So, this is your place. A little small, a tad out of the way but...nice view. A few geraniums might help and maybe...or is it gerania?"

"How 'bout shuttin' the fuck up, O.K.?"

Walt surveyed the cityscape appreciatively. Jack unlocked, opened the door and went in. Walt followed. "I forgot a house-warming present. Sorry," he muttered under his breath."

Jack tossed a duffel bag into his arms.

"Guess that means breakfast is out," Walt cooed, pretending to be sulking,

"C'mon, we're already late getting back to Madison's. Gotta get a move on."

Jack turned back around to heave up another duffel and slung it over his own shoulder.

"I just love it when you get butch like this!"

"Honey, I am butch like this. You just never took notice."

Jack turned around to face Walt, face to face. Walt dropped the duffel bag he had been carrying and clutched Jack's biceps and smiled. Unexpectedly, he started to croon, weaving in a sultry Lauren Bacall impersonation.

"Isn't it Romantic? Music in the night, a dream that can be heard."

Jack had to admit that Walt had a capable singing voice. He managed a gratuitous smile, but wanted to keep his mind focused on the task at hand. He admonished Jack,

"C'mon Romeo, keep it moving. Pick up the bag and let's get the car loaded."

"What? I rescue you like a damsel in distress and I don't even get a thank you?" Walt repeated his hurt, sulky demeanor.

"You never quit do you?"

Walt laughed. "You've never indicated that you want me to

quit".

Increasingly annoyed, Jack snapped a little too harshly, "Walt, Japanese troops have taken over my city. Your city! This morning I saw a guy I've worked with for two years get executed. For no reason. For no good reason whatsoever!"

Walt planted a long, passionate kiss on Jack's lips. Jack almost responded, but then broke it off.

"Walt, I'm only going to mention this once so listen carefully."

"What?"

"We are at war. You need to get a grip on all this or you're never gonna get out of it alive. And I, for one, want you alive. Clear?"

Walt was speechless. Jack pulled Walt closer to him and gave him another passionate kiss. After a brief moment, Jack again broke away.

"There. You happy?"

"For now."

Walt picked up his duffel bag and headed out of the shack. Jack followed him, another duffel bag over his shoulders.

"Good kisser," Walt allowed.

"Yeah, you too," Jack Maxwell responded, wishing the time and place were entirely different.

Los Alamos, New Mexico

The short walk to the Fuller Lodge from his quarters at the end of the row of short, squat military barracks was always exhilarating for J. Robert Oppenheimer. Oppie, as his friends called him in a mixture of familiarity, love and respect, reveled in the clean crispness of the high desert of New Mexico. The sky that afternoon was the thin blue of the desert, broken only by gossamer streaks of white clouds that seemed to be frozen in place. He ordinarily relished the tall, stately mountains that ringed the military compound in the distance and would sometimes simply stop and absorb the clarity of the arid landscape. But today was different. A dark pall hovered over everything; at times he felt he could barely breathe. In a strange way, despite the importance of his job, of the Atomic Bomb, and of the intense, stifling secrecy under which he and his colleagues had to work, he knew that fate or God had chosen him to be in this place at this time. At night, as sleep eluded him, he would ponder the terrible paradox: to save humanity he must create a weapon that could annihilate it.

In a few, short steps, Oppenheimer crossed the quad of the former boys' school and ambled up the steps to the lodge. Before it became a government lab, this was a place where young men were taught to study and respect nature. Ironic, he thought as he opened the massive front door, that young boys had come to this very place for their health, for an education designed to make men in the great outdoors, much in the tradition of Theodore Roosevelt. Once the former President's Rough Riders had been instrumental in founding this serene spot in a world seemingly gone mad with the ambitions of a few men. Now, so many of these young men were probably on their way to death on alien soil. So many would have paid the ultimate price already.

He quietly entered the main library. A dozen or so of his colleagues were already assembled, debating vociferously among each other. At his entrance, the room immediately quieted.

"Thank God you're here, Oppie. Have you heard the news? Dallas surrendered, almost without a shot being fired. They now control east and central Texas."

Oppenheimer faced the group, taking a long drag on one of the elegant cigarettes that had become his trademark. He knew every one of these men either as friends or colleagues or both. Fermi, Teller, Seaborg, von Neumann, they were all here. They were incredibly young to carry such a heavy burden. He was thirty-eight. Glenn was only thirty. The illustrious Italian, Enrico Fermi, was only a few years older than he. The oldest was Issac Rabi, at forty-four. They had come from across the country and from the elite of American universities to this mountainous retreat. He had come from the University of California at Berkeley; Fermi had left his position at Columbia to move to the University of Chicago. Princeton was represented; so was MIT.

"No, gentlemen, I hadn't turned on the radio. What does The Hill hear from Washington?"

"The Hill" was a euphemism for their working, secure retreat in New Mexico's mountains, only about twenty-five miles from Santa Fe. More formally, they were known as "Project Y." Only among themselves could they use the term, "Los Alamos," which meant "cottonwoods" in Spanish, and for which the boys' school had been named.

"Nothing. No one will tell anything without authorization from someone."

"If Germany is going to win this war, we should stop the project immediately," demanded Levy Fleischman. Levy, like many of his colleagues, had fled Europe when it had become clear what Hitler's intentions were. He was only twenty-nine. Like the others, he had top degrees and honors in some aspect of the work that had brought them all together. They had been selected to create the ultimate weapon, the atom bomb.

"Agreed. But not until ..." Oppenheimer's words were uncharacteristically cut short by Edward Teller.

"Of course, we know that we are in a race with Hitler. He will stop at nothing until he owns the bomb. We have known this since 1938. The Axis invasion was unforeseen. Now they are at the doors. It is better that Hitler works on his own bomb. We should not give it to him. I agree with young Levy – let us destroy our research, our papers. Can you imagine what Hitler would do with a weapon of this magnitude?" Teller's stentorian tones rang throughout the room, his heavy Hungarian accent unmistakable. In lighter moments, Teller and some of his Hungarian countrymen were apt to get together, sing a few songs, and enjoy their spicy, native cooking.

"It'll take years for Hitler's intelligence to figure out Teller's handwriting, so we're safe," joked Dick Feyman, the baby in the group at only twenty-four. He was born and bred in Queens, and, like the majority of the assembled men, he was Jewish. Only his brains had allowed him to study and succeed at MIT and Princeton. Only his brilliance at mathematical equations gave him the right to sit with the intellectual and scientific elite.

Oppie, who had listened to the diverse opinions, took center stage again, puffing on a freshly lit cigarette. He exuded an air of quiet strength among his colleagues, as he did in the laboratories or in the machine shops. His patrician air held their attention. Oppenheimer was born to wealth and he had the demeanor and intelligence to go along with it.

"Listen, until we get orders from Washington, we'll do nothing. I agree that we should do everything to prevent Herr Hitler and his minions from gaining access to our secrets. But, let me assure you, they – or their Japanese counterparts in San Francisco – don't know we are even here. We are probably the best-kept secret in the world. As a precaution, I do suggest, though, that we send our wives to safety. Tonight."

The main door to the library had silently opened. General Harcourt Groves, a graying, balding middle-aged man who had been appointed directly by the President to oversee the military and budgetary process of Project Y, came forward and stood in the midst of the scientists. The four stars on his collars reflected the light from the chandelier that had been lit as the sun set over the crest of the Jemez mountains. He was well over six feet tall, his shoulders slightly hunched as he crossed his arms over his chest.

"Gentlemen, I share your concerns. The developments of the past few weeks on the west coast, and now next door in Texas, could not help but make us all concerned. I don't want to minimize the threat General Rommel and General Yashita pose to this project.

"Yet, I have to reiterate that Project Y is the safest and most secure location on the face of the earth. We have taken every precaution to keep it that way. I know that some of you have been very uncomfortable with only going to Santa Fe once a month, and then only by yourselves, rather than in a group. I know some of you have had to get used to living at this altitude. And I know that it has not been easy on your wives, living in the makeshift conditions of military housing, with the muddy streets, and the lack of conveniences."

"Not to mention hiding behind a post office box where we cannot receive our mail directly." Levy Fleischman was petulant, his hands stuck deep in the pockets of his brown suit, the rimless glasses always sliding down his nose. He did not like military men, German or otherwise. He especially did not like this uneducated military man in front of him who commanded so much of their lives.

Harcourt Groves smiled and continued. "Yes, the post office box, too, helps assure your safety." The box at which all mail for the project – some two thousand men strong at this point – was received had become a local joke in Santa Fe. When the project was not referred to as "The Hill" it was simply called "Box 1663."

"Yes. Yes, we know this is for our safety," Fleischman interjected. "So is the fact that half the time when we do get leave to go to town the road is washed out. Fermi can't get his vermicelli and tomatoes and that is the greatest tragedy of all."

The group as a whole laughed briefly. Fermi was known to love his food, and had frequently sneaked into one of the mess kitchens on the odd day to cook up a batch by himself. His own quarters were too cramped to do his cooking justice.

"Exactly the point, gentlemen. You know that we can only get in or out of the project on the narrow road over Otowi Bridge across the Rio Grande. Or we have to take the longer way 'round. Can you imagine trying to get German army tanks and troops across that road? The bridge has a maximum capacity of ten tons, and the timber roadway is only about sixteen feet wide. They would have to parachute into the compound to capture you. Or your strategic materials. This is why we chose the place. Or, rather, why Doctor Oppenheimer chose it."

The two roads into the compound were gravel, with sharp right and left turns that made it difficult for trucks or other vehicles to gather any speed. In some areas, there were precipitous cliffs on one side or another as the road traversed the many arroyos that had been carved out by water over the eons. The

Rio Grande River itself was hundreds of feet below and the small cantilever bridge that connected the two sides of the road looked rickety enough to collapse any second.

"Sure, and so he can be close to his own ranch. Or to his wife, whenever she chooses to come up here. She's too good to be with the rest of us," Fleischmann could not help but add the insulting snippet. He slid his glasses back up on the bridge of his nose. It was widely rumored that Oppie with a one-year old son, was having an affair inside the project compound with a secretary whenever his wife and child took off to California. There was, of course, no proof. No matter how highly educated the men were, rumors abounded like wildfire.

"Which brings me to a point, gentlemen. Doctor Oppenheimer has already suggested this possibility. We believe it is in your best interests to send your wives and children up north. We have a location ready. This is only a precaution, you understand, but a necessary one if the absolute worst were to happen. We would like to have everyone at the Lamy junction by nineteen hundred hours, to catch the connection to Denver. That means we will leave here at seventeen-thirty sharp to take us to Santa Fe. We will have the cars waiting for your families."

"But I thought you were asking," said Fleischman.

"We assumed the answer would be in the affirmative, doctor."

There was a nervous shuffling of feet and clearing of throats. A few of the men got up from their armchairs or cushioned couches and ambled about.

"General, let me say just a few more words," Oppie said.

The general nodded. "Of course."

Oppenheimer raised his thin frame from the chair into which he had sunk. He quickly extinguished the omnipresent cigarette dangling from his mouth.

"Gentlemen, we knew that when we all assembled here in this small corner of God's world that our combined intellects would take us to areas man has never before explored. We do this to preserve our civilization as we know it, and to shape it as it may yet become, for our children and theirs. To save it from a world gone mad. Most of you know that I love to read, and to read widely. As we face the coming days of struggles, I leave with you some thoughts from the Indian classics, the Bagadavita, in which Lord Krishna advises on the field of battle, 'Not fare well, but fare forward, voyagers.' So must we 'fare forward' no matter our individual futures, my friends."

The group was hushed by Oppenheimer's eloquence and slowly dispersed, each with his own thoughts. Levy Fleischman walked pensively across the quad to his quarters and to his young attractive wife. His pockets were thrust deep in his coat pockets as the thin lights from the rickety street lamps cast their growing shadows among the old trees. It was twilight in the mountain valley.

Lost in thought, Fleischman did not notice Aaron Daniels' footsteps until the slight, earnest young man had caught up with him.

"Levy, have a second?"

Fleischman stopped, noticing briefly the military police guard that eyed them.

"Sure, Aaron. What's up?"

The sound of a few planes overhead made them both search the skies warily.

"Germans?" Aaron inquired hesitatingly.

"Doubt it. Probably our boys." As reassuring as Fleischman tried to sound to his colleague, he could no more identify the engine sound of one plane than he could tell one type of cactus from another.

"Well, not much we can do about it. Listen, Levy, I'm worried about Lisa. In her last letter, which I only received this morning, she told me she was taking the train from New Jersey to come see me. That letter was posted six days ago. What with the censors and all, I'm afraid she'll arrive tonight."

Fleischmann furled his brow and chewed on his upper lip.

"Hmm, can't make any calls out, even to check the hotels in Santa Fe. Chances are they would have cancelled the trains from Chicago when Texas fell."

"Maybe. Don't know. Don't even know whether she left the same day she sent the letter." Daniels was truly distraught.

"Well, if she'd arrived a day or two ago, you would have known. Someone would have called you. They didn't cut the phones until yesterday."

The MP, who had moved quietly and unobtrusively closer, now came up to the two scientists.

"Gentlemen, may I see your identification," he said pleasantly but firmly.

Both men quickly yanked their identification tags from around their necks and showed them to the MP.

The man eyed the tags and nodded.

"Sorry. Just procedure. Sure you understand. Listen, I could not help but overhear you. Maybe I can help."

Aaron Daniels was all ears, staring intently and nodding at the young military policeman.

"If you want to find out whether your wife is in Santa Fe, I think I know someone who can find out for you. A bunch of us are going to town on passes in a half or so with some of the wives. I'll be happy to check for you."

NEVER ON THESE SHORES

Aaron was overjoyed, shaking the embarrassed solder's hand, almost hugging him. "My name is Dr. Aaron Daniels, My wife's name is Lisa. Here, here is a picture of her."

He pulled out his wallet and extricated a worn picture of a young, dark-haired and dark-eyed woman.

"Thanks, I'll make sure it gets back to you. Where did she come from, New York?" The MP scribbled a few notes into a small notebook.

"Yes. She would have left no more than six days ago, according to the postmark on her letter."

"O.K., my name's Garret. Garret Beecher. I'll let you know as soon as I know. Of course, if she's in town, she'll have to join the others on the train out. Understand?"

"Yes, sir. Thank you again." Aaron pumped the MP's hand excitedly.

As Garret left, Aaron and Levy marched together to their respective destinations on Bathtub Row, the group of apartments that housed the scientists. As Aaron prepared to enter his small flat, Levy slapped him on the shoulder.

"So, not to worry, young Aaron. The prying eyes of Uncle Sam will find your Lisa for you. Now, I've got to face the Queen of Sheba when I tell her she's going to have to pack and leave. Such a blessing!"

*

At precisely 19:30, the cavalcade of a dozen brown Chevrolets, each with a military driver and an armed guard, left the compound by the narrow, twisting and turning gravel road that would take them to Santa Fe to meet the feeder train to Lamy Junction. The trans-continental railroads did not actually come into Santa Fe. One had to take a three-car feeder from the city to Lamy, a junction less than a half hour south.

Half an hour later, the entourage stopped at the small railway terminal in Santa Fe, unloading their female cargo. The soldiers, including Garret, stood at attention as the women climbed from the cars and entered the station. They followed them and again stood at attention at the platform as the group boarded. Within a few minutes, the engineer blew his whistle. The locomotive ejected a massive burst of steam, and the three-car train was on its way.

Garret approached his superior, a beefy, red-faced Irish master sergeant who had driven the first car in the caravan.

"Sarge, we have some time to pick up a few things?"

The Irishman looked at Garret disdainfully.

"Not too many shops open at this hour," he said sullenly.

"I've got a friend who stays open late," Garret retorted, not impolite, but firm.

"We're pulling out at 20:30. Not a minute later."

"Yes, sergeant."

Garret threw the sergeant a quick salute and sped in the direction of a small tourist shop, only seconds away from the railroad station across the square. He entered the small storefront, a tinkling of bells announcing his arrival. Garret felt awkward with his heavy M-1 rifle slung over his shoulder. He briefly looked at the collection of turquoise beads and bracelets and necklaces.

"Hey, Garret! Want some joe?"

A young American Indian boy of about fourteen looked at Garret inquisitively across the back counter, holding a steaming cup of coffee. His was dressed in dungarees and a blue shirt with embroidered sun and stars and moon covering his shoulders. His jet black hair was tied back from his face with a broad ribbon of light brown leather.

"Hey, Whispering Eagle. Sure." Garret moved toward the back of the store and accepted the hot cup of coffee from the young boy.

""What's with the bean shooter," the boy asked, eyeing the gun across Garret's shoulder.

"Oh, I'm on duty. Just have a few minutes. Listen, can you find out if a lady's come to town from back east, say, in the last two or three days?" Garret pulled out Lisa Daniels' picture. The boy inspected it appreciatively.

"Hey, she's a Jane dame! Sure, I'll find out. Got a butt?"

Garret searched his uniform trousers and came up with a pack of Camels.

"You're too young to smoke, kid," he admonished the boy as he handed him a cigarette. Instantly, Whispering Eagle lit up, deeply inhaling the smoke.

"Sure. The kitten in dutch?"

Garret always marveled at the kid's use of the latest slang. He must spend half his time and all of his meager earnings at the local picture show, he mused. He sipped cautiously at the cup.

"No, not at all. Husband thinks he missed her train and you know us. Can't get a word in or out unless it's official. Here, take the picture. There's a code word on the back. You can use it if you need to come find me. Or, if you get into trouble here. Someone will get word to me."

"Hey, duck soup! I find her, I'll let you know"

The entrance of a bent, older man followed a rustling of the beaded curtain that separated the store from a back room. A colorful serape covered his thin shoulders; a cigarette dangled precariously from his lips.

"Ah, Garret, he who drinks from my spring, I hope it is not bad new that brings you to us?"

Garret liked the old man. During his few off-duty hours when he was permitted to be in town, he would spend them listening to the man's tales. He knew that many of them were colorful fabrications. But true or not, the stories never ceased to fascinate him. At the same time, he knew that the man's intelligence information was better than his sergeant's.

"No, Chief Soaring Eagles, no bad news. Nothing, anyway, that the radio has not already reported. I just asked Whispering Eagle to find one of our men's wives."

"And, grandfather, she's a truly hot tomato!"

The old man looked at his grandson and shook his head.

"He reads well, but he reads the wrong things. His world consists of gangsters and detectives. His language, too. Garret, many trains filled with munitions have come from the north. Other trains from the south bring troops. And there are many more airplanes in the skies."

Garret digested the information though he, too, was in the dark as to the specifics. If troops were coming from Ft. Bliss, he thought, Santa Fe was being reinforced. That meant only one thing – Los Alamos was being reinforced. That, in turn, meant that the project was in danger of being attacked by the Germans. That's why the women had to leave, he reasoned.

"Thanks, Chief. I have to get back. Orders. See you soon, kid." He patted the young boy on the head and turned to leave.

"Hey, Garret, another butt?"

Garret shook his head, grinned, and tossed the nearly full pack of Camels at the boy.

"Thanks!"

Garret set the half-full cup of strong, black coffee on the

counter, adjusted his rifle and, waving at the pair of Indians, left the store. Checking his watch, he was relieved to find that he still had plenty of time before the master sergeant would throw one of his explosive temper tantrums. The dry air and the distinctive incense-like smell of the desert brought him back home to Texas, to his mother and to his little sister, Hannah-Lee. And then he thought of his brother, Travis, and the argument. Nothing he could do about that now. At least they were safe in that one-horse town, out of the way of anything important. He wished he could phone them, just a few words. He knew when this fracas was over he'd go home like it had all been a bad dream.

San Francisco, California

The five story Belmonte Hotel at the corner of Mission and Ninth Street, just south of Market Street, was a classic "Style Moderne" building. The hotel had been built by an eccentric young millionaire who had spared no expense in its construction and furnishings. The young man was enamored of the modernistic building style that had been the rage for nearly two decades. Its faux-Egyptian exterior was washed in a gold hue, accented with black. The large windows were framed in chrome. A monstrous set of stylized gargoyles stood watching from each side of the huge portal where, in more prosperous days, the nouveau-riche youths of some of San Francisco's finest families would gather for their all-night parties. The Belmonte had become a welcome new watering hole after its completion in early 1930 and, despite its location, quickly became one of the city's most notorious, but elegant speakeasies. By the time of Prohibition's repeal, however, the hotel had quickly declined in popularity.

On the day of San Francisco's surrender, the Belmonte had been taken over by Japanese occupation troops. They herded the women they had taken captive during the day into the hotel, unloading them from jeeps or trucks. Most of them had been working at jobs in the warehouse district. The Japanese systematically had gone through each street just below Mission, executed at least one person in charge of the warehouse or retail operation, and bundled away young women whom the soldiers fancied. It was part of their strategy to clear the area south of Market Street and cordon it off with barbed wire. This would hamper the easy movement of the resistance. The prize to be garnered by the occupation of the area would be stockpiled food, machinery, and a few manufacturing operations the Japanese could use after their takeover was complete. The women were just a bonus.

Among the captives milling in the hotel's grand lobby were Angie Puzzo, Harriet Millgate, and their coworkers from the Safeway. Harriet clung to Angie in sheer desperation as the Japanese roughly shepherded the quartet into one of the three small elevators. A solder pushed a button to the fifth floor, and the metal cage slowly ascended.

The hallway was filled with women, most of them in their twenties. As the soldiers shoved Angie and the others toward the end of the hall, Harriet, separated from the group by her captors, ran into the arms of another woman. The contact at first startled her. But in an instant she felt safe, hugging, sobbing and quivering in the arms of the stranger. Angie was prodded further down the hall. She tried to look back at Harriet, but, with the throng of people between them, she could no longer see her friend.

Unlike Harriet, whose southern belle innocence had been legendary in their neighborhood, Angie knew what fate awaited them all. Despite the nausea she felt at the very thought, she held herself with decorum, bowing and avoiding eye contact with the Japanese. She quietly and unobtrusively took every slim opportunity to assess her surroundings, to know where she was, and how she might get out. She had watched her older brother many times on the streets and learned how he handled himself.

At the end of the hall, in the very last room on the right hand side of the corridor, her Japanese captor opened the door and pointed to an unlit room. The man flipped a switch, and gave Angie a final push into the room that sent her sprawling onto the bed. The Japanese man slammed the door. Angie ran to the door and opened it, only to see a rifle barrel sticking in her face. She slowly closed the door again and wandered back into the room, looking at the neatly made bed, not daring to even sit on it. She paced to and fro, looked at the window, and went over to try to open it. It was nailed tightly shut. She peered out the fifth floor window into the darkness, lit only by the garish neon light of the hotel's sign. She saw barbed wire strung along the fire escape. As she pondered her situation, a series of a woman's panicked screams somewhere down the hall pierced the silence.

In the end room, Harriet had been stripped and shoved onto the bed, her cheek pressed into a pillow. She stared vacantly out the window, avoiding looking at the Japanese officer who was raping her. She was too emotionally and physically exhausted to resist. The man straddling her and grunting in time with her movements was no longer a part of reality to her. Her mind was back home. "Oh, Daddy, I'm so sorry! This is not the way I thought it would be. Please, forgive me," she thought over and over again.

*

Carmine had dozed off, quietly inebriated by the vodka and by the tension of the day, in the storeroom of Dodge's bar. Through the haze of alcohol, he heard a quiet but incessant tapping. It stopped momentarily and then started again. He groggily opened his eyes, feeling pain shoot through his left shoulder as he moved gingerly. He stood up from the makeshift seat constructed of liquor crates on which he had fallen asleep. Listening more intently, he realized that someone was at the front door knocking. He staggered to his feet and walked to the front of the bar unsteadily. He reached the front door, and whispered, "We're closed for remodeling."

Only seconds later, he heard a familiar voice.

"It's Lindy. Let us in!"

Instantly Carmine was alert.

"Where's your key? You're supposed to have a key."

"Carmine? Is that you? Let us in. Dodge never gave me a key. He gave it to Jimmy and he doesn't have it."

There was a small commotion outside as Jimmy Aoki looked through his key ring for the key. He cursed silently as he failed to find it.

"I swear to God I had it," he said flatly, but loudly enough for Carmine to hear him through the shut door.

"Japs don't believe in God, they're Buddhists or some shit like that."

Jimmy retorted sullenly and protested, "I'm Catholic."

"Right! Jimmy, you are so full of it! You never went to church a day in your life," Carmine shot back.

"That may be true but I was still baptized which means...Ah! I found it".

Jimmy pulled a chain from around his neck at the end of which was the key. Without removing it from his neck, he turned the key in the lock and the door opened. Carmine pulled it open wide enough for his head to poke through.

"What's the password?" Carmine demanded.

Lindy, wanting to get off the quiet street, snapped angrily, "Great! Tweedledee and Tweedledum...and, uh, tweedle fuck you."

She pushed the door open, pushed past Carmine, grabbing Jimmy and pulling him into the interior of the bar all in one movement.

"You the only one here so far? What about Dodge?" she asked.

"No word," Carmine replied.

"Did you try him on the radio?"

"Oh yeah, the radio," Carmine said, still feeling boozy.

Lindy instantly understood Carmine's behavior.

"Dammit, Mary! What good are you? You're drunk. You're first to report in. Don't you even remember what you're supposed to do?"

"Yeah, I remember."

"Shut up," Lindy snapped.

"It's not that simple, girl. You don't ..."

Lindy cut him off. "The hell it ain't!"

Lindy pushed Carmine out of her way and charged down to the basement. Momentarily fiddling for the light switch and finding it, she moved some boxes and quickly found a concealed shortwave radio. She turned the instrument on, grabbed the microphone and pressed the button to talk.

"Marlene Dietrich to The Gipper, come in."

Carmine slumped down on the stairs and watched in silence, sitting on his haunches.

Lindy kept trying the radio, focused on her task.

"Marlene Dietrich calling The Gipper, come in. Ronnie baby, talk to me!"

For a second she looked to the stairs. Carmine squatted and looked sad.

"And don't try to give me no poor puppy dog face. You screwed up," she said in annoyance at him and her inability to reach Dodge.

"They got Angie," Carmine said quietly, tears welling back in his eyes.

Lindy stopped cold, staring blankly at the radio dial. There was silence except for the static from the radio. She turned to Carmine whose lip had started to quiver uncontrollably. She dropped the microphone and threw herself into his arms, hugging him gently. She started crying.

"Oh shit, no."

"Oh shit, yes!"

From the top of the stairs, Jimmy had heard Carmine's simple statement. He looked into the cellar, thought about making the climb down the narrow steps, then decided to afford the two friends a moment alone to grieve. He lit a cigarette and sat in the dark watching its glow cast small shadows on his hands. As he was about to take a drag, the now unlocked door creaked open and two figures slipped inside.

"Oh, shit!" he thought. "The Japs have found us."

*

On Treasure Island, Dodge and Carlton had loaded up the dingy to capacity. The small boat bobbed up and down on the lapping waves. Less than a foot separated the top of the boat from the water line. Carlton started to throw in one more duffel bag.

"No, Carlton, that's it. We still have to get in. Anything else and we'll sink."

"O.K. Listen, I was coming down from the bridge and saw the stockyards. Completely empty. No jeeps, no trucks. There were at least two dozen a few weeks ago."

The island, the former site of the World's Fair in 1939, had been hastily converted to a military base at the beginning of the hostilities in Europe.

"Must've shipped them out, probably to supply L.A.. It's down to brass tacks at this point. We'll be lucky if we can squirrel away a bicycle."

Dodge climbed into the dingy and began to situate himself. The boat seemed precariously low in the dark water. He looked at Carlton to follow suit.

"What about this?" Carlton asked.

The last duffel bag still sat on the bank beside him.

"Oh, right." Dodge scratched his beard.

"Look, I'll haul it back up to the cave. Just be a few minutes."

Before Dodge had a chance to reply, Carlton had shouldered the duffel bag and started to hike back up the trail. As he disappeared behind the brush into the dark, Carlton said nonchalantly, "Keep the meter running."

Dodge waited alone in the darkness, the sound of water lapping against the side of the dingy. He stared pensively into the darkness of the bay, then at the lights from the city that only a few hours ago had promised merriment despite the war that was raging only a few hundred miles north of them. He suddenly felt very vulnerable. Like summer lightning, a bright beam of light stabbed the darkness over the water sweeping back and forth. It came from a small patrol boat.

"Oh fuckin' great," Dodge thought. "Shake a tail feather, Mary! We got company."

He risked calling out to Carlton who could only barely be up the trail. Carlton had heard Dodge. He turned and rushed back down with the duffel. He looked in the direction Dodge was facing and saw the approaching patrol boat, still at a distance.

"We can't make it. We gotta hide."

"No, Carlton, get in. Get in!"

"They'll spot us, I'm telling you. There's no way! C'mon. There'll be time. Don't be stupid".

Dodge, anxious and frustrated, climbed out of the well-loaded dinghy.

"Help me with this," Carlton commanded.

The two heaved with all their strength to pull the fully loaded dingy out of sight. The patrol boat drew closer as they tried to shield the dinghy from sight, the light sweeping back and forth like the grim reaper's scythe. They secured the dingy behind some bushes at the shore. The pair lay flat on the ground, faces down, as if not seeing the patrol boat would not let the patrol boat see them.

The boat came within twenty feet of the shore. They hardly breathed. The patrol boat motored by slowly, its searchlight scanning the shore. It halted, motor idling, and they could hear two men conversing in Japanese. The searchlight scanned the top of the hill, darting hear and there like a spastic firefly. The engine came to belching life and the boat continued on its way, the basso roar of its exhaust slowly receding in the distance. After the boat had passed and was heading towards the north, the pair relaxed.

"Hmph! Guess they're right. They don't see that well in the dark," Carlton quipped.

"What?" Dodge asked absent-mindedly.

Carlton pulled the edges of his eyes, mimicking an Asian look and sticking out his teeth to mock a Japanese stereotype.

"Hmm, very funny. You'll have to show that one to them if we get captured. I'm sure it'll have them rolling in the aisles," Dodge said dryly. He stood up, easing out of his hiding place and climbed down to retrieve the dinghy. Carlton followed.

"Nobody's capturing me, that's for damn sure." Carlton said, secure in his sense of invincibility. He stood beside Dodge, hands on his hips, before the city, his eyes on the landmark Ferry building. Dodge looked at Carlton with a brief revealing moment of weariness and affection. He sighed deeply. Then he patted Carlton on the shoulder a few times and smiled.

"Damn, Carlty, they probably won't."

New York City

"You don't look well. Are you coming down with something?" Carrie hesitated as she walked by the table where Lillian was bent over a ledger, making frantic entries in the room crowded with artifacts.

"No, no. It's nothing. I'm not sick and it's. . .it's getting hotter every day. There's not a whole lot of ventilation down here with these old dusty things, you know?"

Lillian had been musing about her own parents. Her father had been a WWI hero, or so he told everyone, and a devout evangelical. He often preached extemporaneously in Portland, Oregon where Lillian had been raised. She well remembered his "Christian" whippings and the terrible haze in which her mother seemed to meander every day. Both of them spent a great deal of time avoiding father's displeasure until finally, and perhaps subconsciously, Lillian had decided to marry Dean Marshall. Everything was great until he met the parents and told them his real name was David Gelder, a Jew from New York City. Her father had stopped chewing in mid-swallow and almost gagged on the cake Dean brought with him. Father made it easy after that with his "him or us speech." It was a no-brainer for Lillian who easily took the "him." Her regrets about Dean had nothing to do with her father's implied warnings. But it was dear old Dad that indirectly led to Lillian's short engagement. Now that Oregon was in Japanese hands, she assumed that her parents had taken off for the deep woods. This was always father's idea of a great lifestyle, anyway. It turned out he was right about a lot of things, but for all the wrong reasons.

Carrie slapped a stack of ledgers down on the corner of the desk as if to wake her from sleep. She leaned closer to Lillian's face, studying her expression. "Have you heard the latest news?" She tipped her head toward the small table radio on top of the five-drawer file cabinet against the wall.

"You mean about the evacuations?"

"Yes, yes, of course. Do you think we should maybe think about leaving, too? I don't have any reason to stay here anymore.

My boyfriend and I broke up a month ago. He didn't want to leave his parents, even before the world went crazy, so I decided I didn't need to be a mother or a nurse or a maid. None of the above. I keep telling myself being alone is better than being with the wrong one. . . hey. What's with the waterworks? Did I say something?"

"No, no, Carrie, it's not your fault. My. . .my so-called love life doesn't exist anymore either. Dean was shipped out last week and. . .and my true love had to leave, too, so there you have it. And here we are, the Lonely Hearts' Association of the Met!"

"You're talking about Lucien West, aren't you?"

"How did you know?"

"Hell, I'm not blind. Guilty of bad choices, yes, but not blind. I saw that coming, though. Tried to warn you, if you remember. Married men never work out. They don't leave 'mommy', not usually."

"Yes, I do remember but nothing got through. I was besotted, as they used to say in those old novels. I think that's why they call it 'crazy in love'. I was sick with that disease."

"Well, you're still alive and mending, even if you do look like death eating a cracker."

The announcer's voice crackled from the small radio, sounding artificial and tinny. "We interrupt this program to announce according to sketchy reports, the Axis powers have invaded the coastal regions of southern Florida. Most of the citizens have evacuated to refugee camps in Atlanta and farther up the eastern seaboard and most of those who remained were either killed or captured. Resistance has been sporadic . Two men in the same family managed to sink an Italian troop carrier with a small fishing boat and home-made explosives. The two patriots were killed in the effort. And now for the latest reports on transportation for evacuees heading for Atlanta and points north. . ."

Workers in the room exchanged worried glances but kept on with their filing and recording. A large moving van had been parked outside the lower dock of the museum and men were racing to get it as full of artwork as they could. Someone said the destination for these treasures was an underground weatherized vault in Colorado, somewhere underneath a mountain. Others guessed that it was being hidden in sealed off subway tunnels, not 200 yards from the museum. No one was certain of anything, these days.

"I think we need to talk. I've decided to try and find Susan, Dean's sister."

"The one from Miami?"

"Yep, her. Susan Jamison."

"Honey, you must be sleep deprived. Finding anyone from that part of the country is going to be...."

"I can't be talked out of it. I need to do something meaningful or I'm going to go crazy. Sue was the only one in Dean's family that made me feel accepted. She like me when I needed it most. I owe it to her and to Dean. He's off on some mission somewhere. He could be dead for all I know. I'm her only hope and I need to do it."

Carrie looked at her watch and then thoughtfully into space. "I'm going with you."

"No, I don't want you to do that."

"I'd rather try to help somebody than just sit here or in my apartment, listening to the news. The museum is overstaffed for this job and I won't be missed. I heard the evening trains headed south leave at six p.m. and again at ten. A neighbor of mine took her sister to the station day before yesterday and said it was jammed with servicemen and civilians and didn't leave the station until an hour after it was supposed to."

"I'm not surprised. I have to check on Dean's parents and see if they've heard anything new from her. And I would be forever grateful if you could go with me...if you really want to."

"O.K., it's settled. That gives us a day to wind things up, give things away and pack one suitcase of essentials. That's all they're allowing people to take. And get as much cash as you can. Rumor has it that the banks are going under next and they will have to issue scrip like they did in the Civil War. God, this is unreal, isn't it?"

"I hardly know where to start," Lillian chewed on the end of her pen. "Let's do this. I'll leave today about five and get to Dean's parents' place. I'll come in to work tomorrow, bringing my suitcase and if you can do the same, we can leave here about four, maybe get to the station a little early and get on the first train headed south."

"Sounds like a plan. I know this is the thing to do, rather than just wait around, wondering what's going on. And my broken heart has healed longer than yours has."

She winked at Lillian who wondered why she resented Carrie's implication that her love affair was over. She brushed the thought aside and worked as fast as she could, eating her meat loaf sandwich at her desk, working as she chewed, feeling a little guilty about making plans to abandon these artworks she loved to care for.

*

That evening, Lillian knocked on the door of the Gelders' apartment about five-thirty and they were huddled together in the small parlor, frightened and withered as flowers in a drought.

"I don't know if you're thinking of leaving the city. They say the Germans...."

"Oh, no. That's absurd. I'm too old to leave my house, my things. . ." The elderly woman looked around the room at her faded treasures, her horsehair sofa, the tintypes of long-dead relatives on the faded flowered-paper walls.

"We'll be fine here," Papa interrupted. "And when David, I mean Dean, comes home, he'll know where to find us, right?"

"Yes, I can understand how you feel. Now tell me, have you heard anything at all about Susan?"

"Isn't that horrible about those Italians in Miami Beach? They've taken all of Florida, it said on the radio. Ridiculous! We've got to stop those barbarians. The last we heard, Susan was leaving for a place in North Carolina. Duncan...or something like that...I can't remember."

"It must be Durham. The Duke University campus. That's highly possible because many of the eastern seaboard universities and colleges are housing the refugees. Do you know anything about Susan's father-in-law, Fred and your grandson, Jason?"

"No, and to be honest, we're afraid to think about it. Fred was always such a hot-head. No telling what he would do and on top of that, he could talk Jason into anything. But Susan was always reasonable and such a sweet thing, so capable and compassionate. Are you going to leave, too?"

"Yes, I am. I have to. I promised Dean I would try to find Susan and keep tabs on her for him and for you. You'll be all right here?"

"Oh my, yes. Not to worry." A faint smile played around the woman's lips.

Jonathan suddenly stood up and declared, "I'm going, too.

She's my sister and...."

"Are you crazy? Did you hit your head on a stone or something? You sit down and be quiet," said Papa Gelder. Then, thinking more of it, he added, "We need you here. If something happens to me, you'll be the man of the house. You'll have to take care of Mama and Mariel."

"O.K., Papa. I hadn't thought about that. You're right."

"Good. I'm proud of you both and I'll try to reach you or one of your neighbors as soon as I get into the safe zone in the south and of course, if I find out anything about Susan's whereabouts. And if I do, I'll bring her back here, to be with you." Lillian hugged them both, noticing the thinness of their bony shoulders under their clothing, and left them wiping away a few tears as she hurried down the front steps of their Brooklyn apartment building.

When she reached her own apartment, she dragged her suitcase out of the top of the hall closet and began to pack things she could not do without. When she got to her wedding album, she sat down in the middle of the floor and wept. This uprooting was like a death, maybe even worse, she decided. It was not ending peacefully. And there was so much unknown ahead. Lucien filled her mind and crowded out everything. Still, she had vowed before God to love, honor and obey Dean. She added shame to her guilt and felt worse. She wasn't going to think about that anymore. It would sort itself out. She had to focus on the task before her. It was insanity, she knew, but she needed to find Susan or die trying.

Mayfield County, Texas

Travis Beecher and Jonas Kincaid were kicking up a cloud of dust on the dirt road leading to Doc Peterson's farm as Jonas crawled along in second gear. He dodged the numerous potholes in the road, almost sliding into the shallow ditches that ran alongside. On both sides of the road, to each horizon, stretched acres of land that would eventually be covered in fluffy, white bolls of cotton. At this time of year, the neatly rowed plants were just beginning to sprout their annual foliage. Here and there on the fields stood large irrigators sending thin sprays of water into the air. Up ahead was Doc's farm, its twin neatly painted silos unmistakable against the sunset Texas sky.

As they arrived at the farm, the pair saw dozens of pickup trucks and a few cars parked haphazardly on the hard, packed dirt. Several dozen men, mostly young, were gathered, smoking, joking, chewing tobacco and spitting the chew wherever it happened to land. A few women were in the crowd. Jonas seemed to know almost everyone as he climbed down from the truck. The young men patted him on the back or, in good-natured fashion, gave him a poke in the ribs.

"Late as always," drawled one of the men. "Be late fer yer own funeral!"

"Yup, you gotta wait for the best! Come on, Trav, we gotta see the Doc first."

He pulled Travis into the Doc's spacious foyer and closed the front door behind him. Instantly, he put a finger to his lips, motioning with the other hand to the half-open door to the study. They could see the backs of three tall men in suits, sporting black fedoras on their heads, talking heatedly to a fourth. No

153

question, they had to be Germans, thought Travis. Both he and Jonas had seen movies in which Germans always wore fedoras. They crawled forward silently until Jonas pulled Travis into an adjoining coat closet. In the close air of the closet, they could hear distinctly and Jonas peered through a small crack in the woodwork.

"It's the Doc, alright. He's speaking German, don't ya know!" he whispered.

"What're they talking about?" Travis whispered back,

"Hell, I don't speak no Kraut talk! No, wait. Now they're speakin' in English. Listen!"

As Travis pressed his ear to the thin woodwork, he distinctly heard the heavily accented English of one of the men.

"You have a virtual army at your command, Herr Peterson. Such men are hard to come by, loyal and trustful as they are. They listen to you, honor you, it seems."

The pair heard the broad Texan accent of Doc Peterson.

"You ain't telling me nothing new. I run this show, don't I?"

"So why, then, the change of mind? You gave us your word that you would assist our cause. Should I fear something amiss?"

Doc's voice started to have that edge to it that Travis knew all too well.

"Now don't ya be beady-eyein' me in my own house that-a-way. We've got rules agin that in Texas! This ain't about nobody backstabbin' nobody. I'm jest not sure we're eyeball to eyeball on this here proposition, see? Y'all askin' me to change the rules of my organization, see, Mister Buchner?"

"I'm just asking for your position on this matter. I can assure you this is something you Americans will benefit from greatly." The man identified as Buchner raised his tone ever so slightly.

"Listen now, I'm not sayin' we won't give you whatever help

y'all need when the time comes. But, well, we've got our own set of ideals, see? Good ideals. White America for the white man. Keep it pure."

"And this is our aim, as well."

"Yeah, O.K. But your methods? It's just not our way, see? This is still our country and we aim to keep it that way. Especially in Texas." Peterson's voice actually seemed to hold a hint of pride in it, Travis remarked to himself.

Buchner's tone became supercilious, as he said condescendingly, "Your way? What is your way? You prance around in fields dressed like ghosts. You burn crosses. You hang a black man from the trees, and you hide. You needn't hide any more. You can come out of the shadows and stand proud in the streets. You will have no one to fear ..."

When Doc Peterson became angry or frustrated, he yelled. He yelled now.

"Watch your step, Buchner.! I'd hate fer ya to have to see just how much in command I am! I don't hide from no one!"

"Herr Peterson, perhaps we should begin again. When we first came to you, you assured us of your loyalty to our cause ..."

Peterson broke off the man in mid sentence again.

"And I still am," he said more quietly.

"So, then, you now take back your offer of assistance, do you not? What am I to think upon leaving? Perhaps you do not understand what is at stake in this world? It is not just the intermingling of the races. Believe me, if it were that simple, we would have finished our job long ago. No, it is also an ideology. As such, we must think in terms of more than just – how do you Americans say – 'Spring cleaning?' Communism, Herr Peterson, is still a problem in much of Europe. We have done our part to squash it as best we can, but it still spreads."

Through the slit in the woodwork, Jonas saw the man take down a book from the Doc's shelves. He thumbed it absent-mindedly as he continued his discourse.

"The problem with ideologies, unlike the reproduction of the lower races, is that it is not restricted to race or sex. There is no gestation period that allows us time to find it and kill it. It moves as fast as a plague. You can't simply kill it in the womb; you have to eliminate its culture. Otherwise – a commie country full of genetic abominations."

Buchner had lost Doc Peterson.

"Lookee here, I don't know all them fancy words, but I know we got our problems, same as yours."

The German tried to get back to the issue at hand, but failed as he talked on.

"We are here to liberate you from, what is apparent in this country, an infection that has already set in. We give you the power to eradicate it. And we give you power over your floundering leader to do this. That Jew, Roosevelt, for example."

Even the Roosevelt dig did not seem to accomplish its purpose. Peterson ignored it entirely.

"We're doing our part just fine. Look, I appreciate the offer. It's just, well, I don't think our methods see eye to eye, see? I don't think our men are jest gonna to start kow-towin' to a bunch of krau … Germans. Or Japs, for that matter, especially. Those little yellow bastards. And shit, you're over runnin' the place with fuckin' wetbacks. Shit, you marched in here like Grant took Richmond and now you expect everything to be hunky-dory and I jest gotta think 'bout that some more."

Buchner tried a different tack in hopes of rescuing a hopeless situation. He found it difficult to lower himself to this Texan's level.

156

"Your men would cut off their own ears if you told them to do so, would they not?"

"Sure they would. I'm their leader."

"The Japanese will never set foot in Texas. You have my word on that. And the Mexicans? Well, they were a necessity. They are pigs and like pigs, they will be taken care of when the time is right. But you must understand that we must use whatever tools are available. You do understand, don't you? Then what is not to see eye to eye about?"

"Look, our causes, as you call 'em, match up just fine, But I got a style problem. Texans just ain't used to kissin' ass and my men ... "

Buchner interrupted. "But if your men obey your every command then it is not they that do not accept our help, it is you. Shouldn't they be given the choice?"

"Sorry, Buchner, this dog don't hunt right now. But, like I say, anything you need when y'all get here. You jest let me now. I'll help out the best I can."

Buchner knew that he had lost that round.

"I am very sorry, that we cannot come to an agreement. I think in time you will see the error of your ways. Perhaps you will reconsider in time. Our offer still stands. Auf Wiedersehen."

Buchner clicked his heels, turned on them sharply, and left the room. As the Germans passed the closed closet door, Buchner said to his lieutenants, "Der dumme Esel versteht es einfach nicht! Der will es schon sehen!"

Moments after the men inside the study started to leave, Travis and Jonas heard the thud of the front door. He yanked at Travis' sleeve.

"Follow me. We'll take a back door and double back to the front to join the rally. Should be gettin' started just when the

Doc gets through shakin' hands, that lyin' son of a bitch! Sold us right out, he did. Did you hear that? That motherfucker thinks he can handle this his way. He's wrong, I tell ya, dead fuckin' wrong."

Travis nodded quietly. His respect for old Doc had just increased tremendously. He was, after all, a Texan and an American. He was a stupid bigot, but he wasn't going to let the Germans rule his country.

Moments later they were under the quiet night sky, the first stars appearing on the eastern horizon. Doc Peterson stood on a makeshift platform, no more than two heads above the crowd. Some of the men had donned their robes and hoods and looked eerily like Halloween goblins.

"Hey, by the way, where's Hannah-Lee? She was supposed to be here! Told you to bring her!"

Travis had not forgotten Jonas's crude jokes about his sister. Nor had he forgotten to tell her about the Ku Klax Klan rally. He'd do almost anything to keep Hannah-Lee and Jonas apart. Heck, his sister was only sixteen, for one thing. She could do a lot better than Jonas Kincaid, to be sure, for another.

"She wasn't feeling well. Said she wanted to take a nap," Travis lied.

"Nap, my ass! Tell her I'll be thinkin' 'bout her when she wakes up!" Jonas let flash another of his lewd grins. "Hey, you wait here. I gotta take care of something real quick."

He sprinted behind the group now waiting to see what Doc Peterson's rally was all about. Just briefly, Travis could see him catching up to the trio of Germans who had taken a position at the very rear of the crowd. Jonas was talking to them and looking over his shoulder like a true conspirator. The yips of a pack of coyotes broke the still night air and the moon, an orange crescent, sat on the far deep purple mountains like the devil's grin.

Doc Peterson, resplendent in his white linen Klan robes and hood, embroidered to show his exalted rank, and a Bible clasped in his left hand, raised his right hand.

"In the name of God Almighty and his Son, Our Lord Jesus Christ, we beseech you to guide us along the path of righteousness, and for us to heed Your way in all things. A white America for white Americans! Amen."

A raucous chorus of "Amens" echoed through the night air, the light from the burning torches creating strange, shifting patterns over the assemblage.

"Brethren, members of the United Klans, hear me speak! We got krauts not more than ten miles from here and they're gonna be takin' over, they think. I do believe, and so do you, that we stand for the same ideals. We want a white country for white men. They aim to rid the world of the Jew and his lackey, the nigger. So do we!"

The crowd was cheering and clapping in a carnival mood. Petersen scanned the crowd through the eye slits of his costume. He was pleased. There were more than five hundred people assembled.

"But I feel that they want more'n that. I think we gotta remember that we're Americans, and Texans, born and bred. And if we let a bunch of Wienerschnitzel-eatin' sons of bitches step all over us, well why, we ain't no better'n niggers ourselves."

The crowd had quieted perceptibly and Peterson could see some of the men cross their arms, perhaps in uncertainty, perhaps in defiance.

"We saved the great State of Texas from the taco-bendin' Mexican bastards that the krauts have joined with. I heard tell that they done blowed up the Alamo! My daddy fought in the

Great War against these self-same krauts and I can tell you that
..."

He did not finish the sentence as he saw Jonas, brandishing
a revolver, jumping on the makeshift stage and approaching him
threateningly. Jonas wore no robes. His sandy hair and his white
undershirt and ten-gallon hat made him look like Gary Cooper.

"What in the hell do you think you're doing, son?" Peterson
asked incredulously.

"You ain't in charge here no more, Doc!'

"Put that thing down, son, 'fore someone gets hurt."

"Why did you do it, Doc?"

"Why did I do what?" asked Doc Peterson. He was looking
at the crowd as if embarrassed and waiting to gauge their reaction. He had a gun in his waistband but could not reach it unless
he could find a way to stick his hands into his robes. He carefully laid the Bible down on a folding chair. He was sweating pro-
fusely beneath the hood and robes. He was not going to give the
younger man the satisfaction of removing his hood until the situation was resolved. It was quite a thing to kill a man; it was
more than that to kill a ranking member of the Klan, especially
in front of so many witnesses.

"You turned into a Jew-kissin', nigger-lovin' coward, that's
what!"

"What the hell are you saying, boy?"

Jonas was more a believer in the Germans than even the
Germans were, Travis thought as he watched in awe. What was
Jonas thinking?

"I know about you, you cowardly piece of dog shit! I heard
you sound like we was afraid to join the greatest army on earth!
You made me ashamed to be an American. Damn, you're not
smart enough to know when you've been licked and when to

stand on the right side of God's will!"

Jonas took a couple of deep breaths, then continued, addressing the crowd while keeping his gun trained on Doc Peterson.

"Listen, the Doc was given the chance tonight to join up with the elite of the Waffen-SS. They want to make us members of their organization, with complete control over our own territory, with the power to run it as we see fit. He turned them down! Whadda ya say to that?"

Most of the crowd stared blankly at the spectacle developing before them. They followed the Doc; they trusted him. Most liked him. Quite a few of them also liked and respected Jonas. He'd been the winning quarterback in his senior year in high school. That automatically made him a hero in this part of the country.

Doc felt the division and uncertainty of the crowd. They'd never been called upon to choose between their leaders. It was one thing to get unanimous consent to scare the hell out of a few Blacks on the other side of town. It was quite another to have to think for themselves, to make their own decision.

Somewhat more plaintively than he wanted, Doc said, "You don't understand!"

"Shut up, Doc. I understand everything. You're afraid. You'd have us getting killed to protect this Jew-lovin', Nigger-lovin' mess of a country just when it can finally be cleaned up! You'd have us throwin' rocks at niggers for the next fifty years when we could have the power to pick 'em all up and do away with 'em once and for all! Do you hear me goddammit? POWER! We will have the POWER to make it all right, once and for all! Tell me how I don't understand, you yellow-bellied sidewinder!"

Now somewhat tamely, Doc said, "I offered them our assistance."

"You offered them nothing!" shouted Jonas. Turning to the throng, he said, "He wasn't even plannin' on telling y'all about this little meeting he had tonight. Now what kind of leader don't inform his men of deals concerning them? The Germans offered us a kingdom, and he wants to keep us as slaves."

One of the men in a hood and robes, standing in the front row, spoke up.

"Damn Jonas! Is he tellin' the truth, Doc?"

Without letting Doc respond, Jonas triumphantly held up an official SS armband.

"Here's the truth, goddamn it! Here's the truth! The lord high mucky-muck kraut hisself gave me this. And there's enough to go 'round for all of ya. Just a few minutes ago he asked me to tell you that you're all invited to join. Complete with training and the best weapons. This town is now ours to run, our way, no fucker from Washington D.C. lordin' it over us. It's for the good of the white man. It'll be Texas for Texans. For white Texans."

A cheer surged up from the crowd. Almost to a man, the hoods were removed and tossed in the air. Doc was about to thrust his right hand into his robe when Jonas spotted the movement. Rapidly, Jonas pumped two shots into the Klan leader. The elder man stumbled and fell, knocking his hood off as he propped himself against the folding chair that held his Bible. Blood stained the front of his robe.

"You fuckin' traitor!"

"Fuck you, Doc." Jonas leveled the gun at Doc's head and pulled the trigger. The top of his head came off like a jack-o-lantern hit by a mule. Doc's body fell off the makeshift platform into the dust.

Again hushed, Jonas looked defiantly at the crowd, waving his gun wildly.

"Anyone else got some ass-kissin' ideas? Anyone doubt that I'm the leader of this outfit?"

At that instant, half a dozen SS troops in their black uniforms, machine guns at the ready, marched onto the small stage and stood next to Jonas. Surveying the crowd triumphantly, he saw Travis making his way to the road alone. Good luck, he thought. It's a long walk to your farm, good buddy.

Immediately after the SS troops had taken their places on the platform, Lieutenant Buchner climbed onto the stage. In his accented and Yankee-precise English, he looked at the crowd and said, "Any man who wishes to leave may do so now. All of you who would like to live in an America free of racial impurity, stay and you will this very night become members of Der Führer's elite army, the Texas SS."

Waiting to see whether anyone would leave Doc Peterson's farm, Buchner turned and looked into Jonas's eyes.

"Mein Gott, Jonas, if only we had come to you to begin with …"

Turning his attention back to the crowd, Buchner said, "Those of you ready to serve your country and the Reich for the greater good of the world, repeat after me:

"I pledge allegiance to this flag and to the flag of my brothers, the SS …"

Mindlessly the crowd murmured the words.

"I swear to thee Adolf Hitler, as Führer and Chancellor of the German Reich …

"Loyalty and bravery.

"I vow to thee and the superiors whom thou shall appoint …

"Obedience unto death, so help me God!"

The volume of the pledge had died somewhat when the word "Adolf Hitler" and "death" were pronounced, but Buchner was satisfied.

"Welcome to the Waffen SS Texas."

During Buchner's speech and pledge to the Fatherland, three of the Waffen-SS soldiers had holstered their weapons and unfurled three flags new to everyone at the Klan gathering: the official German red-white-and-black swastika flag, the Waffen-SS flag, and an American flag with "SS" written in black over the field of stars and "Waffen-SS" written boldly over the last two red and white stripes. A soldier brought a small easel and unfurled a picture of Adolf Hitler with two flags in the background. One of the flags was German, the other the new American flag.

The madness of the night culminated in a deafening chorus of "Sieg Heils" as Buchner and Jonas handed out armbands.

New York City

The next morning, Lillian struggled with her heavy suitcase on the bus and managed to avoid the glares of the other passengers who were already crowded without the addition of a suitcase getting in their way. She dragged it into the museum, and worked straight through the lunch hour, and Carrie joined her about two in the afternoon, blinking rapidly with excitement, her own overnight case bulging.

"I'm ready, Lil. Ready as I'll ever be."

"And I'm so thankful I have you to go with me. This would

be twice as difficult alone. Let's wrap up this next batch of entries and then we can head for the station. I think we need to get there real early. I heard people on the bus talking about leaving themselves. Probably everybody wants to get out of here."

The two women catalogued and checked about a hundred more masterpieces and artifacts, then as if by prearranged signal, they nodded to each other, grabbed their cases and headed for the ladies' restroom on the main floor. It was three-thirty in the afternoon.

"We need to stop here because I have a feeling it's going to be a long time before we have access to a clean restroom – or even soap and water for that matter."

"I hadn't thought of that."

After they washed their hands longer than usual, they made their way out to the sidewalk. Lillian turned to look back at the museum and her mind filled with memories of Lucien and their unrequited love affair and the hope she would see him again, some where in her future. She sighed and, glancing at Carrie, walked briskly beside her, headed for the train station shuttle bus.

The shuttle was jammed with people just this side of panic. The nervous tension was contagious; people were motivated by sheer terror and fear, and humane niceties went out the window. They shoved and pushed and scowled and glared and clutched their children close and their belongings as if they were hauling gold bars out of Fort Knox. Lillian and Carrie ended up locking arms in self defense with their two suitcases riding on the floor between their legs as they stood the whole way, hanging to the swaying canvas loops above. The bus driver seemed bent upon trying to make people fall and took corners recklessly, like a teenager who had just learned how to drive. Lillian's hat fell off twice and Carrie lost her grip once, almost landing on two seated passengers who scowled at her. Lillian caught her and held on, until she got her balance again.

They arrived at Penn station about a quarter to five and found the place so crowded there was no way to find their way to a ticket counter much less to a departing train's platform. There was a frantic chill in the air as if everyone wanted to start screaming but controlled themselves and remained quiet. The cavernous main hall with its marble walls echoed and magnified every sound so that four or five thousand people milling about in lines or in groups sounded like ten thousand. Children cried. Dollies, loaded with bags, hustled their way through the crowd pushed by porters in dark blue uniforms, sweat on their brows, exhaustion subdued by fear.

The station master's voice boomed incessantly, but most of the words were unintelligible and the background drone was like distant and incessant thunder. Lillian noticed an electric sign high up near the ceiling. She read the words aloud.

"All persons desiring to reach Atlanta, please go to Track Number Four. All persons desiring to go to North Carolina, South Caroling and Virginia, go to Number Three or Number Two. You can purchase tickets at the gate from a conductor. Please board immediately."

"Let's go. This way." Carrie grabbed Lillian's arm and the two women made their way through people jammed together like a massive school of confused fish, each one heading in a different direction then turning and trying another. It was pure bedlam.

Eventually, they made it to Track Number Three and stood in line for what seemed like another hour to buy tickets and climb into one of the passenger cars. When they finally got inside, the noise from the platform was muffled by the plush upholstered seats and the people, finally on the train that might save them from the hell that was coming, relaxed a little bit and their voices were less strident. Carrie and Lillian commandeered a window seat for the two of them and they wedged themselves together into it, with their cases stowed beneath their seats. They stared out the fixed glass window at the still thronging and frantic citizens trying to escape the unknown. Neither one spoke because they were beginning to realize the truth of what was happening. The conductor that had sold them tickets had said there were no return tickets available until further notice; the government would not be allowing civilians on any trains after three or four more days. Both women thought they might get back in time if they could find Susan. But down deep, where the nightmares are born, neither of them truly believed that it was possible. The attempt had to be made, though.

The train finally gathered strength and began to jerk-tug itself on its way, down the tracks. It moved gently through the maze of tunnels under the city, lights flashing and the glare of sparks shooting from the wheels illuminated the dank sides of the passageway as the train squealed from one turn to another. It burst out into the evening sky in New Jersey. Carrie and Lillian wiggled themselves into more comfortable positions and watched the landscape unfold outside their window. The immensely tall smoke stacks of oil refineries, the hunkering storage tanks, and the vast network of elevated train tracks and highways and bridges became a Piranesi-like maze of twisted metal and concrete. The red glaze of the setting sun lit the fetid pools of polluted water that laced in and out between roadway and factory. The Garden State looked more like the eighth circle of Dante's Inferno.

"Look at that guy on the bike!" The sailor in the seat next to them was leaning forward and pointing out the window.

The rider had what looked like an entire household of items hanging from his bicycle and from himself. The tires wobbled under the weight and the three observers began to laugh.

"He ain't gonna make it to the corner, much less out of town!" The sailor was doubled over, laughing.

"You're right." Carrie nodded in agreement, then stopped laughing, realizing her state of mind was no different. "Poor guy. He should get an A for Effort. This is hell for all of us."

"Well, not me," continued the seaman. "I've been trans-ferred so many times I wouldn't know what it's like to sleep in the same rack twice in a row! Where are you ladies headed?"

Lillian studied the young face and decided he was harmless. "Hopefully, North Carolina. One of the colleges there that's put-ting up refugees. We're looking for my sister-in-law. She might have ended up there, running away from Florida."

"Yeah? I've heard that's been a rough go. Can I buy you ladies a drink in the club car? I don't know if they're serving any food yet."

Carrie looked at Lillian and they both nodded yes and got up, putting the seat sign that read "Occupied" on their seats while they moved through passengers to the club car. The sailor led the way and the roar of the engines and the scream of the wind was a contrast to the silence inside as they walked across the open-air metal platforms between cars. They had to make it through three cars before reaching the diner and then the wait for a table seemed an eternity.

"Wait here, I'll be right back." The handsome sailor grinned and elbowed his way through the people waiting and eventually came back with three drinks. "I hope you girls like bourbon and ginger ale! That's all they got."

"Bourbon and ginger is fine and bedsides, we're headed for bourbon country." Carrie was all smiles.

Lillian was more reserved but she welcomed the soothing effects of the drink. They stood sipping and chatting for a long while, inching forward until at last they were shown to a dining table covered with a white linen cloth and a red paper carnation in a bud vase near the window. The three new friends sat down and soon another sailor, an acquaintance of the first seaman, as if on cue, asked if he could join them. He sat without waiting for the response and they all ordered another round. The war had altered everyone's sense of propriety whether they had one before or not.

As the evening wore on, the sailors kept the drinks coming and Lillian and Carrie barely remembered the meal. The young men kept exchanging looks heavy with expectations and one of them even went so far as to try and caress Lillian's knee under the table. She was tempted to jab his hand with her butter knife but she restrained herself and signaled Carrie to be aware of wolves on the prowl.

By the time the train made its first stop in Trenton, New Jersey, both Lillian and Carrie were warmly tipsy, but their circumstances were of such a sobering nature, it was impossible to drown their self-control. The sailors sensed this and, while disappointed, were polite enough to settle for 'good nights.'"

Both stared at the shadowy landscape slithering by the window.

"We're a tad closer to Durham. I think that's one of the most likely places to find Susan. In one of the dorms at Duke."

"Makes sense, I guess. Much as any of this does."

"We'd better try and get some sleep."

"Good idea."

The train clacked on through the night, passing sleeping villages and townships, small glimmering pockets of people enveloped in the darkness. It was an overcast night and in the distance Lillian could see the low lying clouds near the far hills glowing a faint red from the hidden towns and cities below them. The train rocked to and fro, to and fro until she fell asleep, her whole body, now limp with slumber, rocking, rocking. She dreamed she was in Lucien's apartment in his bed. Lights from passing cars in the street below briefly illuminated the ceiling in moving triangular patterns. He was on top of her, inside of her, rocking on her, rocking, squeezing her tender breasts, her nipples hard, his sweat dripping onto her. She pushed her thighs up against his as he rocked, pushing her head in a rhythmic motion into the headboard which creaked with each thrust. Her eyes looked into his upward. His face taught and tense as he looked down at her, rocking, rocking. He orgasmed inside of her and the shudder passed through her body like an electric current running from her crotch to her nipples and into her throat. She moaned and gasped a few short breaths. The squealing of the train's brakes woke her suddenly, her hand having slipped into her panties. She pretended to switch positions in her sleep, gently opening her eyelids ever so slightly to make sure no one had seen her. Sleep overtook her as the train rolled onwards into an uncertain future.

Mayfield County, Texas

A long string of headlights moved toward the outskirts of

Dallas. Small, ramshackle clapboard buildings and shacks dotted the sides of the road. Most of the electrical power had been shut down and people wisely stayed indoors, peering out of their windows through closed curtains. Three commandeered civilian vehicles that had brought Buchner and his SS men to Doc Peterson's ranch led the caravan.

In the front vehicle, Jonas Kincaid, proudly sporting his newly acquired Nazi armband, gave directions to the SS driver.

"Y'all turn left at the next road down. There'll be a church on the right. We'll circle there."

To Bucher, he smirked, "Always can find niggers at church!"

Buchner just nodded wordlessly.

The driver followed the directions and the lead car ground to a halt in a few seconds. A large assemblage of blacks was gathered in front of the Third Immanuel Baptist Church. Others moved along the road toward the church. Everywhere the eyes could see in the dimly lit street, there were scores of black men, many women carrying babies, and other young black children holding hands, obediently trudging behind their mothers or aunts or neighbors.

As the trucks slammed on the brakes one by one, hordes of white men, some still partially dressed in the white robes of the Klan, clambered down from the vehicles and started to dart throughout the small community. Many sported handguns or hunting rifles. More than one chugged large sips of cheap bourbon from pint bottles being passed around. A few found torches in the truck beds and lit them. Others found a sturdy four by four inch piece of lumber and tied a cross section of smaller branches to it.

"Bring it over here," one young man in white robes yelled out to his companions. The men with the cross moved prompt-

171

ly to the front of the church, began to dig a small hole some shovels from one of their pickups, and firmly set the cross into its foundation. They poured some gasoline on it. With a match, the fire quickly raced up and down the dry wood, creating the feared fiery cross.

Black men and women had started to scatter from the scene when they realized what was about to happen. The minister in his dark robes held up his hands, his palms stretched out in supplication as if to embrace his entire congregation.

"Keep your faith, my children," he admonished. "The Lord is our shepherd."

A united chorus of "Amen" emanated from the crowd.

Somewhere in the crowd a woman started to sing. She had a beautiful soprano voice that carried well over the confusion. It was an old spiritual that spoke of the trouble she saw until she found Jesus. Soon others spontaneously joined in until the song overpowered the wailing and the shrieks and the whimpering.

Jonas clambered over Buchner, who had been watching the growing pandemonium from inside the car. He threw open the door, and fired two shots into the minister as he raced forward in the melee. The older man crumbled and fell, face down, into the muddy street.

"Always wanted to get me a nigger preacher!" Jonas shouted triumphantly. He emptied his magazine at random into the milling crowd. Two younger black women who had raced to assist their fallen minister fell in turn. Someone took one of the torches and threw it into the interior of the small, white-washed Baptist church and bolted the door shut from the outside with his shovel. Within minutes, the building stood engulfed in fire. The flames shot from the steeple into the calm, night air. The tinny little bell rang twice before it fell to the steeple floor. Its plaintive sound was overpowered by the roar that engulfed the small community. People who had sought refuge in the building now tried to flee, slamming their bodies vainly against the barred door. Jonas fired several rounds through the door and shouted, "The devil's a knockin', ya black bastards."

"Where is their Jesus now," said Buchner as he gave orders to his driver to move away from the burning building. The Americans, he thought, would never be as efficient and orderly as his own people in ridding the world of the inferior races. The Americans, themselves, were too soft. Everything had to be debated, discussed and then compromised into a mediocre "solution" that pleased no one and accomplished little. They needed the reinforcement of German discipline. They needed it badly. This hooligan display of violence did not impress him. Soon the Fatherland would solve the problem of the American blacks in orderly fashion. Scientifically, methodically.

Within minutes, other houses started to burn as the hoodlums threw torches and burning branches into the shacks. Bodies of men and women and quite a few children lined the road, falling wherever the bullets had found them.

A group of about fifty black men suddenly appeared from a thicket. They were armed with pitchforks, shotguns, machetes, hoes, anything they could use to defend themselves and their families. They attacked a group of Klansmen that hadn't had time to escape. The blacks hacked them to pieces and started moving toward Jonas and his group. Several hundred rounds of machine gun fire lit up the night casting strobe-like red light onto the faces of the dead, dying and the fleeing. The Nazi SS had opened fire and mowed the blacks down like hay before the reaper. One tall, well-built black man raised his arms to the sky and shouted, "Jesus, my Lord, save us!" The bullets hit him mid-waist almost cutting him in two. He fell back onto his comrades. Screams and shouts punctuated the air as Jonas looked on.

"That's more like it, them fuckers," he said.

It took the better part of an hour before the hatred of frenzy spent itself. Finding a ride with one of his fellow Klansmen, Jonas Kincaid was exuberant. The Germans boarded their trucks and with a nod from Buchner, took off into the night toward the German-Mexican encampment. The Klansmen stood around in groups staring at the carnage. Little was said. No one went to their fallen comrades. A black baby lying near his dead mother was left to wail through the night.

The events of the day had brought Jonas much closer than he ever dreamed to realizing his personal goal of becoming a sort of warlord in control of his small part of Texas. If he needed to be supported by an invading army, then so be it. God works in mysterious ways, he thought. Someday, the Nazis would be gone and he would be the only one strong enough to rule. As he learned in third grade from Mrs. Jackson, "anybody can grow up to be president." He smiled at the thought.

After a time, someone asked, "Jonas, sir, what should we do with the bodies?"

"Fuck'em," was his response. "Coyotes and buzzards gotta eat, too."

They all piled into their pick-up trucks and cars and slowly made their way back to their homes.

"Hey, today the niggers, tomorrow the Jews and fags!" Jonas shouted out of the truck's window into the Texas night.

In the midst of the carnage, the makeshift fiery cross sputtered in the darkness. Eventually, as the first pink and gold light of dawn painted the clouds on the horizon, the cross burned out leaving a thin wisp of grey smoke climbing lazily into the still air.

The baby had stopped crying.

*

"Travis?"

Travis rolled over, still half asleep. He was lying on top of his bedspread, still dressed from the night before. Only his soiled boots had been shed. He blinked the sleep from his eyes, then recognized his mother standing over him.

"Mom? Gee, I'm sorry. I must have overslept."

Mrs. Beecher lovingly stroked her son's hair.

"Whatever time did you get in? I finally went to sleep about midnight. Worried sick, I was."

Travis yawned, then sat up.

"Look, is Hannah-Lee in? We've all got to talk."

"Yes, son, she's downstairs. Is anything wrong?"

He nodded briefly. "

"I'll be right down. Tell you then."

"O.K. I'll have some breakfast for you."

Mrs. Beecher turned, left the room and walked down the stairs. Travis stripped his clothes off down to his shorts and plodded barefooted to the small bathroom they all shared. He ran some water in the sink, doused his head and hair and eyed the growing dark stubble of his beard. He found the tube of shaving cream amid his mother's and sister's paraphernalia, squeezed a small amount of the paste into his hand and smeared it over his face. He briefly stropped the straight edge razor and then began the distasteful act of shaving. It was the one thing in daily life he hated the most, or used to.

After a few minutes, his shave complete – a few red splotches of new blood on his skin – he marched back to his bedroom, found a clean plaid shirt, and dressed. He carefully polished his soiled boots before pulling them on. Then, the job as complete as it would be, Travis went downstairs to the large kitchen. His mother had a pair of eggs in the frying pan and some slab bacon on the griddle. Despite the war, farmers managed to eat reasonably well. The two dozen chickens they maintained on the farm provided them with all the eggs they needed. They traded the rest at Arnie's grocery for things they could not raise themselves.

Hannah-Lee was sitting at the table, a magazine hiding her face. He went up and kissed her on the head lightly.

"Morning, sis."

Hannah-Lee dropped the magazine. She turned her blue eyes toward her brother.

"Did you stay at the Klan rally all night?"

"Nope. But had to walk most of the way home before someone came by and picked me up."

"Did you go to a Klan rally last night? You know that your father could not stand those guys. Especially that Doc Peterson," his mother said, bringing the eggs and bacon, together with some toast and strawberry jam to the table.

"Doc Peterson's dead. Jonas Kincaid shot him last night."

"Good God!" Mrs. Beecher exclaimed as she fell into a chair. Hannah-Lee just sat silently.

"There's more."

As he dug into his late breakfast, Travis recounted the story of what he had seen and heard the night before. When he had concluded, he said, "Mom, Hannie, we've got to leave now. Right now. It's just not going to be safe. We'll make our way to Aunt Susie's in Oklahoma. The Nazis ain't there yet."

His mother's eyed rounded. "But, Travis, that's a long way! And we've got no car, not since we couldn't afford to fix it. It's still down at Greerson's shop."

"We'll take the bicycles. It'll be a hard trip, but it's safer than staying here. I told you, Jonas saw me leaving the rally. He'll come after me, no doubt. The Klan, and worse now, the krauts, don't tolerate disagreement. He'll come after me, for sure."

Mrs. Beecher looked distressed. Although she was only in her late forties, she was beginning to age well beyond her years, Jonas thought. Ever since Dad had gone to the war, she was beginning to show some gray in her hair. Her slender figure was beginning to spread around her hips and waist.

"I just don't know, but I know you're right in one way. Heard talk this morning that they burned down a section of color-town outside Dallas. And that the Nazis are trying to find out where the Jews live. God knows, we don't have that many, not like in New York."

"Mom, you know what happened in Germany when Hitler took over. First came the communists, then the Jews. Then whoever parts their hair on the left. Here. It'll start with the coloreds. That Nazi last night made a big deal – and so did Jonas – about how they and the Klan share the same principles."

Hannah-Lee rumpled her blonde hair. "Look, we're not niggers, or Jews, or even Catholics. Don't even know any Jews in school. So why would they bother with us?"

His sister had struck a chord in Travis.

"Because I'm supposed to be his friend, and Jonas knows I disagree with him. Sure, I don't much care for coloreds, either, but I don't wanna kill 'em! What the dickens would we do for labor to pick the cotton? I don't know any Jews, either, except that feller at the bank. And he's a nice enough guy. Mainly, Hannie, Jonas wants to get you! And he'll try to do that to get back at me."

Hannah-Lee was horrified.

"Jonas? Interested in me? Not in a week of Sundays! He's a creep, even if he is your friend!"

She pouted and crossed her arms across her bourgeoning chest. His baby sister was by no means a woman yet, but she had the makings. For people like Jonas, at sixteen she had all the attributes he needed. In this part of the world, it was not uncommon for girls to marry at Hannah-Lee's age, sometimes younger.

"Well, then, Travis, let's go and get started. I'll see if the phone still works and I'll give Aunt Susie a call to let her know we're coming. How long d'you reckon it'll take us?"

"The phones ain't workin'," said Travis. "That's for damn certain. Figure a day or two, depending on how far we can go."

"We'll have sore backsides, that's for sure," Hannah-Lee piped in.

"Let's get packing," said Travis, suspiciously eyeing the Nazi trucks that were barreling down their road, roaring past and throwing up clouds of dust.

Richmond, Virginia

Lillian stretched herself awake, glancing over at Carrie's head lolling back against the seat cushion. She looked very young and vulnerable sleeping so innocently, with her lips slightly open and her blond hair tousled and falling over her forehead. She seemed to sense Lillian's staring.

"Yuk, what an awful taste in my mouth! What army marched barefoot across my tongue?" She grinned at Lillian.

"I'll second that motion. We had too much to drink, that's for sure. No more of those dangerous games."

"Agreed." Carried stared out the window. The train was slowing down. "I wonder where we are."

"I'm pretty sure these are the outskirts of Richmond. We had several unscheduled stops during the night. I woke up each time and once, an MP walked through the cars, looking at the face of every serviceman. I guess there are a lot of guys going AWOL."

Carrie yawned. "I wonder if I can get in the ladies' room. If you'll watch my purse, I'll be back in a minute and do the same for you." She climbed over Lillian's legs and made her way up the aisle, swaying with the movement of the train.

Lillian watched her retreating back and turned to stare out the window. There were some clotheslines already waving laundry and children swinging books lashed together with leather belts as they walked to school. On the surface things looked quite normal. She wondered if this was the calm before the storm.

Carrie returned, her face freshly washed, her eyes bright. "O.K., it's your turn. Go on, the cold water on the face is great."

"Yeah, I bet."

Lillian smiled and walked stiffly to the restroom, glad to find there was no line. When she got back to the seat, Carrie had brushed her hair and had put on fresh make-up.

"That feels tons better. Someone said the diner doesn't open for breakfast until nine, so we've got a bit of time before we can get coffee."

"How are you holding up?"

"How is anybody holding up?

"You know what I mean . . .West."

"Oh, God, I don't know. I try not to think about it."

"Why? This is a real feeling, isn't it?

"Of course." Lillian felt herself flushing. "He. . .he's wonderful and I think I love him."

"Wow. That's a serious deal, honey, especially with both of you married to other people!"

"I'll probably rot in hell for this but I just can't help myself. I do love him so."

"My God, Lil, you're playing with fire. Dean has such a vicious temper!"

"Mmm. Temper, but no passion."

Carrie nodded in understanding and they both grew silent, afraid to think too much about anything more complicated than breakfast.

*

When the aroma of freshly brewed coffee reached their noses, Lillian and Carrie looked at each other and immediately grabbed their purses and made their way through the crowded aisles, back to the dining car. They managed to get large paper cups of coffee and a courteous porter in a spotless white coat offered them free doughnuts, which they gratefully accepted. Back in their seats, they were reminiscing about the phenomenal art collection at the museum when the train chugged to a stop and the aisle was suddenly filled with men in uniform, all bending under the weight of large duffel bags.

"Where'd you girls get that coffee?" A marine smiled, motioning to their cups. "I'd give a dollar for a cup of joe right now!"

"In the diner car. It's three cars up, and doesn't take long to get there. If you'd like, we can watch your duffel and you won't have to wag it along. . ." Carrie smiled back at the marine and he touched his cap in a salute of thanks and hurried off in the direction of the coffee supply.

When the young marine got back with his coffee and dough-nut, he suggested they reverse the set of seats behind the girls' and then they would have two pair of seats facing each other and could ask for a drop-in table between them and could play cards.

This seemed a great idea to Lillian and Carrie and with several hours to go before they reached Durham, they looked forward to some kind of time-consuming diversion.

The porter was cooperative and soon there was a foursome enjoying card games with plenty of good-natured kibitzing going on all around the table.

"So why are you girls going to North Carolina?

"I think my sister-in-law might have reached there when she escaped from Florida." Lillian's tone of voice was doubtful.

"Are you sure she got out?" The marine corporal's expression was grave. "What's her name?"

"Jamison. Susan Jamison."

"Jamison? From Miami Beach?"

"Yeah.....What do you know about her?"

"Nothing 'bout her. But it's all over the news about two guys name of Jamison. A kid and his grandfather. Sank a wop ship single-handed." His voice and eyes dropped. "They's both killed....I think. But maybe I heard it wrong."

The women were stunned into a rare silence.

"But there's lots o' Jamisons, I imagine. Right?"

They did not respond.

"Sorry, ladies. I'm the messenger, not the mess." With an uncomfortable look on his face he muttered a good-bye and walked away as if in a hurry.

The sailor put the cards down on the table and helped the porter store the table.

"We should be in Durham in about three hours," the sailor said, looking at his watch. "I'm going on to report for duty in… oh. Almost forgot. Can't say." He looked out the window. "Anyway, I'll have to stay on board for a bit longer than you ladies…"

*

The train, now full beyond its maximum capacity, chugged along steadily but left Richmond later than planned. They reached the outskirts of Durham around five-thirty in the evening and the jostling crowds pushed and shoved and both Lillian and Carrie felt like they were being swept along by ocean waves. They both silently agreed that they would not let the news alter their mission. In fact, they both felt that if it were true, Susan needed help all the more.

Lillian kept changing hands carrying her suitcase and although she knew she might be glad she had everything she had brought, she couldn't help but wish she didn't have so much. Carrie's smaller bag seemed much more logical and she moved much more briskly than Lillian.

"C'mon, I see a street car up ahead. We can make it, I think." Carrie pulled Lillian ahead and they got in line to get on. The conductor glared at them impatiently.

"Does your car go to the Duke campus, sir?" Carrie was careful to be extra polite.

"Yes, lady. Eventually every car goes around the campus. There ain't no place else to go in this burg."

"Oh. Well, then, we'd like to go where the most evacuees have been going, if you might know where that is?" Lillian smiled brightly at the dour man.

"Mmm. And that would probably be the Medical Center. I can drop you a few blocks from there."

"Thank you."

The two young women dropped coins in the receptacle and held on to the overhead grips, trying to navigate the crowded aisle with their luggage. Carrie and Lillian edged slowly back to the middle of the bus. Every seat was taken and people from all walks of life were jammed inside, not talking to one another, apparently not even aware of their surroundings. The frequent stops and the jerky starts made everyone standing cling to the handholds as tightly as possible. Conversation was impossible and eventually the conductor craned his neck around and signaled to both Carrie and Lillian he was nearing their destination.

The streetcar wheezed to a stop and the mid-car folding doors sighed open. The girls stumbled down the two steep steps onto the street. As the streetcar hustled away, they looked around and were sobered by the quiet beauty of the verdant campus. Many of the apple trees were in bloom and bulbs were poking up out of the rich loam of the flower beds.

"Look, Carrie. There's a 'You Are Here' sign. . .on that post." They struggled to orient themselves on the graphic campus map in the fading light. "There. The Duke Public Safety Office seems the best place to start. But we're at the intersection of Erwin Road and Hospital Drive, and look, Duke Hospital South is not too far from here, south along this curved street. If we hurry, maybe someone there can steer us to a dorm where we can unload these suitcases and get a shower."

"Sounds great to me, Kemosabe. Let's get there."

Los Alamos, New Mexico

Garret sat at a small desk in his barracks room. He was off duty, but his squad was not in rotation to go into Santa Fe. Most of the fellows mingled about in the pool hall or the recreation room, playing cards, foolishly discussing whether the baseball season would proceed despite the war. Garret was not feeling particularly sociable and had opted to stay by himself at the barracks. He had been listening to his radio and heard through a dispatch from Washington that the situation on the West Coast had grown worse, especially in San Francisco. Following the fall of the city, the Japanese had virtually sealed it off, carefully monitoring any traffic going across the bridges, and reducing ferry traffic on the Bay between Oakland and the city to one every three hours. Sections of Chinatown had been systematically burned or looted by Japanese soldiers, resulting in the deaths of hundreds of Chinatown's residents. According to the report, the Japanese military had pushed as far south as Monterey Bay. Unlike San Francisco, the Presidio at Monterey and Ft. Ord were engaged in a major battle, with nearly thirty thousand American troops participating. The troops, principally trainees briefed in beach and jungle warfare, put up strong resistance. There was little doubt they would all perish.

Garret took out some stationery and, lost in thought, tapped his pen methodically against the desk. He did not even know whether the mail would get through to his friends, let alone the censors. He was just going to write a personal letter. He knew the security regulations. There would be nothing about his job, nor about his location. The security fellows seemed to know how to send mail with different postal addresses. It was confusing to his friends, since they often received postmarks from widely differing locations. Perhaps after the war he could explain. But who would care?

At that moment, he heard a slight knock on the barracks door, followed by the creaking of the old hinges. Aaron Daniels, looking disconsolate himself, stood in the entrance.

"Hi, Garret. Do you have a second?"

"Sure, come on in," Garret replied, replacing the unused stationery.

"Just wanted to see if you had heard anything about Lisa," Aaron stumbled.

"No, sorry, nothing yet. Hey, it's only been a day. But if anything comes in, I'll get a hold of you immediately. We do know that Lisa was not in town in time to be on the train with the other women."

Aaron went from looking disconsolate to downright depressed. His shoulders sagged even more than usual.

"Gee. I don't know what to do. Are we getting phone calls again?"

"Nope, we're shut down very tight. Only official matters get through, and then only to top brass. Though I would think that Lisa would be able to get a message through, don't you?"

Garret tried to console the young scientist.

"Well, I can only hope for the best." Aaron did not make any attempt to sound brave.

"That's all we can do," agreed Garret.

Aaron shook the young soldier's hand and meandered back.

He never realized how very much Garret shared the uncertainty of this new reality.

Mayfield County, Texas

Travis, Hannah-Lee and their mother waited at Arnie's grocery store as Doris Hawley prepared large sandwiches of ham and cheese and bologna for their trip. She sliced the ingredients on the cutting machine somewhat on the heavy side, and smeared gobs of mayonnaise and mustard on the rich brown slices of bread spread out before her.

A woman in her late fifties, her massive bulk was enveloped in a flowered dress covered by a food-stained apron. Her gray hair was tied in a large, untidy bun at the top of her head. She talked non-stop as she prepared the food for the Beechers.

"Don't blame you a bit for taking off. Not one bit. At least you've got somewhere to go. I got kinfolk up in Ohio, but who'd mind the store if I took off? And Arnie's somewhere in Africa, last I heard from him. Army don't tell us much, and we don't get mail the way we should. Used to be I got a letter from Arnie every week. Now, I haven't heard from him ever since the Germans came marching up from Mexico and invaded us. Guess that's to be expected."

She barely paused to suck in a large, noisy breath, and then rapidly continued.

"Those krauts are no better! Tell you what I saw this morning? Went into Dallas for some supplies – what with the rationing gotta be careful with the gasoline, you know – and apart from the fact that the town's almost closed down tighter than a tick with kraut patrols at every intersection and them asking for your license and everything – they write everything down. Everything little thing! – anyhoo, I had to go by the Centennial Stadium on the way to the farmer's market, and what do you think I saw?"

She stopped in her rambling and looked inquisitively at the trio of Beechers standing in front of them. Hannah-Lee, who was slurping on a bottle of NeHi, cued the older woman.

"What?"

Mrs. Hawley, who did not need encouragement, looked appreciatively at the girl.

"Well, first there was a smell in the air that I've never smelled before. Mind you, I've been to the slaughterhouses in Dallas. Smelled some awfully bad smells there. You ever been at a chicken ranch? There's some bad smells! Remember visiting with Arnie once when we went to see his buddy in Arkansas. He had a chicken ranch. Had about a thousand chickens. Now, that was a smell!

"But that weren't nearly as awful as I smelt this mornin'. Couldn't make it out at first. Then, as I was coming near to Centennial, the smell got worse. You know, they got the old incinerators there, the ones they shut down when the fair was being built? Well, the krauts must've opened them up again, for the stacks were spittin' out the darkest, nastiest clouds of smoke I've ever seen, except'n that time I was in Pittsburgh, long time ago. Those steel mills stank nasty, but still, this stuff smelled worse!

"Well, I'm stuck in the truck waiting for another kraut stop, when I see a string of garbage trucks coming out of the stadium, all in a row. They came right past me, from the right, you know, the entrance to the place. Their machinery was a-pumping away,

187

digestin' the garbage, I thought, when I saw an arm danglin' from the back. A human arm! A colored folk's human arm! Then, when the second truck came by, I saw legs and seemed like other pieces of bodies, all of them from colored folks. I tell you, thought I was gonna be sick right there in my truck. Rolled up the window and nearly fainted from the heat. But the smell...."

Mrs. Hawley stopped and shuddered, her eyes filling with tears. She wiped them away and continued, her voice breaking a little here and there. Mrs. Beecher cried, while Hannah-Lee's jaw sagged in disbelief. Travis remained stoic. He had heard of the stories of the gas chambers in Germany. Like most people his age, he thought it was just anti-Nazi propaganda. Now, the terrifying truth seemed to have come to their home in Texas.

Before anyone had a chance to say a word, Mrs. Hawley ran on in her narrative.

"Well, I just wanted to get away from there as quick as anything. My husband always said I was built for comfort, not for speed, but God Almighty, I wanted outta there, you can bet your sweet life. I'm sure you can understand. Went to the farmer's market that end of town and saw Grady. You know, the man who sells me the corn meal and such. Well, we were talking about what was going on, and he heard tell that the krauts are roundin' up and gassin' all them negroes. Told me Bob Dawson, the plumber, built some makeshift shower stalls, big enough to hold about a hundred of them. Then when they herded them all in, instead of turning on the showers, they turn on the gas. Grady said it's some kind of chemical gas, not the kind you use for cookin'. Grady was in the Big War, and he said he'd seen some of that gas. Takes just a little bitty tablet in water or some such, and you're dead."

The woman appeared to shiver for an instant, then resumed

non-stop while she was putting the finishing touches on the Beechers' sandwiches, wrapping them in sheets of white paper.

"Well, seems that, after they gas 'em all, they just heave 'em into the backs of the garbage trucks, and let the trucks pack 'em in like so much trash. Then, I reckon, they take the poor souls to the incinerators and burn the lot!

"Well, I tell you, all the years I've lived here, I never had no problems with our negroes 'round here. Now, Arnie, he sort of went with the Klan in earlier days, but he swears he never did anything except scare some black folks. Never did see no one killed. I'm a good Christian woman; don't hold with killing no one. Can't believe them krauts be such Godless creatures as to do something like I seen! I just can't believe it! Seems like the end o' the world, I tell y'all, the end o' the world. And why not? I say, why not? God must be more'n angry at all this and us Americans not bein' able to do nothin'."

Apparently Mrs. Hawley had finally run out of steam. The emotion of relating the story to the stunned trio drained her. Mrs. Beecher silently took the wrapped packages.

"Thank you, Doris. Thank you so much. Hannah-Lee, would you put these into the bikes' carriers? Make sure you cover them up with the blankets so's they don't get too hot."

Hannah-Lee took the packages and left the store. Travis, in dazed silence, helped his sister stow the provisions for the first leg of their trip.

"Doris, thanks for taking care of the farm. You don't really have to do anything other than pick up the eggs every morning. Sure you can sell them all. We'll be at Susie's in Norman. Doubt whether they'll keep the phones up for long, but you've got the number, just in case. If you change your mind, come on up and stay with us."

The two women hugged at length and cried a little. Outside Mrs. Beecher joined her children, already astride the bicycles, as Doris Hawley stood in the doorway of the country grocery, crying silently.

The trio had not pedaled more than two miles on the hard-packed gravel road when Travis spotted a German army truck in his rear view mirror. The truck was speeding, catching up with them rapidly, and kicking up clouds of dust.

"Mom! Hannie! Let's pull over!"

His mother and sister turned their heads. Seeing the racing truck, they nodded, backpedaled, and came to a halt. They moved their bikes to the far right side of the road in the weeds and grass that bordered the ditch. They disturbed a group of bullfrogs that had sat in the small rivulet of the ditch, stopping a symphony of deep-throated croaking.

The truck sped past, the driver not bothering to apply his brakes. German soldiers sat hunched in the open back of the vehicle, their steel helmets catching rays of the sun, their guns slung across their backs. A second truck sped by, then a third. Each was filled with regular German Army troops.

The Beechers were enveloped in a cloud of rising, choking dust. Hannah-Lee rubbed her eyes wordlessly. Travis looked concerned and silently shook his head at his mother. Bringing up the rear of the convoy was a pick-up truck, its bed filled with hollering and whooping teen-aged boys.

As the last vehicle sped by, Travis instantly recognized Jonas' truck. A second later it jammed on its brakes. Its driver leaned heavily on the horn and waved out his window at the trucks ahead of him. The Germans understood the signal and stopped while Jonas climbed down from his pickup and came walking towards the trio by the side of the road. He was wearing his Nazi armband conspicuously tied around his bare, muscled arm.

"Howdy, Travis, Mrs. Beecher, Hannah-Lee," he said, eyeing the young girl lasciviously.

"Howdy, Jonas," Travis replied.

Jonas eyed the bicycles and the small bundles each had in its carrier. Several armed soldiers came running towards them from the trucks ahead.

"Going somewhere?"

"Just out for a little picnic," Travis lied.

Jonas scratched his head.

"Y'all left kinda early last night Missed all the fun!"

"Yeah, well, you know how it goes." Travis scratched his boot in the dirt, his hands in his pockets. Inside, his fists were balled tightly.

"Well, Travis, reckon we all didn't get to swear you in. We're all part of Der Fuhrer's army now. We're in charge of this county, don't ya know."

"Look, Jonas, its still a free country. No one's got to join anything. The German said so last night. He invited anyone who didn't choose to be sworn into his group to leave. He didn't threaten nobody."

Travis rubbed his hand over the stubble of his blond beard.

"Yeah, but seein' as you're my friend, I was mighty disappointed. So were my friends." He pointed at the young men who were milling about, some with hands deep in their pockets, embarrassed, others with their eyes on Hannah-Lee. None of he boys would look at Mrs. Beecher, whom most of them had known for many years.

"Come on, Jonas, let's go," urged one of the young boys.

"Yeah, if'n he don't wanna be part of the group, let him be," said another. They were a different bunch of ruffians in the sunshine of the day than they had been the night before. A few climbed back into the pickup truck.

Jonas felt that he had to exert his leadership.

"Look, anyone's not with us is against us!" he yelled. Quickly he crossed the few steps to Hannah-Lee, grabbed her arm and yanked her forward. Surprised and frightened, the girl struggled to get away. Mrs. Beecher screamed, while two of the German soldiers moved cautiously forward, un-slinging their rifles.

"Let me go, you son-of-a-bitch!" Hannah-Lee protested. She kicked hard at the much larger boy, lodging one quick kick at Jonas' left shin.

"Shit, bitch!" Jonas exclaimed.

In a flash, Travis let out with a yell and landed a solid jab to Jonas's jaw. The unexpected punch caught Jonas off guard and knocked him to the ground. Getting up, fury filled his eyes and he could barely get words out.

"Get her. Get the girl!" he stammered.

"Run, Hannie!" Travis shouted at the same time.

Hannah-Lee stood frozen in fear long enough for two of the German soldiers to run to the girl, slap her harshly across her face and pin her arms behind her back. The slap had been hard enough that her head sagged and she went limp. The soldiers dragged her away just as Travis lunged at Jonas again. The pair rolled on the ground, kicking and punching at each other. A swift kick from one of Jonas' boots caught Travis on the right temple and he blacked out.

"Put the girl in the truck with me," Jonas commanded. Realizing that the soldiers probably did not speak English, he pointed and gesticulated. The Germans understood the gestures and dragged the limp girl to Travis' pickup, momentarily forgetting about Travis lying on the ground.

Through the fog of her tears, Mrs. Beecher saw her daughter being dragged away by the Germans. Instinctively, she ran after her girl just as Travis reoriented himself.

"Hannah-Lee!" the woman cried as she ran after her and the soldiers. Jonas stood in her way, watching the spectacle. She reached him in an instant and pummeled the startled Jonas with her small fists, all the while crying hysterically. Startled by the ferocious onslaught of the small, older woman, Jonas threw a punch between her breasts that knocked the air out of her. She doubled over. As she tried to stand up again, a single shot rang out. Looking surprised, Mrs. Beecher looked at the rapidly staining front of her dress, then collapsed on the gravel road. The German soldier who had shot her raised his rifle and waved at his comrades in the convoy.

"Gehen wir," he yelled. He motioned to Jonas. "Schnell!"

Travis, lying near the ditch, knew numbly that his mother was dead. Seeing Hannah-Lee dragged away, he almost retched. He knew what Jonas had in mind for her. Nonetheless, he calculated that he was vastly outnumbered and could do more good if he could somehow get away. He quietly rolled down the shallow embankment into the creek. If he could traverse the small field between him and the woods standing less than half a football field away, he might have a chance.

Seeing Jonas walking toward his truck and hearing the German trucks starting, Travis took the chance. Climbing quietly up the far embankment, he crouched low as he reached the cotton field. He moved forward as rapidly as possible when he heard Jonas' voice crying out.

"Hey, wait a minute! Hold it!"

Travis did not know, nor did he care, whether the shouts were directed at him or at the Germans. He only knew he had to reach the woods. He broke into a run, crouching as low as possible and still maintaining some speed. Suddenly he heard the whistle of a bullet flying by. Then another and another. He zigzagged between the cotton plants. Looking briefly backwards, several German soldiers were now following him. He panted from the exertion. Ten yards to go, he thought feverishly. The pain in his side was excruciating. Eight yards and touchdown! His mind thought back as he had always prayed his friend Jonas would score a touchdown on Friday nights. Jonas always had. Travis had never made it even to the junior varsity team. Now it was his turn. Five yards! He heard the Germans thrashing through the young cotton plants some ways behind him, yelling at each other in their guttural language.

Suddenly he reached the welcome shade of the trees. He knew that he had made his touchdown, but he kept running, dodging branches and underbrush, mindless of the briars and poison ivy scratching his bare arms. Suddenly, a pair of arms yanked him off his feet and upwards into the branches of the trees. A hand was firmly clasped over his mouth before he passed out.

Durham, North Carolina

The two women began to walk as fast as they could, south on Hospital Drive and as soon as they walked up a steep hill, the sprawling complex of the hospital buildings came into view. Their jaws dropped and they stood perfectly still, staring at the myriad of choices below.

"Well, that third building on the left looks like the main hall. Let's try that."

They walked with a renewed spring in their strides and once inside the waiting room, were chagrined by the number of people waiting. Some were sprawled on the floor, some were leaning against walls, and no one was speaking to anyone else. Carrie and Lillian eased their luggage near an opening against the wall and stood patiently.

The harried volunteer behind the desk was processing people as fast as she could. There were no emergency injury cases here, that was obvious, but as nearly as Lillian could tell, most of the people were evacuees from farther south, which filled her with hope. With about twenty people ahead of them, the girls were becoming aware of their fatigue and their hunger and suddenly, two more volunteers showed up. The woman who had been working said, "Thank God!" stood up and walked out of the anteroom as the two others took over.

With two people registering the needy civilians, Carrie and Lillian were soon facing their interviewer and telling the young man their story. He listened and took notes, then referred them to Wannamaker Hall, a dormitory formerly reserved for male students but now open to evacuees. He couldn't guarantee a bed, but there were mattresses and plenty of open floor space. Any safe and clean place to sleep was a godsend.

The man gave them a slip proving they had registered and then told them where the nearest diner was. Any greasy spoon would do. They got there just before it closed, ate, and headed back to Wannamaker Hall. By the time they climbed five flights of stairs, they were both glassy-eyed with fatigue. They were shown to a metal cot and with their clothes on, squeezed in and drifted off.

195

Dreamless sleep was their reward and they both awoke the next morning as day broke and a spring rain brushed the rooftops. Coffee was available on the first floor in the waiting room and the girls left their suitcases locked under their cots and started walking as fast as they could toward the Public Safety Office. Another helpful evacuee told them there were extensive files on people coming in from the beleaguered south and they hoped, if Susan had made it out, that she was registered there.

The rain had abated as they made their way up the slick steps of the government office and entered another crowded waiting room. By the time they reached the desk, half a day had evaporated and Lillian was growing impatient with the red tape. The female clerk studied them over her rimless reading glasses and cleared her throat.

"We have many, many people from the Miami area, you know. We've had so many injured our hospitals are full and the overflow, of patients not as seriously hurt, have been relegated to the art museum – the Nasher Museum of Art, right across Campus Drive from here. I see no patient named Susan Jamison listed on our admittance lists but you might check the museum. That was the only place we had left after the gymnasium filled up and the museum has huge rooms of space…"

Lillian and Carrie thanked her and left quickly, before the woman could prattle on. When they got past the receptionist in the museum entry, who had told them to look in the modern art section for a Susan Jamison, they worked their way through hundreds of people on stretchers, many wounded, some just staring at nothing. One man was lying on the hard floor, next to his empty stretcher, and Lillian approached him to try and get him back up on the gurney. He was missing an arm and had a bandage over most of his head. Carrie tried to pull Lillian back away from the man but she motioned for her to let her go.

"Hello." She smiled at the man.

"Margie, is that you?" The man's voice was almost a whisper. "I'm so thirsty."

Lillian looked meaningfully at Carrie, who nodded and left to find a nurse.

"We're getting you a drink, soon now."

'You found me!" The man coughed up blood and Lillian wiped the phlegm off his chin with the edge of his torn shirt. He caught her wrist in his bony hand and held on, as if to a life pre-server.

Carrie returned handing Lillian a paper cup full of cool water and said, "The medic is swamped in the other room but said he'd get here as soon as he could. . ."

Lillian held the cup to the man's lips and he drank grateful-ly, then began coughing up blood again. He stared at Lillian's face, squinting his eyes.

"I thought you were my. . .my wife. . .my Margie"

Lillian smiled. "I'm sorry, I'm not her. . ."

"Then. . .then you must be an angel sent to. . ." His cough-ing became more pronounced.

"Go find a nurse or somebody who can help this man. . ."

"There isn't anyone, Lil! They are just bogged down in the other rooms. There are too many injured here. . ."

"I feel so helpless. . ." Lillian leaned over the man and stroked his forehead. The soldier whispered something to her and opened his clenched fist, holding something out to her.

"No, I can't take. . ."

"Yes, please, angel. . ." He pressed a silver St. Christopher medal into her hand.

Lillian's eyes brimmed over as she and Carrie left the dying man and continued searching the endless cots for Susan.

They wandered in and out of rows of people, some sitting up, some unconscious, some muttering unintelligible words, some moaning and weeping as if they would never stop. Suddenly, Lillian halted and held one of her hands over her mouth, pointing with the other.

"There! Back there, the woman sitting up and facing the wall. See? I think that's Susan."

They crawled over bodies and outstretched legs and arms and got to the woman's cot. It was Susan but she seemed to be in deep shock.

"Susan! Susan, can you hear me?" Lillian put her arms around her sister-in-law. "My God, Carrie, look at her!"

Susan stared unblinking at Lillian, then abruptly began to cry, putting her arms around Lillian's neck, pulling her close. "Oh God, Lillian, they're gone, they're gone! Dad and Jason both! Dead! And I'm sure Ryan is, too! I have no one, no one!"

"Oh, hon, I'm so sorry, so sorry." Lillian sat holding Susan close and rocked back and forth, as if she were a mother holding a child.

Carrie sat on the other side of Susan, stroking her hair, tears of sympathy flowing down her cheeks.

Over Susan's bowed head, Lillian looked at Carrie. "We've got to get her out of here and somehow back to New York, where her folks can help her heal."

"But do you think she can make the trip?" Carrie was dubious about the prospect of Susan surviving the uncertain journey north.

"She's got to make it. She's got to." Lillian continued stroking Susan's shoulders and gradually, Susan's sobs quieted and she began to talk.

Susan told them of the fear in her old neighborhood and the disbelief as they were told to evacuate and the stubborn bravery of her father-in-law, then the horror of finding out it was he and Jason on that suicide mission, ramming the huge battleship with two old torpedoes that sank the ship and killed them both. After that, the Italians, furious and apoplectic with humiliation, stormed the beaches and wreaked havoc even though many civilians remained behind trying to defend their homes. Not a building on Miami Beach was left standing. The bombardment lasted two days. Then the troops stormed the beaches.

As soon as Susan found out what had happened from Fred's fishing buddies who saw the whole thing, she had run to her neighbor's house and they had talked her into leaving with them in an abandoned hearse and that was how they made it to Atlanta. The facilities there were overrun with people. Susan left her friends and kept going north, ending up in Durham, at the Duke campus. She had been there for nearly a week and was coming out of the first stages of her terrible grief and shock.

The three women walked to the cafeteria near the art museum where more volunteers were serving food, then they took Susan with them back to Wannamaker Hall, where they gave her a clean pair of pants and a blouse after she took a long hot shower and washed her hair. She was coming back, albeit slowly, and that was the first sign Lillian and Carrie had that she would recover.

Lillian pulled a crumpled road map from her and huddled over it, showing the other two where State Highway 15 intersected with Interstate Highway 1, which would take them north to New York. And the more they looked at the map, the farther it seemed.

At the edge of the campus, they stopped at the diner. They

NEVER ON THESE SHORES

hoped to be able to hitch a ride with some good Samaritans if they were at the right place at the right time.

They went inside the diner and sat in a booth, sipping coffee and waiting for someone that looked like they'd have room for three strangers as passengers, someone heading north.

After an hour and too much coffee, Carrie nudged Lillian with her elbow and pointed her chin toward a middle-aged man sitting down in a booth across the room.

"Hey. I just saw him get out of a pick-up, one of those big mamas, and it has New Jersey plates." She glanced pointedly at a dull green truck on the parking lot, loaded with hundred-pound bags of plums, tomatoes and onions, obviously headed for northern markets where fresh produce was impossible to find. The man had removed his straw hat and was running his thick fingers through his sparse hair, staring at the menu. Lillian stood up.

"I'm going over there and see if he'll take us with him, if he's headed north. He might like to have some help with the cost of the gas." She swallowed visibly and walked briskly through the tables to the booths on the other side of the L-shaped dining room.

"Uh…sir? Excuse me?"

The man looked her up and down, his watery blue eyes staring and insolent. "Yep?"

"My friends and I. . ."she motioned to Carrie and Susan, across the room, "are desperate to get a ride to New York City. The trains are not taking civilians north, not regularly, and we have to get our friend Susan back to be with her family. . .she escaped from the invasion of Miami Beach. . ."

"Yeah? Did she escape with anything valuable?"

"No. Nothing as valuable as her life. Her father-in-law and

son were killed by the Italians trying to help protect the rest of us. . ."

"Mmm. You think that's gonna make me feel obligated or some such? Everybody's in some sorta shit...excuse my French, ma'am, but these is tryin' times."

"No, I didn't mean it that way. But we are just trying to help her out. And we'll be glad to share the cost of the gasoline. . "

"Now that's more like it. Yep, I'll give ya'll a ride. I could use the company. Let me finish this here burger."

"Of course and I can't thank you enough. My name is Lillian and my friends' names are. . ."

"Pleased to meet ya. You can call me Dutch."

Lillian nodded and hurried back to Carrie and Susan, telling them the news but feeling some vague misgivings about the man. But beggars can't be choosers, she thought.

The others were overjoyed at having a ride back and Lillian shrugged, attributing her fears to the pressures they had all been enduring. They watched the man eating his hamburger. He wiped at his mouth and stood up, jerking his ticket from under the sugar canister, and walked up to the cashier's counter, signaling for the three young women to follow him outside.

They had already paid for their coffee so they hurried outside with their two suitcases and Susan's laundry bag of belongings, which was everything she owned in the world.

Dutch got in the driver's seat and Carrie got in front beside him. Lillian and Susan crammed in the back with the luggage partly on the floor and seat between them, adjusting for as much comfort as they could manage, as the truck left the parking lot and headed for the freeway, going north.

At first, they talked about the war, but after a time they all fell silent and simply watched the countryside glide by as the truck made its noisy way north.

"You gals all Yankees?" he asked.

"No, I'm a Dodgers fan," quipped Carrie. The girls laughed, but Dutch didn't get the joke.

"My family's from Alabama, 'riginally, my great granddaddy fought in the War Between the States. He'd be turnin' in his grave if he knew I has yankee girls in ma truck. But times is changed, I reckon. Times is changed. "

"We're all in this together, Mr. Dutch," said Susan. "And I can't thank you enough for…"

"Never you mind, girlie," he said. "Bygones is bygones, I know. But still…"

As the afternoon wore on, Susan dozed in the back seat and Carrie squirmed as her bladder began to signal she needed to relieve herself and soon.

"Dutch?" Carrie's voice was softly pleading. "Dutch, I have to. . .I have to go to the bathroom."

"Ha! There ain't nothin' along this stretch of highway for miles, missy. You jes' gonna have to hold it. I can pull to the side o' the road and you can piss in the bushes. Shit, I don't mind if you don't."

"It's O.K. with me. I'm sorry. I just can't wait."

"Well then, I guess when you gotta go, you gotta go, right?" He laughed and suddenly jerked the wheel sharply to the right, turning up a dirt road that was barely visible from the highway. "I drive this road about three times a month, so I know every nook and cranny. . ." He was leaning forward, looking for something. "There's what I was lookin' for."

He slowed the truck while he eased it into the edge of a heavily wooded area, with the nose of the hood almost pressing itself between the slender trunks of young willow trees. He cut off the motor and opened the driver's door, stepping outside.

"Oh, there's no need for you to get out, too. I'll be fine." Carrie opened the passenger door and, holding a tissue she had dug from her purse, stepped out onto the rough grass.

Dutch laughed again, that same forced and threatening sound. "You other little ladies wanna get out and stretch?" He leaned inside the cab, crooking his index finger, inviting Lillian outside. Susan was still asleep but had begun to stir.

"No. . .no, we're fine."

He was fishing in one of the pockets of his coveralls, then turned to walk in the direction Carrie had taken, deeper into the shadows of the trees. At that precise moment, the sun peeked out from behind a cloud, and glinted on a piece of mirror-like steel Dutch was holding in the palm of his hand.

"I likes the smell o' yankee bitch's piss," he mumbled. "You little cunny cunt. Start yer pissin'."

"My God, he's got a knife! Wake up, Susan!" Lillian elbowed Susan's back and opened the door and jumped out, racing to catch up with Dutch. Susan froze and would not move from the truck.

"Stop! You sonuvabitch! What the fuck do you think you're doing?"

Dutch wheeled around and punched Lillian in the face. She fell into the bushes, in a daze.

He straightened up and found Carrie about twenty yards ahead. She was squatting and urinating with her panties around her ankles. She saw him and turned sheet-white, lunging upward, trying to pull up her pants. Her legs got tangled up in her underwear and pants and she pitched forward on her stomach.

"That's it, baby, just leave them trousers down and let me

have at that sweet little yankee ass! Then I'm gonna have me some lovin' from your cunny cunt buddies, too. And if you don't do what I tell ya', I'll slice y'all open with this and fuck you any-where I want!"

Dutch grimaced as he unbuckled his belt and unzipped the fly of his work pants, his erection popping out as if it had been a trapped animal. He kept one hand on his penis as he pressed a knee into Carrie's back and stroked her buttocks with the razor-sharp hunting knife. A line of brilliant ruby red followed the point of the blade.

"I'll gut you like a hog, ya little bitch."

Carrie screamed.

"Shut the fuck up, bitch!" Dutch tried to mount Carrie while she squirmed and twisted beneath him. He stuck his fore-finger into her anus.

"How do ya' like that, Miss Yankee Prissy?"

"Please, no...." Carrie cried.

"Say pretty please, ya little cunny cunt."

Susan came up behind him holding up a jagged rock about the size of half a loaf of bread and, with all her strength, she slammed the rock into the back of Dutch's greasy head. He jolt-ed upright for a split-second and then, as he reached for his scalp she raised the rock again and again, smashing his head to a pulp. He fell over on top of Carrie who was struggling underneath his weight.

Lillian had revived and staggered out of the bushes.

"Lillian! My God, Carrie. . .Carrie isn't moving!"

Lillian and Susan rushed to pull Dutch off of Carrie, but they were too late. Dutch had never lost his grip on his hunting knife and while he had the point of it pressed to her buttocks near her waist, the force of Susan's blows on the back of his head caused him to pitch forward against his knife-wielding hand and this drove the knife into Carrie's back. She was still alive but her bleeding was so profuse, they knew she was beyond help.

The gushing blood was turning the brown dirt to copper-stained earth. Carrie opened her eyes for a minute, looking at Lillian with recognition but not saying anything. Her face was gray and her breathing was labored. Suddenly, spittle frothed on her lips and she exhaled with a long sigh. She was dead.

Lillian rocked back on her heels and wept into her hands. Susan was so stunned with this unexpected horror she could only stare at Carrie's face and the widening pool of red.

Gently, Lillian reached over and closed Carrie's eyelids and looked at Susan.

"Hold on, Sue. We gotta get outta here."

Susan was silent.

"Sue! Come on."

Susan stood up and, zombie-like, started walking back to the truck.

As they approached it, Susan said, "What about Carrie? We can't just leave her there."

"We've got no choice. I'm sorry, we've got no choice. Let's get going. It's getting dark."

The truck refused to start at first but with a little coaxing and a vicious verbal threat, the motor coughed to life and the girls bumped along the dirt road leading back to the highway. Lillian didn't turn on the headlights until they entered the main road. She turned left and headed north. Susan stared out the window at the yellow moon that had risen in the east.

"The moon. It's following us," she said.

Santa Fe, New Mexico

Some miles away in Santa Fe, Whispering Eagle continued his one-man search for the missing Lisa. Yesterday, the first person he had talked to was Jim, the young, black shoeshine boy who had his own regular stand at the train station. He was no more than a year or two older than Whispering Eagle, but stood nearly a foot taller.

"No siree, didn't see no tomato like that get off a train. Keeps my eyes peeled all the time. I'se meets all the trains, 'cause that's good business. Hey, what's a pair of legs like this want with a young redskin like you?"

"Nothing. Just doing a favor for a friend of mine, you know."

Later he had made his way through the hotels where he thought she might stay. The concierges and bellboys whom he knew shook their heads. No, sure would have remembered this one, most offered, in one way or another.

Today, he went to the army depot just on the outskirts of the town.

"Hi, Sergeant," he yelled to the man at the gate.

"Hey. How's things?" the older man responded good-naturedly as he waved to the young boy.

"Oh, you know, little bit of this, little bit of that."

The Indian lad crossed the tarmac to the guard shack, pulling Lisa's picture from his pocket.

"You seen her lately?" he asked the sergeant. The man looked at the picture, gave a brief whistle of appreciation, then shook his head.

"Can't say I have, though I'd like to have seen her. What a

dish! She a friend of yours?"

"A friend of a friend," Whispering Eagle replied.

"Sure, I know. Hey, do you want to take a letter for me?"

He looked at the sergeant, a smile crossing his thin face.

"Sure! You know the cost, Sarge." The smile grew broader.

"Yeah, I know. A cigarette."

"Two." Whispering Eagle held up two fingers.

The sergeant shook his head. "Thief!" he said, again good-naturedly, and handed the Indian a small, stamped envelope. Then he pulled out a pack of cigarettes, withdrew two, and handed them to the boy. Whispering Eagle stuck the envelope inside his shirt, and slipped the two cigarettes into his shirt pocket. He waved as he walked into the army depot.

He repeated the routine of asking about Lisa. He had had no luck. No one had seen the young woman. Whispering Eagle had collected a dozen cigarettes and took back with him half a dozen envelopes stuck in his shirt as he sauntered out of the army depot.

San Francisco, California

Jimmy tried to hide the glowing tip of his cigarette in the palm of his hand as he watched the two shadowy figures standing in the closed bar entrance. He stopped breathing and simply waited, his mind racing and no solution appearing to him. In a millisecond he realized that if he called out, he'd expose his friends to certain capture and probable death and, if he didn't, they'd all be caught anyway. Could he take them himself? He had no weapon. It was then that the cigarette started to burn a hole in the palm of his hand.

"Fuck me!" he yelled at the top his lungs.

"Oh, Mary, what the fuck is that?" said one of the figures. All three of them seemed to jump at once, one of the strangers backstepping and tripping over a broom on the floor. He toppled in a heap.

"Ben, are you all right?" said a voice.

Jimmy said, "Who the fuck is Ben?"

"Jimmy? Is that you?"

"Oh, shit. Ben? And Phil? Phil, is that you?"

By this time, Carmine and Lindy had heard the ruckus and had come running up the stairs.

"Very dramatic, girls, " said Lindy. "How about knocking first."

"It's us," said Phil rising to his feet and dusting himself off. "Is Dodge here?"

"Looking for drink tickets?" said Jimmy.

"Not exactly," said Ben. "Let's go downstairs. We need something."

"Let me lock the door first," said Jimmy. "And my hand smells like a hamburger. Thanks guys."

They ambled carefully down the old steps and huddled in the storeroom.

Ben Shaw had been a university English teacher, but didn't like the low pay or the conflict he faced daily about out-of-classroom relationships with students. Phil Smith was a bartender in the bar they were all sitting in. He had met Ben over a year ago and they were living together a few weeks later.

Just after arriving in San Francisco from Minneapolis, Ben had run for a seat on the city council and had been thought a shoe-in as a Roosevelt-style New Deal democrat. Unfortunately, he let his wry sense of humor pop out at inappropriate times. Once, at a debate with the reactionary republican candidate, the moderator asked him who his favorite author was and why. Spontaneously, he responded that Sinclair Lewis was his favorite because, "he wrote some readable books, had been the first American to win the Nobel Prize for Literature, and managed to get laid in every small town and big city on the planet even with a face that looked like it had caught on fire and been put out with an ice pick." The other guy picked Margaret Mitchell and Gone with the Wind. Ben lost in a landslide and Phil's only comment was, "I think you lost the acne vote. Next time pick God and tell them how nice the Bible is. This is still California, USA, not the second moon of Uranus."

"So what brings you here?" said Lindy half-heartedly. Carmine sat in a stupor mulling over the news about his sister and feeling more impotent than ever.

"We need some of the dynamite," said Phil matter-of-factly.

"Dynamite? What dynamite?" asked Lindy.

"The pile you're sitting on."

They all stared at the floor simultaneously as Phil nudged everyone aside and reached down to pull the round iron handle on the trap door in the floor.

"No smoking, please," he said looking up at them.

He opened the door, set it back on its hinges and jumped in landing only three feet down.

"They used to hide moonshine down here in Prohibition days. Dodge showed me this spot. Some local gangsters used to run this joint and they had stolen dynamite from some construction project to use in a bank job. They didn't need the space for booze, so they stashed the TNT here. Dodge told me all about it. Can't vouch for the story, but it sounded good to me. Yepper, here 'tis."

Rural North Carolina

"There! A mileage sign, on the right. See it?" Susan was squinting through the windshield. "Slow down so we can read it."

"I see it. Twenty-five miles to the intersection with US 1, which is what we want. That takes us right into the City…but…we're almost out of gas."

"The sign said Dinwiddie is off to the left, in about five or ten miles? I'm not sure."

"O.K., we should make it there. Pray they have gasoline."

They drove in silence for the next few miles and saw only military vehicles, all heading south to the front.

"Here's the cut-off." Lillian slowed the truck and exited the freeway, turning into the main street of a sleepy little North Carolina town.

Three blocks down, just past the A&P was the red, black and white Texaco star beaming down from its rusty sign post. There was a large, hand-printed sign leaning on the pump, which read "No Gas For Civilians. Military ONLY." Lillian turned to the right and pulled close to the pump, turning the motor off. The red gauge of the gasoline indicator shuddered to a stop, hovering over the black E.

"I think I see someone inside. Look." Susan leaned toward Lillian, pointing to the small building. A figure moved around inside. She opened the passenger door.

"C'mon, let's go in."

Lillian pulled the keys from the ignition and the two bedraggled travelers walked up to the plate glass door, pushing it open.

"Sorry, ladies." Behind the counter stood a man about 25 years old.

"I can't sell you no gas, not a drop. We been told it's all restricted to military vehicles only and that there truck don't look like no military vehicle to me." He grinned at them, flashing brilliant white square teeth and sparkling deep-blue eyes. A shock of jet-black hair fell across his tanned forehead and the thickness of his neck and the definition of his biceps bulged under the rolled-up sleeves of his blue work shirt. He kept wiping at the glass counter with a polishing cloth but his eyes never left the two exhausted young women.

"Ya'll look mighty beat down. Where ya'll headed?"

"We're trying to get back to New York." Lillian put her arm around Susan's shoulders and they edged closer to the counter. "She's been through hell, mister."

"That's been goin' around, I guess." His polishing cloth had stopped moving. "Hey, my name is Walter." He walked from behind the counter and it was then his artificial leg became visible, jutting out from the bottom edge of one leg of his cut blue trousers.

The women couldn't help staring. "Yep, I lost a leg, but not in a war. I was helping my uncle tree a big ole' coon that had been stealing all our chicken eggs two years ago and when I shinnied up that tree, I was lookin' up at the coon, not at where I was putting my damned feet, and so I slipped. Fell eighteen feet. Broke three ribs, ruptured my spleen, and my leg got skewered on a jagged trunk of an old pine that had been split by lightnin'.

My leg bones looked worse'n that damned tree. Nothin' they could do."

"I'm sorry," Lillian Said. "Look, we've just got to get to New York as soon as possible. "Couldn't you spare us some gas? We'll be happy to pay you double."

"Double? Gosh, that'd be a lot of money. . ." Walter hobbled over to the doorway and stared out at the truck. He smiled. "I guess I could make an exception for you two. Wish I could do more for the war effort." He led them back outside, where he filled the tank.

"That oughta get ya' close."

"How much?" Lillian pulled out her wallet.

"Nothin'. Y'all owe me nothin'."

"We've got to give you something," said Lillian.

"I'm a married man, ma'am, but thanks anyway."

"No, I mean, well, we've got some apples and plums in the back. You're welcome to some."

"Well, that's right kindly. Foods a might scarce although we're doin' O.K."

He walked around to the back of the truck and looked in the sacks. "I'll take these here apples. That all right?"

"Of course. And thank you."

"Thank you," he said hefting the sack out and nearly falling over. They acted as if they hadn't noticed. As the two women climbed back in the truck, Walter leaned against the driver's door and lowered his voice. "Ya'll best take the back roads. It's all farm country thataway." He pointed out the route on the map Lillian was studying.

"See that road? After you pass Colonial Heights, stay on US 1 till you see the cut-off to 295, then take that north toward Richmond, but don't go there, take state road 301, due north."

Walter waved as they pulled out onto the roadway. By the time they got to the small town of Hanover, they were fighting to stay awake. Lillian pulled into a gravel driveway of what appeared to be an abandoned old barn with one of its huge wooden doors hanging askew and the other stubbornly closed. She stopped the truck and turned off the engine.

"You know, if we could get that other door open, we could drive the truck inside and it wouldn't be visible. That would buy us a little safe down time so we could get some rest."

"Sounds good." Susan opened her door and climbed out of the truck, walking up to the old barn door,

Lillian looked around the area cautiously, walking behind Susan, preparing to help her wrench the door open wide enough to drive the truck into the barn.

A sudden burst of a scrambling, screeching noise startled them as four or five nesting owls shot through the opening, flapping their wings wildly as they headed for another roost. Small paws scratched against the clapboard floors as rats scurried under the hay.

"It's O.K., Susan. We're bigger than they are." She patted Susan's trembling shoulders and they began to wrestle the leaning door out of the way, finally forcing it open.

"Walk carefully. I don't want to have to pull you out of a hole. This whole damn barn looks like a fart would blow it down."

Susan cracked a smile as she tiptoed around the edge of the inside of the barn and Lillian inched the truck inside. The floor creaked and moaned but held.

Lillian climbed up into the back of the truck and got some tomatoes, apples and a head of kale. Susan kicked and pulled stacks of sweet-smelling hay into a thick pallet. They ate without talking. After tossing the remains of the produce out the door, Susan returned and said, "I just need some sleep. I don't think I've slept in weeks. And I don't think tonight is going to be any different."

They lay awkwardly next to each other. Lillian was weeping softly.

"Lil? You O.K."

"I was just thinking about Carrie. She was such a good person. She would never hurt anyone. She was here because of me...she...now..."

"Stop thinking about it. Try to put it out of your mind. We have to take each day as we find it. There is no yesterday and probably no tomorrow. Only today. We're just going through the motions, just the motions. Death is everywhere. It is so horrible, but...but....Carrie may be the lucky one...God forgive me for saying it. She may be the lucky one."

They said nothing further but silently listened to the cacophony of crickets, frogs and night birds.

*

Lillian was naked and chained by her wrists to a wall, her hands pulled over her head. The room where she found herself was completely dark except for the conical beam from a hanging lamp over a small table. On the table were lancets, tooth extracting pliers, a thumbscrew, a vise that would fit around a skull and countless knives of all lengths and sharpness. Empty picture frames and torn paintings littered the room. A uniformed man, dressed like a Gestapo agent was shouting at her.

"Will you tell us?"

"My name is Lillian Marshall. . .I'm only a. . ." She shrieked as the German shoved a burning cigarette into the small of her back. She twisted and turned, pulling against the shackles holding her by the wrists.

"Perhaps you did not hear my question?" He burned her again with the cigarette, smiling broadly as she screamed in pain.

"I'm thirsty. Please, water, please."

"Water, water, everywhere and not a drop to drink!" The man laughed hysterically and poured water all over her hanging head and her bare breasts.

Lillian sputtered and coughed. "Please, please, please stop!"

"Where are the paintings?"

"I don't know!"

The German slid a long, shiny knife across her back, drawing blood that oozed down across her buttocks. She screamed with all her might, her teeth bared with the excruciating pain.

"Shut up, bitch! Stop your useless noise before I have to kill you!"

She struggled against her manacles, fighting for her life, and in one fierce lunge, shoved against her torturer who fell back against the hanging lamp. Its beam swung from one side of the room to the other as it swirled side to side. In the spinning glare she looked up and saw her tormentor's face. It was Lucien West, her love. She heard someone screaming and realized it was herself. She awoke suddenly, sweat pouring from her body into the hay.

She looked out through the gaps of the barn siding. The sky was turning a pale turquoise as dawn approached. Susan lay beside her soundly asleep. Lillian closed her eyes and prayed to make it through the day.

Dallas, Texas

General Erwin Rommel reclined in a large, comfortable velvet armchair as he listened to the finale of Beethoven's Ninth Symphony. He had closed his eyes, luxuriating in the strains of the choral piece. He never understood why Hitler preferred Wagner to Beethoven. Perhaps Der Führer preferred the chaotic times in Germany during which Wagner had written to the relatively peaceful ones of Beethoven. Times were reflected in music, he mused. More simply, perhaps Hitler simply preferred Wagner's nationalistic themes. Perhaps, there was no sense to Der Führer's likes and dislikes. Beethoven was full of power, but imbued with a serene, mystical air. Schiller's words to the Ninth were full of the hope he, Rommel, also held for the world.

As the solo voices joined with those of the choir, a furtive knock disturbed his reveries. Rommel snapped, "Come in!" and a small, mousy man in a regular army tunic came into the room. He drew himself up to his full, short stature, and saluted. His insignia showed him to be a lieutenant. Rommel perfunctorily returned the salute, then immediately placed a finger over his lips, motioning the man to remain silent. The soldier did so and remained obediently at attention. Rommel waved to the man, inviting him to stand at ease. Rommel returned his attention to the music and listened to the remainder of the Beethoven. When the piece had concluded, Rommel looked at him inquisitively.

"Yes, then, what is it?"

"Sir, I am Lieutenant Schreiber with Signal Corps Intelligence. We have intercepted transmissions that indicate a much larger than usual amount of air traffic in and around Santa Fe, New Mexico."

Rommel scratched his chin while lighting a cigarette.

"Santa Fe? There is nothing of importance there, as far as I know. It is a dusty little town in the mountains, no?"

"Yes sir, here." Schreiber walked a few steps to a map displaying the southwest United States in political and topographical detail. He pointed to the small city represented by a tiny blue dot.

"What kind of traffic?"

"Mostly small aircraft. Their transmissions are coded differently than normal military traffic. Also, and this may be of special interest, sir, they appear to be ... well, sir, circling! They are not simply going from point A to point B. They appear to be circling the city."

Rommel's interest became evident by the rapid puffs of smoke on his cigarette.

"Why would they circle this town if there is nothing there? How much of a military presence is there in Santa Fe?"

"Nothing, sir. There is just a small token defensive unit to guard the city. A typical unit for a town this size. They seem to be monitoring the rail traffic coming through just south of the city. The rail traffic has increased over the last several days. It seems to be shoring up against the eventuality of us moving west, or the Japanese coming east."

"That's it, then! They are monitoring the rail traffic. Thank you, Schreiber!"

The lieutenant hesitated, then spoke up nervously.

"Sir, there is one more thing..."

"Yes, then, go ahead," Rommel said somewhat impatiently.

"Well, sir, this is not substantiated by any hard evidence. Just rumors. But it is said that just north of the city, less than thirty miles away, there is some sort of government installation – not military – but with quite a few civilians. Our intelligence people cannot be more specific than this. They have just seen many strangers in town. In a small city like this, sir, strangers stand out quite distinctly."

"Yes. Get me more details, Schreiber."

Schreiber gave his superior a smart Sieg Heil salute, turned on his heels and left. Rommel rose, stamped out the cigarette in an ashtray, and walked to a large stack of books piled on the floor. He scanned the titles then pulled out a large atlas. He bent down, extricated the book and scanned its pages, coming to rest on a detailed map of New Mexico.

San Francisco, California

The LaCosta Hotel had seen better days but its recent conversion to a condominium apartment building in the heart of the Castro section made it a hotspot for young gay men to acquire their first real estate. Seven stories high with a turn of the century lobby that had been refurbished with estate furniture and artwork of British hunting scenes, gave the structure a real sense of permanence. It had survived the 1906 earthquake and the residents lovingly referred to the LaCosta as 'The Unsinkable Molly Brown."

Terry Sinclair and Robert Aldrin had met in Cleveland and decided to leave middle-America to the middle-Americans. San Francisco was their hope of an open and free lifestyle where they could live the way they wanted and be themselves openly. They bought a third floor apartment in early 1941 right after Terry had been turned down by the Selective Service. Robert had tried to join the Navy and was also rejected. Both in their mid-twenties, Robert was a bartender at a fashionable wharf watering hole, The Green Leopard, and Terry worked as a dental hygienist. Both of them were out of work since the occupation by the Japanese.

Two stories up from them was Gino Rossi, a gay doctor in his fifties who had been arrested in Memphis, Tennessee for soliciting sex with an undercover officer outside a known gay hangout. He "pleaded out" to charges of "sexual misconduct and public lewdness" and agreed to leave town in exchange for an expunged record.

The Japanese had decided to take over the United States Postal Service building just next door to the LaCosta and used the vast squat fortress-like building as an ammunition storage depot. With its numerous loading bays for bulk mail and Parcel Post, it was ideal.

"Not like cruising the mailmen in their summer shorts, is it babe?" said Terry gazing down at the Japanese soldiers guarding the granite steps at the front of the post office. "I used to think Asians were cute. But these guys...I dunno."

Robert was clearing the lunch dishes. "Never cared much for rice queens. Now the thought of it makes me shiver."

A rapid-fire knock at the door made them both stand bolt upright. They stared at the door as if waiting for the butler to arrive. Terry motioned Robert to answer.

"Uh, who is it?"

"It's Gino from upstairs. Let me in."

Terry jumped to the door and opened it. Gino was standing

there in coveralls and a leather flack jacket.

"I thought Halloween was in August, girl. Aren't you a little early?"

"Very funny. We need to talk. And it's October, dumbass."

"Bet you don't talk to your patients that way."

"Don't have any more of those. The Japs are rounding up doctors, nurses and everyone who can put on a band-aid. Listen, do you remember Ben and his boyfriend, Phil?"

"Yeah," said Robert.

"They're coming up to my place just before curfew."

"A party?" asked Terry.

"Listen you dumb queen. This is serious shit. They found out that the fags are all being rounded up and sent somewhere. Where, no one is quite sure, but rumor is the Japs are killing them."

Silence entered the room and hung in the air like smog.

"No way."

"Yeah, way. Believe me it's true."

"We gotta get outta here. Are we all leaving together?" said Terry.

"Look, escape is not a viable option. The city is surrounded and there's no easy way in or out. It's only a matter of time before they clean out this building."

Robert walked to the window and looked down at a large Japanese truck that was unloading wooden crates next door. "So what are we supposed to do?"

"A bunch of queens are gonna board Jacky Allen's boat at midnight tonight."

"Aren't they patrolling the harbor?"

"They should, but they're not. Most of their ships are still tied up in Portland. A bunch of he-men types launched a counter-attack on the coastal batteries and did the Japs some damage so they've kept most of their light patrol vessels up there."

"I thought Jacky's boat was for partying. That's all I can remember about it. I remember it's big, I think."

"Big enough. It'll hold about fifty people and it goes like a bat outta hell. We need to set up a diversionary action to bring the Japs here."

"Oh, that's fucking great. I went from being jailbait to being Jap bait in only ten years," said Terry. "Are you crazy?"

"Terry, be quiet for a minute," said Robert. "What do they want us to do?"

"Ben and Phil got their hands on some dynamite and a few handguns. We're gonna blow the shit outta that building next door at 11:45 PM. That'll give us fifteen minutes to make it to the pier and get on that boat. Every Jap for a mile around is gonna make for this place. That'll give the guys a chance to run for the pier."

"That's your plan?"

"Roughly. That loading platform in the alley," said Gino walking to the widow and pointing down. "That's where they store the howitzer shells. A little dynamite in there will bring that whole fucking building down, fuck up their ammo for weeks and maybe buy MacArthur and the army in L.A. a little time."

"And if we decide to pass?"

"Then stay, watch the fireworks and wait for the little yellow fellows to use you for target practice."

"I never thought I'd say it," said Terry. "But I'd rather be back in Cleveland."

*

Gino, Terry, Robert, Ben and Phil met at 11:00 PM in the basement of the LaCosta. Two drag queens came with Ben and Phil; Diego, known as "Latina Satina," and Greg called "The Czarina in Exile." Both brought their street drag clothes in duffel bags along with two 45 caliber automatics. Ben Shaw held the sack with the dynamite from Dodge's bar and Phil Smith looked warily on, sometimes more afraid of Ben's bag of dynamite than the Japanese.

"I love your gun, sweetie," said Terry.

"Wanna rub it?" asked Greg.

"Enough of that bullshit," said Gino. "Tell me the plan again. I want to make sure you've got it straight."

"Yeah, straight to the nearest man," said Diego.

"Listen, you dumb shits. Have you got the plan down?"

"We're gonna be two girls lost after curfew. We make a fuss with the Japs out front, nothing too serious, but enough to make the motherfuckers come and watch the cat fight. While they're watching, getting their teeny-weenies in an uproar, Ben and Gino sneak into the alley and chuck the bomb into the loading dock. Terry and Phil will keep them covered. When it blows, we girls run like hell. We all head to the pier, every girl for himself. See, I'm not only beautiful, but intelligent. Momma always said that someday I could grow up to be the First Lady."

"Yeah, the first lady with a ten inch dick."

"You flatter me, darling."

"Enough," Gino said. "It's time to get moving. Listen you guys. I need to say this. I love every one of you. We've had our ups and downs, but we could always count on each other, more even than our own families. No matter what happened to us back home, this is our country and as much as I'd like to see some of those assholes that used to kick me around in high school get their asses kicked, I wanted to be the one to do it, not some fucking fascist barbarians. Anyway, good luck, Godspeed, and don't break a heel."

They all hugged each other in silence. Ben doused the light, opened the door letting the drag queens out into the dark alley. Diego and Greg looked more radiant than ever as they strutted out toward the street.

Rural Virginia

Susan decided she wanted to drive for a while and by the time they had eaten more tomatoes and apples, the sun was climbing up into the morning sky and the highway was almost deserted. They had been driving nearly an hour when they spotted a woman running out from the woods and waving both arms in a panic.

Susan slowed the truck and as they approached the stranger, she could see it was a black girl, about twenty four years old, wearing ragged clothing and a terrified expression. Susan pulled over and the girl ran up to the truck.

"I need help."

"What happened to you?" Lillian was skeptical, afraid to trust anyone or believe anything anyone said.

"At the college...some men....I don't know who, they just attacked us. It was awful, awful. I just ran, kept running." The girl's knees suddenly buckled and she grabbed at the door handle of the truck for support.

"My God, let's get her inside." Susan got out of the truck and caught the girl just before she slid to the ground.

Lillian had already hopped out of the cab and raced around to the driver's side to help lift the girl into the back seat. "What's your name?"

"Sarah. Sarah Hamilton."

"You're with friends, now, Sarah. My name is Lillian Marshall and this is Susan, Susan Jamison."

Sarah's dark eyes opened wide. "Please get me away from here."

They crowded into the truck and slammed and lock the doors.

"Susan, drive." Susan wiped Sarah's perspired face with her shirt tail.

"The world's gone crazy, crazy. Thank God you were here."

"You're safe now. Don't worry. We've got to get you some clean clothes. I've got some stuff here you can have."

She opened one of the suitcases and gave Sarah a few things to wear. She struggled to change in the truck and kept looking out the windows as if they were being followed.

"What town is your family in?'

"Philly."

"O.K. What we've got by way of food is yours, too," said Susan.

"We're going to New York. We could take you to Philly; it's on the way, sorta."

"I don't know. I guess. I can't think just now."

"All we've got to eat is fruit and onions. It'll give you the craps, but it's better than nothing."

They laughed and the truck headed north, the sun setting behind the trees and casting shadows across the road as if they were climbing a ladder.

After a few hours they saw signs for Washington D.C. It was dark and there was a lot of traffic, both military and civilian.

"Look, we'll stop in D.C. It's probably the safest place to be right now."

The closer they got to the city, the slower the traffic moved. Lillian began to worry the truck would overheat when suddenly, a guarded checkpoint loomed ahead. Each vehicle was being investigated by two marines.

When their truck reached the guards, the young marines asked them where they had been, where they were going, what they were doing with a load of produce.

Lillian as usual started to explain and the soldier simply looked at her as if he had heard it all a thousand times over.

"All right, ladies, get moving. And good luck getting to New York. The roads are crowded but you should make it fine if this old truck can hold together."

"Sir?" asked Susan. "Is there a place to stay? It's late and we'd rather travel in daylight."

"Can't blame you," he responded. "There's a refugee camp up ahead about four miles."

"Thanks."

"Move along, move along."

Lillian, Susan and Sarah were given makeshift sleeping quarters on the second floor of the county library building. The building across the street, an old warehouse, had been converted to a makeshift hospital that was handling overflow wounded from the battle of Florida. Atlanta was under attack and several thousand civilian casualties had been moved up to Washington by train.

The girls looked out the window at the ambulances pulling

up and leaving.

"Maybe we should help," said Sarah.

"Maybe you need to get to a hospital…or maybe the police."

"No. Nobody can do anything for me now except what you two did. I just want to forget about it?

"What were you doing there, Sarah?"

Susan shot a glance at Lillian as if to say, "shut up."

"No, it's O.K.," said Sarah. "I was assistant to the Dean at MacNichols College. The all black teachers college. They shut down and those of us who wanted to, could stay. I decided to stay. I thought it would be safe." She started to cry.

"Let's not talk about it now. You need to rest up," said Susan glaring at Lillian

"Maybe we should just get some sleep for now. Let's talk in the morning," said Lillian.

They all fell asleep quickly to the sounds of squealing brakes and distant groans.

First thing in the morning, Susan found a working telephone and was lucky enough to get through to the Gelders.

"Thank God, you're safe. And Jason? How is Jason?" asked Papa.

"He's….."

"It doesn't sound so good. Susan, what's wrong?"

"I can't talk anymore, Papa. I'll be back soon." She had hung up on him rather than talk about it.

She went out the front door and sat on the steps. The clouds had thickened overnight and the air was heavy. She watched the frenetic activity at the "hospital" and felt useless.

A half hour went by and Sarah and Lillian sat down beside her.

"What's up?" asked Lillian.

226

"I'm tired of being a victim."

"What do you mean?"

"I'm tired of running from the fucking Germans and the fucking Italians. I'm tired of running from the fucking white trash this goddamned country sprouts like weeds. And I'm tired of missing my husband. I can't stand thinking of Fred and Jason. Such a terrible waste. When they died, I thought I died. I wish I had died. But I didn't have the guts. And now I'm running back to I don't know what."

"But Susan...."

"But nothing, Lil. I've got to do something to help. Mama and Papa, they've got their home. They're safe in New York. I need to do something positive. You go back. I'm staying here and helping out in there!" she pointed at the converted hospital.

"Look, Sue, I told them I'd bring you back and that's what I intend to do. You can help the war effort there and help your parents as well. Got it?"

"This is no argument, Lil. I'm fucking telling you, I'm staying here until I have a better reason to leave."

"Have it your way, goddamn it. Goddamn this whole war."

"Can we get some goddamned breakfast?" said Sarah. They looked at her, at each other and all of them laughed.

"Listen, Sue, seriously. Let's put a few days in here. Get your thoughts in order, O.K.? We can all help," she looked at Sarah who nodded in assent. "Then let's decide where we can best help. Together."

"O.K., let's get some eats. Sarah, you are one hungry chick."

The three of them started volunteer work that afternoon. It was a hodgepodge of duties, everything from bedpans to assisting in the operating room. They worked tirelessly and, as Susan had thought, it was a way of fighting back, not just at the invading armies but at the terrible undercurrents that ran through American life. Their devotion to the sick and wounded, to the homeless and displaced, calmed their personal demons.

A few days turned into a few weeks and by the time anyone stopped to talk about it, a month and half had come and gone. They had become old hands at the process and were becoming more and more confident.

One evening, Lillian had gone to visit a young girl she had been reading to, a girl who had been shot as her family escaped up the Florida coastal highway. It was not a serious wound, but like all the others fleeing Florida, the journey to Atlanta and then the move to D.C. was just too much. Infection has set in. She was a precious spirit of a girl and Lillian had taken particular care of her, spending time reading, telling fairy tales and playing bedside games.

When she approached the girl's bunk for their evening reading session, there was a young boy in the girl's bed. Lillian stared and immediately became alarmed.

"Where's Patty? Where'd they move her?" No one answered her, but finally a harried nurse put her arm around her shoulders and drew her aside.

"I'm so sorry to have to be the one to tell you, but little Patty Aronson died during the night. Nothing more could be done for her. I'm sorry. She truly loved your visits, though. You helped so much."

"Oh God, no." Lillian collapsed into a chair and that's where Sarah found her an hour later.

After holding her in her arms a little while, Sarah whispered, "Lillian, Lillian. This is terrible I know, but honey, we had us a miracle. A real one."

Lillian looked at Sarah as if she'd lost her mind. "What are you talking about?"

"It's Susan! She found her boy, Jason, up here in the midst of all these wounded folks. He's been here for almost two months and nobody knew it. That boy didn't even remember his own name for a while. They say he had amnesia. He has a broken collar bone and ribs from the blast and is deaf in one ear, but they think that he'll be O.K. in time. He's thin as a bean pole, of course, but seeing his mother has made a big difference. It's a miracle and I thank God for the both of them."

"Jason? Alive? My God, that's just wonderful. Where are they?"

"In the men's ward they set up way across town."

"Let's go. I can't wait to see them!"

They hurried outside and caught the tram that made its rounds every hour or so. They found Susan seated beside her young son, her face shining, her smile disbelieving. When Lillian called out Susan's name, they both ran at each other and cried into each others' shoulders.

Washington, D.C.

In order to ensure the Black vote in urban centers in his home state, Senator Reilly carefully selected an up and coming young Black aide, a strapping young man named Jackson Delacorte, from Chicago. Jackson was a bit of an enigma to Rooster. He was impervious to insults, to sarcastic put-downs, to borderline racial insults, to glares and embarrassing corrections in front of others. In short, Jackson was a handsome attribute to

Rooster's shenanigans, always obsequious, always respectful, always mannerly and sharp as hell. Rooster used him perfectly and Jackson knew it. He played the part well and Jackson would lull Rooster into trusting him completely. The invasion changed all this. Reilly had hopes for a settled peace with the Axis. He had been promised an important position in the occupied territories west of the Mississippi. Jackson knew that the Nazis intended mass deportation of his people, or worse. Neither took the other for granted. If the Axis invasion failed, Rooster Reilly wanted to appear the patriot. If it succeeded, Jackson Delacorte wanted to save his people. Each had to bide his time and not alienate the other.

On one of their forays into the public arena, they visited the refugee camp outside D.C. city limits. Rooster had made certain he was accompanied by two adept photographers, who could be depended upon to chronicle his good-will mission. The photographers loved Jackson, who was film-star handsome and had an innate ability to know just when to turn toward the camera with a smile and when to hold the young amputee close or when to smile beatifically as he helped a wounded mother try out her crutches for the first time. The more he worked the scenes, the more familiar his face became to the public. This was a Black man every white American could love, they thought. Rooster did not mind sharing the spotlight with his aide.

"Senator! Oh, Senator!" A matron of ample girth was shoving through the press corps and ignoring the flash bulbs, waving her freckled, chubby fingers like an undulating flesh-fan. Her pink cheeks were covered in a soft down and minute droplets of perspiration covered her lined forehead as she huffed and puffed with her exertions, her wispy white bangs lifted and fell, lifted and fell. "Senator! You've GOT to see this miracle! We've got a national hero here, right here!"

"What the hell's she yammering about, Jackson?" Rooster spoke out of the corner of his mouth and didn't lose a beat, smiling at his audience.

"I don't know, sir, but I'll find out." Jackson stepped between the senator and the approaching woman.

"Madam, how can we help you?" Jackson smiled and folded his arms across his chest, waiting to rebuff another over-zealous fan.

"That. . .that young man, the one they thought was dead, you know? The one that helped his grandfather torpedo the Italian battleship, the one that saw his granddaddy die, you know who I'm talkin' about?" The woman was hanging on to Jackson's lapel, pulling his head down closer to her face.

"Mmm, just a minute, Mrs. . uh. . .what did you say your name was?"

"Cornelia. Cornelia Brookstone Harrison. My family has been here. . ."

"That's fine, Mrs. Harrison, no need to explain. Just a minute while I get the senator's attention. . ."

Jackson wheeled around and grabbed the senator's arm, leaning in to inform him of the fantastic photo opportunity right here under their noses. Within minutes, the senator had waved away all the well-wishers and had Cornelia Brookstone Harrison firmly by her dimpled elbow and was following her closely as the woman led them to the men's ward.

The congressman and his entourage entered the room with a great whoosh of the double doors, startling everyone inside.

"Back there! Back against the wall. . ." Cornelia pointed, her bulging chest heaving with the physical effort of racing ahead of the Senator through the door.

"There he is. That's Jason Jamison, and his mother sitting beside him. They were just re-united this morning!"

The senator motioned for the reporters and photographers to wait and signaled for Jackson to move across the room with him and Cornelia. Flashbulbs popped and Susan and Jason were front page news.

*

Jackson Delacorte watched all the media hubbub from a distance, but he could not help but notice Sarah Hamilton jockeying her way through the maze of cots in the men's ward. What a beauty, he thought.

Sarah entered the ward carrying two paper cups of water and was concentrating on not spilling a drop, as she navigated toward Jason's cot. She felt someone staring at her, and when she looked up and looked straight into the black marble eyes of Jackson Delacorte, her knees immediately turned to jelly. She looked away from his probing stare and resumed her path toward Jason and Susan.

Senator Phillip Taylor Reilly was practically filibustering, trying to convince Susan he wanted only the best for her and 'the boy', after all they had sacrificed for the country. Susan had begun to look shell-shocked and Jason himself was growing restless, dangling his legs off the side of the bed and accepting the paper cup of water gratefully. The handsome black man seemed to be accompanying the important-sounding man, but Sarah didn't dare ask.

"Excuse me, ma'am." Jackson smiled warmly in Sarah's direction. "I'm Jackson Delacorte, aide to Senator Reilly here, the senator from Illinois. We're here to... well, to boost morale and see if there's anything we can do to help. And what might your name be?"

"Me?" Sarah could hardly speak.

"Yes. You."

"Mmm. Well. My name is Sarah. Sarah Hamilton."

"How long have you been here helping out, Sarah?"

"We've been here about a month now, doing the best we can."

"Well, I think you're about one of the nicest and prettiest young things I've seen in a long time. Do you think you might be able to get away this evenin' and have supper with me?"

She looked at Susan who was watching the whole thing but acting like she was still listening to Senator Reilly.

"Well, yes. That would be real nice."

"I'll be back here about six, if that's O.K., and we'll find us a fine supper somewhere around here and you can tell me how we can help you. How does that sound?"

All Sarah could manage was a gentle smile and shining eyes. She nodded yes as Jackson shook her hand.

"It's been fine to make your acquaintance," he said staring into her down turned eyes. He joined the senator in the photography session with Jason. It was going to be an exhilarating weekend, thought Jackson, as he watched Rooster preen himself around the mother of the injured young hero and listened to the bombastic senator prattle on about the defense of the nation.

Jackson Delacorte had long been suspicious of Senator Reilly's reasons for rallying behind the majority leader and the Democratic Party. Jackson had honed his antennae to a fine throbbing sensitivity which had been one of his greatest assets in obtaining the appointment as senior aide to the senator. Jackson knew he was the "token" black and did not object. If that's what it took to climb the ladder, then so be it. His devotion to details stood him in good stead as time progressed and he had secret dossiers on many people who were, inexplicably, in regular contact with the senator, for which Jackson could find no logical explanation.

One of these strange affiliations intrigued Jackson. The senator's gardener was a man of indeterminate age, always dressed in baggy clothing, always wearing a large, straw hat that hid his features. Jackson had routinely scrutinized everyone Reilly met with. One day, he spotted an exchange of envelopes between the two. So what, Jackson asked himself, was being exchanged when it seemed anything other than a check for landscaping needs was all that was needed?

The gardener turned out to be Hans Strauss alias Harry Schaefer, who was a German emissary that relayed messages from the Third Reich to Reilly and vice versa. Every lobbyist that had a potentially progressive idea was either declined or encouraged, depending upon the decisions of the people who sent the messages to Reilly via Hans. The Germans, it seemed, were very much in control of Rooster Reilly.

Jackson played dumb because it enabled him to have access to developments he would never have had access to. When Reilly began to receive orders from the Germans to accumulate records of American Jews and Blacks and "known homosexuals and Communists", including their first and second generation family members, their addresses, their genealogies, their contact information, their affiliations, civilian, military and religious, Jackson knew what the purpose was. It was only a question of time as to what would come of all this and how Jackson could use this to his advantage. He suspected the senator of high treason, but he was in no position to do anything yet. His only task was to act ignorant and subservient. He had a great deal of practice at both.

As Jackson Delacorte and Sarah continued to become more and more interested in each other and as Jackson became more and more attuned to Reilly's treasonous behavior, he was painfully aware of his own precarious position. If he was wrong about Reilly, he would be back on the bus to Chicago to a job flipping burgers; it might even earn him a prison sentence. If he was right, but told the wrong people, he'd be floating face down in Chesapeake Bay. He was close to power, but had none. He had no official position or rank, no ability to command an arrest, no authorization that would protect him if he was in error. No one in D.C. liked whistleblowers, even if it was treason you were blowing the whistle on. And being black? That was the icing on a terrible cake. He felt he had to act on his own, in secret. He could strike when his own position and life were not in jeopardy. An affair with Sarah Hamilton wasn't likely to help matters. But, like the invasion itself, there were things that were way beyond his control. This he had to accept. Time was running out rapidly. Of this one thing, he was certain.

Cottonwood Township, Texas

Travis Beecher blinked his eyes and tried to orient himself. His upper left arm was bandaged. It sent flashes of pain through his entire body whenever he tried to move it.

"What the hell ..."

As his eyes became accustomed to the dim light, he could

make out nearly a dozen black faces huddling in the light from a single candle. He was in a small, no more than six by nine foot room, its ceiling less than five feet high. It seemed to be carved out of the earth itself. Ends of roots had been roughly lopped off on the walls of dirt. Night crawlers moved slowly along the ground. A spider had begun to spin a huge web in one corner. A rough-hewn ladder ended at a small tunnel just large enough for a man to squeeze through.

"Don't move that arm too much," a large black man addressed him. "You been shot. Not too bad, just a flesh wound. Sure did bleed some, though!"

"I remember running. The Germans were after me. Killed my mother and took my sister away. Where am I?" The shock of what he just said, his mother dead, hit him in the brain like an iron fist.

"You'se safe. This a hidin' hole we built a time back to get away from the Klan. I'm called Randy. That feller over there is Carl. He saved you. Whisked you up into the trees and you was gone! The Germans waited just a little while. When they couldn't hear you no more, they went and drove away. White devils."

Carl, a powerful, muscular man, smiled a broad smile as he shifted and extended his large hand. He was missing several teeth and hummed as he shook Travis hand. Travis reluctantly returned the handshake. He had very strong misgivings about being this close to black folk.

Stunned inside and out, Travis said, "I'm Travis. Travis Beecher." "Have some supper, Mr. Travis," Randy offered.

His growing sense of hunger overcame his reticence at sharing a meal with a group of black men. "Don't mind if I do," he offered.

Some of the men shifted their positions. As they moved,

Travis could see a large iron kettle hanging on a makeshift tripod over a small, open fire. One of the men ladled a good por-
tion of liquid into a tin bowl and handed it across to Travis.
Another handed him a spoon. Travis dipped the spoon cautiously into the dark liquid. He tasted the concoction gingerly as
some of the men, getting their own supper dished out by the
cook, laughed.

"It ain't gonna bite! Don't have possum tonight. Just some
greens and carrots we done stole!" The man laughed again, a
big, deep laughter.

"Not bad," Travis allowed.

"It'll have to do. You'se lucky we was sitting in the woods.
Saw the whole thing. We escaped last night when they came and
burned our neighborhood," Randy said. "Killed our minister. He
never did nothin'. Jest asked the Lord to take care of us. Them
rednecks workin' with the Germans did most of the killin'. It was
the Klan, sure enough. So a bunch of us just hightailed it out
here. Used this place to hide from the Klan many a time in the
past."

A tall wiry black man named Nat Watkins stepped out of the
shadows.

"How do we know we trust this cracker. How we know he
ain't gonna hightail it outta here and bring those motherfuckin'
kluxxers back wif' 'im?"

"Don't know it," said Randy.

"I sez we cut his throat right here, right now. One less white
devil. I do it myself." He moved toward Travis.

"No you won't," said Randy, rising to his feet. "I trust dis boy.
He may be white trash, but he got just the same reason we does
to hate dem kluxxers. They kilt his kin and we in it together. We
can use all the help we can get. So sit yo black ass down, Nat,

237

fore I knock ya down, hear?"

"I still say that cracker is trouble. I still say kill him."

"And I sez to sit down. I ain't sayin' it no more," said Randy, gripping his knife tightly.

Nat sized up the hulking Randy and backed into the shadows against the wall, his eyes focused on Travis with a seething hatred.

Travis looked uncomfortably around and was about to say something encouraging to the men that saved him when Carl started to hum rhythmically to the slap of his hand against his thigh. Some of the other men joined in, clapping. Soon the men broke into a spiritual. Travis had heard it often, wafting across the fields at harvest time. This was the first time he had understood the words. "I'm troubled in mind, and if Jesus don't help me, I surely will die."

Travis watched in fascination as the men swayed to and fro, singing, seemingly not a care in the world, unless one looked deeply into the men's eyes and listened to the sad strains of their weary voices. For the first time in his life, Travis felt a sense of comradeship with black men.

He nudged Randy. "How come this feller Carl don't sing?"

Randy shot Travis a brief glance.

"Cause one time, some years back, some of the Klan caught ole Carl. They didn't like his singin', so they just cut out his tongue. Right there. Ever since, he can't speak. Just hums. And when everyone else is a-singin', ole Carl, he just hums along. In his head, he's singin', though. Look at his face."

Travis knew something was odd about the man who had saved his life. For a second he could picture the horror the Klan had inflicted on so many innocent people.

"What are you going to do now?" Travis asked. He knew

that he could not simply go back home. Jonas would certainly come for him. He wanted to find a way to see if Hannah-Lee had survived her ordeal. He shuddered when he thought of Jonas, and the anger rose in him again. So did the pain in his arm. Involuntarily, he clenched his fists,

"Well, Mister Travis," said Randy, "last night, after they got through killin' a bunch of us, they carted the rest off to jail. We's heard that that leader of the Klan, the young feller's killed Mr. Doc, he's having his fun at the jailhouse. We's gonna break into the jailhouse and free our people."

"What?" Travis asked, stunned. In Travis's world, black men did not bring a fight to white men; it just didn't happen. Very few, if any, even risked fighting back in the streets if there was trouble. Did these men have a death wish? "You jokin'?"

"No, Mister Travis, I ain't jokin'. We's only got us a handful of us left. And much as we don't mind our soups, we had a little talk and decided we don't rightly plan on spendin' all our days down here. If we don't get our friends and family back, well, might as well jest lay down and die. Sure, we freer than before, but not so free we won't be found and kilt. Best way to survive now is in numbers. So that's what we's gonna do. We already know exactly where they are. And we know the back roads bet-ter'n anyone. Jest a matter of gettin' 'em now."

Travis thought for a bit, chewing the inside of his cheek. He was amazed at how information spread so rapidly through the Negro community. Most of the families had no telephones, and yet they knew almost instantly whenever something important happened in the place they all lived. If he had not been there to witness Jonas's murdering of Doc Peterson, it might have been hours or even days before he had known.

A thought suddenly struck him: if Jonas was there, Hanna-

Lee might be there too.

"Can I come?"

The black man looked at him and pursed his large lips.

"I was takin' you anyways. You betcha you comin'," Randy said.

"Good. That's the way I want it. I want to see whether my sister's O.K.. And I wouldn't mind putting a slug into Jonas' belly myself, for what he did to her and to my mom."

"Music to my ears, boy. Music to my ears."

Washington, D.C.

Spring had evolved into early summer and the numbers of casualties had increased for a while, then subsided, only to repeat the cycle over again as the war news ebbed and flowed. To the medical teams, now alternating with volunteer medical units from all over the United States, the constant tension from having to take care of people with less than adequate supplies was causing erosions in the optimism they had maintained so well for the first few weeks. When the ambulances and trucks arrived with more wounded and dying people, blind frenetic energy flowed through the med staff like a tidal wave. Volunteers and staff moved like the possessed through their duties. Sleep was a luxury and emotions were left at the door.

A warm rain fell in sporadic bursts and thunder rumbled in the distant gray clouds. Gusts of wind fluttered the curtains in the wards. News from the fronts was whispered, but ignored. No matter what happened on the battlefields, everyone was dedicated to the job at hand.

It was Friday at noon that Lillian, Susan and Sarah managed to eat together for the first time in weeks.

Lillian pushed her tray forward and dropped her wadded-up paper napkin in the middle of her plate. "I am so damned tired my hair hurts."

Susan reached across the table and patted Lillian's hand. "I thank God every day for what you did and for Jason's recovery."

"You think he's ready to leave?"

"Yeah, as ready as he'll ever be for now. I think it's time I got him home, back to New York where we can help take care of my parents and each other. I'm . . .I'm homesick. For family."

"I'm not surprised. I always felt that happiness is a big happy family that lives in another city. But I do understand. Sarah, you're awfully quiet today. What do you have to say about this? Are you ready to leave?"

Sarah ducked her head and dabbed her eyes with her napkin. "I think I'll be staying here. I'm doing important work. I want to get certified as a nurse and..."

"Jackson?"

"Well, yeah, there's Jackson, too."

"I think that's fantastic, Sarah." Lillian sipped her coffee and winked at Susan.

"Well, maybe not. You never know what God has in mind for you, but I think he's the one." Sarah said.

"I'm happy for both of you and we're going to miss you but we'd better get over to the commander's office and find out if their volunteer services people can get us train passage to New York. We'll be back later and let you know when we're leaving. Are you gonna be all right?"

"I'll be fine. Just missing you two a whole bunch. But we'll see each other again. I know it."

None of them thought this was likely. The war had shaken everyone's soul to the core. Lillian and Susan stood up and leaned over in turn to hug and kiss and Sarah.

"It's farewell, not good-bye," said Susan.

Without another word, they left and hurried to the field office. They stated their wishes to the young lieutenant with far too much to do. In a few minutes, though, they were booked on the afternoon train to New York City.

They were quiet when they walked back to their dorm room. After they packed, Susan rushed to the ward to tell Jason the good news. Lillian spent the time refilling water pitchers and smoothing pillows and, as always, listening to the lonely words of the wounded.

*

"Here you are ladies and gent," said the shuttle driver. "I know a lot of people are gonna miss you."

Susan, Jason and Lillian were delivered to the platform at the railroad station and the former commuter train, pulling nine extra passenger cars, left in a cloud of steam for New York City. They sat across the aisle from one another, Susan and Jason in one pair of seats and Lillian in another, next to a young mother holding an infant in one arm and holding the hand of a toddler of about four. They were all jammed in the seat with them.

Jason's physical recovery was good; youth has its advantages. But there was a dullness in his eyes. He hadn't heard from his father in months. He might not even be alive. He missed his grandfather and was still trying to cope with his traumatic death and the loss of his gentle wisdom as well as their happy life in Miami Beach.

Susan kept telling him he would make new friends soon, but that didn't take care of the old friends he missed so much.

Lillian managed to organize her purse, even counting the money she had left from Dutch's stash in the truck. It seemed to be enough to tide her over until she could manage to access her's and Dean's savings if the banks were open. She sighed and leaned her head back on the cushion, her mind full of Lucien's face. Her pulse quickened as she fantasized about seeing him again and making love to him. Still, her guilt over Dean was a cloud on it all. She was still married to him, even if she didn't feel that she was. And was he such a bad husband? Isn't it to be expected that the passion of first love wouldn't fade but would evolve into a mature and long lasting love? Maybe she just didn't give it enough time. Dean was a great guy, even if they were at different levels. Levels? She mostly felt they were on different planets. Her head spun.

*

What was the matter? She was screaming at the top of her voice, but Lucien didn't seem to be able to hear her. He was fading away, moving into the distance without moving, not walking, not running, but drifting into a smallness she could not follow. He was speaking earnestly to another woman, and then that woman turned into a young man, a cadet, wearing a strange uniform she didn't recognize, with epaulets and a peculiar helmet with a pointed finial on the crown. What was that about?

Lucien was looking back at her, not seeing her, but looking backward through her as if she was invisible. Then he handed the young cadet a black leather-bound book that resembled an address book and he shoved it inside the younger man's jacket.

The cadet stepped back from Lucien, clicked his boot heels together and when he shot his arm up into the air stiffly, Lillian saw the black swastika armband he was wearing. She shrieked for Lucien to be careful, this was the enemy. Stop, hear me, come back! What is going on? And finally, finally Lucien heard her, and spun around to glare at her and it was only then Lillian saw he, too, was wearing a swastika armband and he was sneering at her from that cloudy place and he suddenly had a sword in his right hand, which he raised up as if to strike her and he rushed at her menacingly, his eyes red, his teeth bared, his lips pulled back in a grimace that made Lillian shiver uncontrollably. "No, no, no, no! You don't understand!"

"I'm sorry, lady, he was just trying to be friendly." The mother in the next seat pulled her toddler back away from poking his toy soldier's bayonet into Lillian's arm. "We didn't mean to wake you. Please. I'm so sorry." The woman cradled an infant in her arms and it was nursing hungrily; the harried mother was close to tears.

"Please, don't worry about it. I was having a nightmare and none of it was your fault. We've all had some tough days. Weeks, actually." She smiled at the woman and glanced across the aisle at Susan and Jason, both sound asleep. "Are you going to New York ?"

"No, I'm going to get off in Jersey. Newark. My cousins have a large apartment there and they've never seen the baby, so with my husband off in the Navy, they insisted I come there, so I'm anxious to get the kids settled for a while, with a clean place to sleep and not be so frightened all the time."

"Yes, that's the hardest part." Lillian let her head drop back again, took a deep breath and closed her eyes, hoping for some rest.

Lights flickering from the passing landscape danced on the ceiling with more frequency as the train shuffled and creaked through tunnels and past the outskirts of the more populated areas. Passengers were beginning to wake up and stretch, gathering their belongings. At the first stop, about a fourth of the people in their car detrained and without much of a delay, the train moved on to Penn Station in New York.

The station was utter bedlam. Some of the people in the jammed waiting room looked like they'd been there for months. They were lounging on the benches, some even stretched out on their own luggage with clothing draped over their legs as makeshift blankets. The odor of unwashed bodies permeated the air.

Lillian led Susan and Jason out to the street. There weren't any cabs available but someone had told them the busses were still running. They found a bus stop with a destination within blocks of the Gelders' apartment and they parked themselves on the bench nearby and waited.

After the sun had set, a bus with the street designation they sought pulled up and wheezed to a stop. Lillian and Susan, assisting Jason, boarded and rode in silence during the final leg of a very long journey.

After a time, they climbed down from the bus onto the darkened streets.

"This way. We have to walk about four blocks. Down this street then left at the next corner." Lillian pointed, gathered up her bag and led the way.

A few flickering street lights began to come on before they reached the door of the brownstone. Susan rang the bell.

"Yes? Who is it?" said the tinny intercom speaker.

Susan started to cry, recognizing her mother's frail voice.

"Mama, Mama, it's me. Susan. I'm here, with Jason."

"Mein Gott. It's Susan, she's here! She made it! She's alive! And Jason.!" The woman began to weep. "Prayers heard, prayers answered. This is a miracle. We need to call the Rabbi. I'm going to faint, I'm going to float away on a cloud! Happy I am this night!"

"Mama, open the door." Susan couldn't help laughing and when her mother pushed the electric lock open, they rushed upstairs and enveloped the older couple in their arms.

They sat up most of the night, catching up on all that had transpired in Florida and finding out how Jason had stowed away on the boat and how he had been spared from death by the force of the explosion and had floated unconscious on a piece of debris like the Biblical Moses. Some men taking turns watching the Italian convoy found his unconscious body at first light and had taken him to safety.

"God was watching over you, my child," said Papa.

By morning, the humble apartment of Susan's family was full of concerned and supportive neighbors and friends. This was the first good news any of them had heard in months.

Lillian asked if anyone had heard from her husband, Dean, but no one had. She waited until a reasonable time had elapsed and excused herself, leaving the Gelders' apartment for her own.

It was four a.m. when Lillian let herself into her own apartment and she was shocked by how little things had changed. She picked up Lucien's photograph from the drawer and stared at the face she loved so dearly, straining and literally willing him to call her or to at least think of her.

She fell asleep, holding his picture close to her breast, her mind full of hopeful plans for the future, nothing else.

Los Alamos, New Mexico

Garret walked his patrol of the compound grounds slowly and methodically. He checked an open door and shut it, making a short note in the small book he carried for that purpose. One of the dim streetlights on Bathhouse Row was out. He noted that. The last house on the Row, the one occupied by J. Robert Oppenheimer, was dark. He turned back up the deserted street. At the quad, he turned left and marched down to the industrial section. Here, there was a guard, rifle slung over the shoulder, roughly every ten yards. A few of the men recognized Garret and said a brief but cordial hello.

Before reaching the high security area, protected by a ten-foot tall chain link fence with barbed wire strung along its top, Garret pushed open the door to the communications center. A fat sergeant, feet propped up on the desk littered with papers, his uniform tie undone at the collar, looked at Garret.

"Something wrong?" the man asked in a harsh, clipped accent that belied his New England heritage.

"No, sergeant. Just wanted to see if I could get a message through to San Francisco on the radio. I know the phones are shut down."

"Not unless you have a priority clearance."

A young private with a pockmarked face who had lounged at a desk toward the back of the room chimed into the conversation.

"What's the matter? Got a love in Frisco?" he said mockingly.

Garret tried not to sound annoyed.

"Fuck you," he replied and turned to go back into the street to resume his patrol.

Cottonwood Township, Texas

Travis sat cramped between the two black men in the seat of the old truck the men had stashed in the fields behind the woods. Behind them, nearly a dozen black men huddled, holding on to the canvas wherever they could. The truck, moving no more than twenty miles an hour over the rough gravel roads, bounced and jolted, its transmission groaning and straining with each painful shifting of the gears. The springs and axles creaked at the punishment of being loaded with as many men as it was carrying.

They were running without headlights, and in the dark Travis could hardly see six feet ahead of the vehicle. To help him see better, Randy had dropped the windshield and fastened it to the hood of the truck. The cool, night wind made the ride more bearable. He knew, though, that the straight farm road would lead them directly into the outskirts of what had been known as Freedmen's Town, an all-Black area on the fringes of Dallas. No lights twinkled in the darkness.

"We're almost there, aren't we?" Travis asked Randy. "Where's the jail?"

Randy nodded quietly, his eyes remaining intently on the road.

"Yeah, we's gonna leave the truck by a friend of mine's and walk the rest of the way."

Carl hummed, flexed his broad shoulders and squeezed Travis even tighter than he was in the small space in the front seat. Within minutes, Randy strained and turned the steering wheel hard to the right, pumping both the brakes and clutch as they slowed to a crawl. The wheels clattered briefly on an old, wooden bridge that covered the ditch. Ahead, Travis made out the outline of a shotgun shack, pitch-black against the intermittent clouds. Then they stopped and the men in the back of the truck scrambled to the ground. Carl dropped easily to the soft, wet grass as Randy jumped from the driver's side. Travis climbed down, favoring his numb right side. The group assembled, crouched low on the ground.

"O.K., we'll take both sides of the road. The jail's about four blocks from here, on the left side of the street. Sure it'll be lit up like a Christmas tree. And there's likely to be lots o' guards. Probly it'll be mainly dem boys from the Klan, but some Germans, too. We don't stand a chance if they open up with the machine guns. Gotta surprise whosever there! Use your knives and don't shoot unless you gotta and if ya gotta, make it count."

Travis and the others nodded silently. Two of the men cradled shotguns in their laps. A wide grin spread across Carl's face as his humming increased in pitch. He fondled a huge, twelve-inch blade.

"Travis, you gotta cover your face with some dirt. You stand out like a full moon at harvest time! Go down by the ditch."

"O.K.," Travis murmured.

"See, there's some advantages to bein' colored," Randy said good-naturedly.

The men started off slowly, following the small road the truck had just covered. At the drainage ditch, they stopped as Travis clambered down the embankment. There was enough water in the ditch for him to scoop up a handful of mud from the bottom and spread it across his face and neck. He only hoped that he would not disturb a rattler in the process.

Travis heard a noise on the other side of the ditch and gingerly crept over the water and up the other side of the embankment. His camouflage was complete and he blended into the night like an invisible man.

Just beyond the woods that hid him there was a huge field. The wheat in the field was taller than a ten year old girl. The blond leaves, sinewy and flowing, knelt before the wind. The field stretched from the tracks to the horizon; at the farthest edge, dim foothills swelled under the light of an almost full moon. The wheat, swaying like ocean waves, seemed to break upon the shore of the distant hills.

Nearby, there was a thicket of live oak and wild sage. A platoon of some seventy-five German SS storm troopers stood oddly in a circle of about 150 feet across. They stood around a depression in the ground. It was a pit actually and the two bulldozers that had created it sat on the perimeter like yellow hulking beasts asleep. As if to awaken them, shouts and screams bellowed from the deeper part of the woods as some 250 men, women and children ran from the tree line, shots ringing out behind them as they came, forcing them on. Each of them was completely naked, stripped of every semblance of civilization. Barefoot they ran, falling and rising again as storm troopers nudged them with cattle prods and bayonets. In short order, they were forced into the pit where their shouts echoed dully off the earthen walls. The sky was full of stars as black summer clouds floated effortlessly on the warm southern breeze.

"Silence," shouted a commander. The throng, panic stricken, did not become quiet but continued to wail and plead.

"Silence," he shouted again. Still they went on.

He raised his hand and simultaneously the platoon that surrounded the pit raised their submachine guns, aimed them into the pit and looked at the commander's face.

He stood frozen against the sky with his shiny black boots, the perfect fit of the trousers, tight against his shins and lower thighs, ballooning out into jodhpurs. The tight black jacket and silver-encrusted epaulets, the black patent leather-trimmed cap. A glint of moonlight caught the death's head emblem on the rise of his cap and, as he stood there, the earth seemed to stop in its rotation as if the world had taken a deep breath.

Silence, finally, except for the whimpering of small children. The commander's black, empty eyes surveyed the mass of humanity before him, but they were no longer human in his eyes. This was the enemy of civilization, the bane of the Fatherland, everything that Der Führer had spoken against. This was the blight, the plague, and he was the exterminator. Surely, he thought, his job was the will of God.

His arm dropped and the sputterings of the machine guns cracked. Bullets filled the air of the pit like hail in a terrible Great Plains thunderstorm. The maelstrom had been unleashed. The torrents of lead penetrated flesh and bone, mother and child, father and grandfather. Bodies split apart, shredded and burst in a torrent of blood and gore. This rain knew no mercy, but dropped dumbly and deadly upon the helpless victims below. The beautiful oak trees and sage devoured the sound as if a pillow had been placed over the gun muzzles and the mouths of the hapless victims. In less than a minute, almost all within the pit were dead.

The smell of gunpowder filled the air and the wisps of smoke from the gun muzzles hung over the pit like the tendrils of some massive phantom jelly-fish in the oceans of hell. Travis thought the frogs and crickets had started up again, but it was the whimpering and gasping of the nearly dead in the pit.

"Finish them," said the officer.

One of the guards pulled out his luger and walked the circumference of the pit, aiming and firing at anyone who looked alive. Travis winced with every shot.

When he holstered the pistol, the engines of the bulldozers started up with a roar that made Travis jump from the hypnotic trance his mind had fallen into in an effort to block out the images before him. As the soldiers started to leave, Travis, crouching, turned and crossed back over the ditch to his waiting friends. He vowed to tell them nothing.

He climbed back up the other side of the embankment and down again, joining the men as they marched cautiously, single file in two columns along the county road. The acrid smell of burning wood still hung in the air. Here and there they could make out some standing ruins of shacks that had not completely been devoured by the flames. There was no evidence of life in the burned-out, deserted community.

Randy, Carl, Travis and the squad of a half dozen men that had marched on the left side of the road crossed over to join the other group. Coming from a block ahead, the group could make out the faint, raucous laughter of men. As Randy had predicted, two or three buildings were awash in lights. Numerous trucks were parked on the packed gravel. Advancing slowly and crouching on the ground, Randy silently pointed ahead.

"That's the jail. There's a white folks' bar next to it. I know there's a back entrance, unless'n they's got it guarded."

"I know where it's at," said one of the men. "Been in dat jail plenty o' times." He laughed.

"O.K., you take three men. Sees if you can break the lock and come in through the back. Carl and me and Travis here will come in the front. If we can surprise 'em, we may get the keys. Dat's the point. Get our bothers out."

"And Hannah-Lee," Travis said heatedly. My God, he thought, dear God, I hope she was not in the group he had just seen slaughtered. Her rescue was his sole motivation in coming along; this and wanting to kill Jonas.

"Right. You find that white girl, you protect her," Randy cautioned. "Dem of us make it, we meet back at the truck. May the Good Lord take care of us. We's gonna need it."

Four of the men peeled off, heading for the alley running along the left side of the jail. Each of them knew that these could be their last moments in this world. As the four men disappeared into the alley, Randy led his group down the road towards the one story granite building on the left side of the street. The building took up nearly a fourth of the block opposite them. "COUNTY JAIL – FREEDMENS' TOWN DIVISION – 1882" was engraved in stone above the entrance. The front doors were opened wide, and Travis could see dozens of young men, most wearing the new armbands of the SS that the Germans had issued the night before, ringed around a central spot, clapping, cheering and jeering. He could see dollar bills being thrown into the ring. He could not see what the men were gambling on. Occasionally, though, he could see two black heads bobbing in the circle. Perhaps they were gambling on which of the black men would win a fight.

"Go, nigger, kill him. I've got five on you," croaked a harsh, angry voice.

"Don't you let me down, hear?" yelled another.

The two windows on the front side of the building were protected with iron bars, but wide open from the inside. There was no sign of the Germans or of the cars they had commandeered earlier.

Randy signaled silently, pointing to the left side of the gray wall. The group moved cautiously across the road, and pressed themselves against the cool granite. More than ten feet above them were the small, barred slits that served as ventilation for the prisoners. Peering around the corner, Randy raised his arm and brought it down in a rapid slashing motion. As he felt the adrenaline pumping through his system, Travis felt Carl's hot breath and the clucking noise as his throat wanted to yell out.

The team sprinted around the corner, rapidly surmounting the three steps, and raced inside. The men yelled a primeval wail, swinging their knives menacingly and setting ferociously upon the hated Klan members. Randy hacked at the first man he reached, grabbing the man's hair, pulling his head back and slashing his throat through to the spine. In an instant, the man fell to the ground. Another quickly fell, the broken tip of Randy's knife blade protruding from his eye socket.

"Jesus, niggers!" someone yelled.

Travis lunged blindly, the blade from his knife meeting the soft resistance of flesh. For a moment his mind did a somersault, thinking on how effortlessly he'd just taken away a man's life. He knew he should feel something, some kind of regret or remorse, or even horror, but he felt nothing, just the instinctual need to keep moving and keep killing. And so he did. Quickly, he withdrew the blade and instantly it found its mark as another man rushed at him. Travis was not used to fighting, but in the small battle that ensued, his reflexes were quick, instinctive. He saw Carl hurl his huge bulk at three men simultaneously, bouncing them to the ground easily and effortlessly. Carl's knife slashed at their legs and stomachs. Blood and gore ran in a stream on the oak floor.

When they saw a chance to do so, several of the Klan members ducked through the front door into the street. A few ran to the bar, swinging open its door.

"Help us! Niggers! They're attacking the jail!"

"Where the hell is the Krauts?"

Young men, half of them drunk, stormed into the street. A few ran to their trucks, quickly retrieving shotguns and rifles from their racks. Most ran the few feet to the jail. Instantly they were embroiled in the battle raging inside.

Travis made his way past the front desk, then turned sharply left to race to the small hallway leading to the cells in the back of the building. The iron grates of the cellblock door were wide-open, keys carelessly left in the lock. Travis pulled out the keys and moved forward to the center of the cellblock. He found the mechanism that unlocked all of the cells, pushed it to the right and felt it give. Over the noise of the prisoners inside, he heard the grating of the sliding cell doors. Instantly, dozens of Blacks crowded out of their cells and stormed out of the cellblocks, pushing, shoving and blocking each other.

Not sure what to make of a white man freeing them, some of them skirted wide of him. "I ain't here to hurt you," he shouted. "Your friends and family are outside right now, killing them that put you in here. I'm on their side, on your side. But we need your help if we plan on getting away alive. You hear?"

Understanding now, they nodded, made their way outside with sneers and balled fists.

As they joined the battle, nearly a hundred prisoners that had been held in the jail, and nearly an equal number of Klansmen now fought each other ferociously. The battle had

NEVER ON THESE SHORES

moved outside into the street. Intermittent shots were fired, and both whites and Blacks lay on the ground, moaning, holding their wounds. Many lay motionless in their own blood.

Travis moved along the narrow hallway along the cellblocks to reach the back door, unlocked it and slammed it open. He did not see the four men of his group. They must have joined in the fray out front. Where was Hannah-Lee? he thought feverishly, his mind racing. Where was Jonas? Looking back to the front where the battle was raging, he heard a door open to his right. Jonas stood enraged, his hair disheveled, his shirt open and torn.

"You a nigger lover, too?" he asked sarcastically. "What the hell you doin'?"

Travis could hardly contain the revulsion that overcame him. The picture of his mother lying dead in the road and the image of his sister being driven away were like a white hot poker in his brain.

"Where's Hannah-Lee?" he growled, hatred sparking from his eyes.

At that moment, his sister's small voice cried out. "Is that you, Travis? I'm in here. I'm in here!'"

Travis could no longer contain himself. In a wild fury he lunged forward, brandishing the knife high above his head. His left side was throbbing and spasms of pain shot through his entire body. He ignored it and tried to see through the bloodshot haze that now clouded his vision as a few steps brought him face to face with his former friend.

Jonas had anticipated Travis' lunge. With a quick sidestep and a sharp blow to the back of his neck he knocked Travis to the floor, the knife skittering out of reach. Kneeling down over Travis, Jonas did not see the gigantic shape that bore down on him from behind. Carl almost crushed Jonas as he leaped at him, pinning him to the ground, and pummeling him mercilessly. His eyes were wild and the fury of his attack unleashed all the hatred he had felt ever since white men had cut out his tongue. Carl bent down as if to kiss Jonas and bit a chunk of flesh out of the side of his face, spitting it out onto the floor. Jonas yelped like a wounded animal and Carl's fist came down on his face.

Travis rolled to his left side, picked himself up, and ran as best he could into the small private office. Hannah-Lee, her hands tied behind her with rough rope, lay on the small cot at the far side of the tiny room. Her dress was pushed above her waist and one small breast protruded from the bra that had been partially dislodged.

"Sis!"

Hannah-Lee gave a small moan.

"Are you alright?"

The young girl nodded, tears falling from her eyes across her battered face.

Travis moved to her side, hugged her and untied the rope that bound her hands. He modestly pushed her bra strap back over her shoulder. Then, supporting his sister as she unsteadily came to her feet, the pair made its way back. Carl was gone, and the seemingly lifeless body of Jonas lay on the ground in the small hallway. Travis steered his sister gently to the back door. As they stepped into the sweet-smelling night air, they took long, deep invigorating breaths and held each other, both trembling. From what seemed miles away, the sound of a man's deep voice intruded their consciousness.

"Gotta go. Now!"

Randy's rough hands grabbed Travis and his sister at their shoulders. He placed his fingers over his lips and quietly moved them along the far side of the alley, through some bushes and into a clump of trees. As they reached the main road, they stopped, hidden by the foliage. Only yards away they could see scores of black men lined up in the street in front of the jailhouse, Klansmen with rifles at the ready guarding them. Standing at the top of the three steps, propped up by three white men, his hands behind him in handcuffs, was Carl. Randy strained to move, his muscles rippling. Knowing what was going through his mind, Travis shook his head.

"Nothing we can do, Randy," he whispered, shaking his head sadly. He knew the huge man was doomed.

As the trio quietly waited for the Klansmen to leave, Travis heard an unmistakable voice bellowing from inside the jail. It was Jonas.

"Lock the niggers back in the cells for the night. Post a guard around the jail in case some more niggers decide to be uppity! We could shoot them all tonight, but reckon we'll let the Germans gas them tomorrow. And get the dead niggers outta here. Get a move on! And get me a fuckin' doctor!"

Under the watchful eyes of the armed Klansmen, Travis, Randy and Hannah-Lee watched as the black men tromped up the stairs and inside the jailhouse. First to disappear back into the jailhouse was the manacled and bruised Carl.

*

Travis, Hannah-Lee and Randy hid in a copse of trees until all signs of life at the jailhouse had subsided. The shouts and screams from within had ceased. The thin clouds thickened and the moon no longer shone. Only a few of the trucks were left parked on the street, presumably those of the men assigned to act as guards inside the jail. The lights had been doused, and the glimmer of a dim light bulb could be seen through the smashed glass of one of the front windows. The bar next to the jail had shut its doors and the garish neon sign had been switched off. Travis looked at his watch and could barely make out the fact that it was just after midnight. Although it had seemed like an eternity, the fight at the courthouse had taken less than an hour.

Peering up and down the deserted street, Randy urged Travis and Hannah-Lee to come quickly with a wave of his hand. They joined him and ran down the right side of the road to the farm where Randy had left the old truck. Within minutes, they covered the short distance along the road and crossed the bridge to where the truck was parked. Randy ran ahead and cranked the vehicle to life. It took him several tries until the engine sputtered to life. In the stillness of the night, the engine's noise seemed deafening. Travis and his sister climbed aboard, and Randy carefully steered the ancient car in the direction of his hideout.

None of the three felt much like talking, each lost in his own thoughts. Hannah-Lee leaned limply onto Travis's shoulder and he held her closely. It was not until they climbed safely into the underground hiding place that the tension that had enveloped them slowly began to subside. Randy stirred the embers of the banked fire, bringing a few furtive flames to life. He suspended an old pewter coffee pot over the flames on a tripod and waited. Travis broke the silence.

"Hannie, are you sure you're alright?" he asked, his arms protectively around his sister's frail shoulders.

"I am alright," Hannah-Lee responded somewhat testily. "I just wish you'd stop asking me."

"I wish I'd killed Jonas!"

"No, you don't. You're not a killer."

"When I think of … "

Hannah-Lee stamped her feet and looked at her brother. "Just get it out of your mind! He didn't do anything. He didn't have the chance." She was lying as much to him as to herself.

Travis was relieved and puzzled at the same time.

"You mean it?" he said in amazement.

"Yes!" she almost screamed. "He only came into the room a few seconds before I heard you and the noise outside. I was tied up, sure. I was scared, scared out of my wits. And seeing Momma shot right before my eyes…" Her tears overcame her and she broke into long sobs that shook her entire body. The memories of what Jonas had done to her lay like a black fog upon her soul.

"There, missy. You was awful brave tonight. Y'all were. I'se sorry about yo' momma. We all lost friends and kin. Jes gotta trust in the Lord, specially at times like dis."

Randy's voice was calming and soothing. Travis could not believe the man's strength. He had lost most of his comrades that night, and knew that the rest would die in the morning. He could think of nothing else to say to the man except "Thank you."

"What y'all gonna do? Can't stay here forever," Randy asked as he poured cups of coffee.

"Well, we can't stay here, that's for sure. We were headed to kin in Oklahoma. But that's out now. Even if the Germans left our bicycles up on the road, we couldn't make it out of the county, not after tonight," Travis replied. He looked at Randy and added, "Besides, they're going to round up every black person they can find after what happened. I know Jonas. He never liked black folks, and now the Germans gave him the power so that he doesn't have to hide behind his white sheets! No, we can't stay here, and you're coming with us."

Randy shook his head. "No, sir. You'd be a lot safer without me. Two white folks traveling with a nigger? No, sir! You'd be caught before you got out of the county!"

The coffee had restored some of Hannah-Lee's self-confidence.

"No way. You're coming with us, after what you did for us! Look, why don't we figure out a way to get up to Santa Fe? No one will suspect we're heading in that direction," she suggested.

"Santa Fe? Why Santa Fe? What's there?" Travis asked incredulously.

"Garret!" the girl said simply.

Travis winced involuntarily as the wound in his left arm sent a new wave of pain throughout his entire body.

"Garret? When did you hear from him?"

"A few weeks ago, I think. What does it matter? Got a postcard from him, and it was stamped in Santa Fe."

Randy looked at the two quizzically.

"Who's he?" asked Randy.

After an awkward silence during which Travis and Hannah-Lee looked quietly at each other, Travis stammered, "Garret is my ... my brother."

There was another brief silence .

"It's a long story," Travis said. "What's he doing in Santa Fe?"

"Well, it was only a very short card. Guess he's with the Army," responded Hannah-Lee. "Now, how are we getting out to New Mexico?"

"Guess y'all don't got no car, huh?" Randy had felt the tension between brother and sister and remained silent. "Guess we'll jest have to borrow one. Man owns these fields, he got a nice car, and he ain't usin' it, I know."

"You mean steal it?" Hannah-Lee said somewhat naively.

Randy yawned and avoided her eyes.

"You got any money?" he asked.

"Some. Not a lot. Don't know how much Mom took with her. I've got maybe twenty bucks," Travis stuck a hand in his back pocket and retrieved a worn leather wallet. He unfolded it, checked its contents and, for the first time since the Germans and Jonas had found them on the road, he smiled a genuine smile.

"Yup, got the wallet, and got about twenty five dollars. Think that'll at least get us there."

Hannah-Lee nodded at Travis. "And Mom gave me ten, but I stuck it in my purse. The purse is bundled in the bedroll in the bicycle. Think we ought to go get it?"

Randy looked hesitantly at Travis.

"If they left the bicycles, won't hurt to see. Gotta meet you up on the road anyways when I get the car."

Randy snuffed out the fire, making sure this time that all the embers were extinguished. He doused it with the remaining coffee, and, in the darkness led the way up the narrow staircase to the tunnel. They had no lights of any kind, but Randy knew the narrow tunnel as well as if it was broad daylight. Hannah-Lee followed Randy and Travis brought up the rear. The climb up the stairs and crawling on his belly brought back his excruciating pain. He bit his lip hard enough to draw blood to stop him from yelling.

"O.K., what time is it?" Randy asked Travis when they reached the soft night air.

Travis tried to make out the faint luminescence on the dial.

"About one a clock," he whispered.

"See you at the road in fifteen minutes."

In seconds, the black man had become one with the trees

that surrounded them, slipping silently away further into the woods. Travis grabbed Hannah-Lee's hand and guided her to where he thought he had first entered the woods from the cotton fields.

Within minutes, they entered the field and gingerly made their way towards the spot where their mother had been killed. Neither showed any emotion while they climbed up and down the shallow embankment. They crouched on the road in the darkness. There were no lights to be seen anywhere. The world around them had gone to sleep. Even the crickets and night birds were silent. Driving high clouds drifting across the Texas landscape obscured the stars.

"Alright, stay here," Travis commanded. "I'll check a ways to see if the bicycles are still there."

He moved carefully to the left and immediately stumbled over the bikes.

"Shit!" he exclaimed as he fell to ground. "Guess I found them."

Hannah-Lee joined her brother and Travis carefully undid the straps that had bound the first bundle of bedding to the carrier. He handed it to the girl who accepted it wordlessly.

"This must be yours."

Travis crept a few feet further.

"Here, here's the second one. That must be Mom's. Can you take this, too?"

Hannah-Lee accepted her mother's bundle, cradling it next to her chest with one hand while she held her own with the other. Travis could hear the faintest sound of sniffling from Hannah-Lee as he moved a few feet more. Lying in the grass was his bicycle. Swiftly he undid his bundle from the rack.

"O.K., let's just lie low until Randy shows up," Travis suggested.

"He'll show up," Hannah-Lee replied bravely.

Less than five minutes later they saw a single pair of head-lights coming from the north. The two huddled close to the ground and close to each other, their hearts racing. It won't be Jonas or the Germans coming from the north, Travis reasoned. Jonas' farm and Dallas were south of them. It had to be Randy. Who else would be on a country road this time of night? Trust in the Lord, Randy had admonished. For once, Travis said a silent prayer while holding fast to his sister.

The approaching headlights moved closer and the sound of the engine became audible. It was not the whiny, high-pitched, stuttering sound of a typical farm truck. Let it be Randy, Travis thought fervently, please. The car, a black silhouette against the night sky, slowed, then came to a full stop only a few feet from where Randy and Hannah-Lee were lying. A door opened.

"Travis?" Randy's voice, though hushed, seemed to carry across all of Texas.

"Yeah," Travis replied. He rose, pulling his sister to her feet. The two sprinted across the tarmac, carrying their bundles. Randy held open the driver's side door and pulled back the front seat. Hannah-Lee scrambled inside and sank into the rear seat. Travis followed, sliding across to the passenger's side. Randy climbed behind the wheel, closed the door, and started a u-turn. The faint dashboard lights illuminated the inside of the car just enough to let Travis see the black man's firm, set expression.

"You O.K., Randy?" Travis asked.

"Yeah, man, no sweat!" Randy grinned. "No sweat!"

Dallas, Texas

In the opulent suite of rooms at the Adolphus Hotel that Field Marshal Erwin Rommel had appropriated, the general held a hastily called staff meeting. Standing with him on the expensive carpet was Field Marshal Dietrich Himmel and Lieutenant Manfred Buchner. Rommel motioned the two SS men to sit on the elegant antique sofa. An easel in the center of the room held a colored map of New Mexico, with markings around the Santa Fe area.

"Gentlemen." Rommel began in his measured, cultured German accent, "our intelligence has determined that there is some extraordinary level of air and rail traffic in the area of Santa Fe, New Mexico, here." He pointed at the map with a silver pen.

"At first we thought that the Americans are merely monitoring their military rail traffic. Since there is no appreciable military installation in this area, this option makes no sense. We then found that there was also an influx of many civilians arriving in Santa Fe from various parts of the country, both by car and by rail. This would indicate civilians of some importance. Why are they there, one might ask. Finally, the other night, many women – we suspect the wives of some of these civilians – were sent by train away from the area."

Rommel paused to let the words sink in, then continued smoothly.

"I want closer investigation of this matter. Lieutenant, I would like you to take a group of the local civilians you have recently acquired and drive to this area. It will be less conspicuous than if I dispatched a full military squad. I want you to go with them, since you speak English and since these civilians are happy to obey you."

"Yes, sir!" Buchner replied immediately.

"And I want you to go in civilian clothes. You will receive a special commendation for this. Of course you know, if you are caught, you will be considered a spy. But I have every confidence that you will carry out this mission successfully."

"Yes, my General! You can depend on me." Buchner seemed ready to stand up and salute. Himmel sat, slightly bemused at the junior officer's eagerness.

"Now," Rommel unrolled a larger map showing the paved roads of the southwestern states. "You will take the highway to Amarillo, here in Texas, where you will then intersect Route 66. This will take you directly into New Mexico here. This Route 66 will then take you within a few miles of Santa Fe.

"To back you up, I will also dispatch a unit of troops, going across country. Most of our regular troop movements are going to come from San Antonio and going to Ft. Bliss in the El Paso area. We expect some resistance in El Paso, so this unit I am sending with your mission is going to move independently from the north. They will also be acting as a scouting team and will communicate with us here. Now this is important – if you happen to meet this unit, you will not make any communications with them. You must at all costs seem to be Americans. Tell these 'cowboys' not to wear their insignia. And advise them of Der Führer's appreciation for their loyalty."

Himmel looked sharply at the general.

"You think it is wise to send untrained Americans to do this job? Can we trust them? And the lieutenant here, well, do you not think a more senior person would be more appropriate?"

Rommel shot his SS counterpart a look that instantly conveyed what he thought of the man.

"Himmel, if I did not think it was wise, I would not have suggested it, now would I? These Americans are part of what is known as the Ku Klux Klan. They are an ignorant rabble and they are young, yes, but they are committed to the Fatherland and its objectives. Lieutenant Buchner assures me that they are more than capable. What they lack in skill they make up for in violence. And they will be under Buchner's direction."

"I just thought ... "

"Enough, Himmel!" Rommel abruptly cut the man short. "Any questions?"

Buchner looked questioningly at Himmel, then addressing Rommel, said, "Sir, the other night the Texas SS proved their loyalty and their dedication. They took an entire section of Dallas, burned it, and arrested many Negroes and Jews. Last night, an attempt was made by some Negroes to release their compatriots. They failed miserably. We will be sending hundreds of Negroes to the chambers today. This young man who leads their 'Klansmen,' as they call themselves, has done an admirable job."

Rommel stood pensively for a second. Then he said, "Good! Contact their leader. You will leave immediately. It will take you the better part of a day at best to reach your objective. Stay in contact with us. I will arrange a special code to be assigned so that you will have direct access and I will be notified immediately. That is all, gentlemen."

Dismissed, Himmel and the lieutenant saluted and left the room. Rommel strode to a window, opened it, and stared at the city under his control. In the distance he could see the continuing plume of smoke rising from the city incinerators near the Centennial Stadium.

San Francisco, California

In front of the post office, three Japanese soldiers saw the two girls approaching and did their best to watch them without turning their heads. They'd been warned not to let their minds wander. This was war and as quick as their victory over America was going, they were never to become complacent. The Americans were still a potent enemy.

The guys were dressed revealingly for the night—slim jackets open in front, dresses that rode a little high near the knee. Not the most attractive girls, but for men like the guards, who were charged with standing up for ten hours at a time, female flesh was female flesh.

As they walked, they scanned the buildings around them, pointed down the side streets and then shook their heads. They appeared to be lost. A brief exchange stopped them in the street and their voices rose. Finally, one of them made a rude gesture to the other, and the Japanese soldiers couldn't help but look; if the girls fought in the street, there would be cause to arrest them. And if they arrested them, there would be cause to get close to them.

"This is not the street we need," said Diego, affecting his best female voice. "You got us lost."

"I didn't do nothin'," Greg replied, "you said we should come this way. Don't blame me, Helen."

From the corner of their eyes they saw the guards watching them like hungry dogs. That was good. Now all they needed was to draw them away from the direction of the alley. If only it was this easy to get guys' attention during normal non-wartime days, life would be grand. Just a little further and they'd be on the far side of the post office and the others could make their moves.

"I'm going back," Diego said, storming past the guards whose heads swiveled back and forth between the two arguing girls, as if they were watching a tennis match. "Don't follow me."

"I don't think so, hussy," Greg said, almost on the verge of laughing. Not that he necessarily thought this performance was amusing, but his nerves and his emotions were jumbled as hell. Laughing was better than peeing himself in fear. And considering how many guns were around him right now, it was a wonder he hadn't already.

Diego stopped, turned back. "Girl, if you come over here I will just scream."

"Then here I come." When Greg got close enough to Diego, he winked, their signal that they needed to step things up a little bit and really give Ben and the guys a chance to get in position. "You are such a bitch," he said, raising his voice again.

"Oh I can't believe you got us lost!" Diego faked crying, covered his mouth with his hand and whispered, "Too much?"

"You're not getting an Oscar, but keep going," Greg whispered back.

"The guards are coming over."

"Where's Ben?"

Diego looked past Greg's shoulder and nodded. "I see them. They're coming out now. Quick, slap me."

"What?"

"Just do it."

"But..."

"Oh for crying out loud." Diego hauled off and slapped Greg

in the face. The smack resounded off the post office façade.

"Ow, you bitch," Greg said, losing character for a moment. He quickly regained it and slapped Diego back, getting much the same reaction. The guards came running over to see the fight, making jokes in their native language and giggling.

Watching from the service door of the La Costa's basement, Terry could see Diego and Greg shoving each other. They looked like they were really fighting. When he saw the guards run up to watch the girls, he turned back to Gino, Phil and Ben. "O.K. Go now, go now." He waved Ben and Gino through the door, then followed with Phil in the rear. They kept their guns pointed straight ahead at the guards. Robert stayed behind, his gun aimed out of the door into the alley as back-up cover.

Ducking low, Ben made sure not to jostle the small backpack that carried the dynamite. He'd been told that dynamite was unstable, and if it wasn't kept in the proper conditions it could sweat. If it sweats, it could explode whether it was lit or not. He hoped his own perspiration, currently streaming down his back, was not as volatile.

They entered the alley and darted straight across it, plastering themselves against the post office wall. Phil and Terry took up a position at the corner, their guns peeking out around the edge. Ben looked back once and put a finger to his mouth, a way of telling everyone to be extra quiet. They all knew the Japanese ammunition was inside the loading dock, but there was no telling if any additional soldiers were inside. How could there not be? Ben thought. Too late to change the plan now.

Creeping lightly, he drew up to the platform where a concrete staircase lead up to the top of it. He took off his backpack, reached inside and took out the sticks of dynamite. In the near distance, he could hear Diego and Greg arguing. Any other day he'd be mildly amused by it; now he just hoped he lived to see them again.

"Here," he said, handing the bundle to Phil. "Hold these while I light the fuse."

"My heart's racing," Phil said.

"Mine too. Just focus." Ben took the Zippo from his pocket, snapped open the top. "Ready?"

"Ready."

He lit the fuse. It came to life with a spark, then began to hiss as the glow moved its way up toward the dynamite. "Quick, c'mon." He ran up the stairs, grabbed the handle for the rolling dock door and pulled up on it. It wouldn't budge. "Shit, it's locked."

"This one," Phil said, turning the knob on the access door at the top of the stairs. It opened, revealing the interior of the depot, which was illuminated by a wan yellow bulb that made the stored ammunition glow eerily. There were enough shells to blow half the block up to the stars. He slid the dynamite across the floor, watching as it came to rest near some very large shells. "Time to go," he said.

Ben nodded, made his way back toward Terry and Gino. "Easy peasy," he said.

"Not quite," Gino replied. "Diego's wig came off."

The night screamed to life with gunfire.

The guards stood motionless for a second as they tried to make sense of how the girl's hair had fallen off all at once. Then it registered that what they were watching were not girls, but men, men trying to trick them. They raised their weapons to shoot, aiming at Diego and Greg's heads, but before they could get a shot off, a bullet came from the alley and burst through one of the soldier's skulls. Even before the dead man hit the ground the other two soldiers were spinning and firing back at the alley. The front door of the post office flew open and more soldiers swarmed out like hornets from an attacked nest. They were shouting orders, waving guns, desperately trying to figure out what was going on.

Diego kicked out and caught the nearest guard in the groin, yanking the gun from the man's hand. Greg was already charging another guard, a very young soldier who was frozen in fear. By the time he saw Greg coming it was too late. They crashed to the ground and fought to get control of the gun. Greg felt the man bite his shoulder and screamed in pain. A second later, Diego ran over, put his pistol to the soldier's head and blew the back of his skull out, spattering Greg's face with pulpish gore.

Wiping his face Greg said, "Thanks, fuck 'im."

"C'mon, honey, move your ass! No time to smooch," Diego shouted. Greg snatched the soldier's gun and fired at the soldiers who were firing on the alley. One of them went down before the other soldiers got a handle on the situation and positioned themselves to shoot in both directions. Diego and Greg ran across the street and raced down an alley, firing back as they went. A group of soldiers ran after them, but dropped back as bullets zinged by their heads.

"Down here," Greg yelled, referring to another small alley that ran along the back of a building. He waited for Diego to rush by and then fired a burst of bullets back the way they'd come, just in case anyone was following. At the end of this alley was a side street that led up toward the La Costa; he could hear Ben shouting that everyone had to get out now. "They're leaving," he said, ripping his heels off. "We gotta sprint."

"Honey, my legs are moving right now. I can't stop 'em."

Together, they raced down the street, saw the La Costa

looming familiarly ahead of them. The street was being strafed with stray bullets, many of which hit the buildings on both sides, sending bits of brick and wood into the air. Ducking low, they peered out and saw Phil up at the next corner, crouched in the alleyway beside the post office, firing at a cadre of Japanese soldiers. "Our guys are trapped."

"But we're not, babe. C'mon, say it with me."

They both shouted, "God save the queens," and ran out shooting.

From the alley, Ben saw two more Japanese soldiers go down, the angle of the attack from somewhere across the street. He looked over and saw Diego and Greg firing back with machine guns, their faces pulled taut in twisted delight. "Crazy fags," he said.

Phil tapped him on the shoulder. "Seriously, guys. Time to run."

And so they did, everyone racing out into the street, taking cover where they could. In the darkness, and with mailboxes and trashcans and cars in the way, most bullets could not find flesh. But some came close and that meant there was no time to lollygag. Ben was sure they'd make it to the next street and be able to get away safely when more Japanese soldiers came out of the building, along with two officers. He signaled to Robert to come out. Robert started across the alley crouched and running when a bullet hit him, sending him to the ground, the momentum of his run causing him to slide in a heap. He was dead.

"Robbie! Robbie! Are you all right? Robbie!" shouted Terry who stood up and ran to where Robert was sprawled. As he reached him, a burst of submachine gun fire splattered mortar and granite from the building façade. Terry took a direct hit to his chest and fell over onto Robert. With his last breath he

273

hugged him.

Bullets flew in all directions in random bursts. A hand grenade landed ten yards away and blew two trash cans into the air scattering debris.

Then there was a low boom. It was followed by a brilliant flash of light. Japanese soldiers went flying through the air on fire, the gunfire ceasing. Ben, Gino and Phil stood up from their hiding spots and watched the giant fireball rise toward the moon. Diego and Greg were still some distance away hiding in the alley between them and the Japanese. The post office had collapsed and a large orange ball of flaming smoke rose in the air, momentarily casting long shadows on everything. Lights flickered in adjacent buildings and then all went dark.

Four Japanese soldiers jumped out of the shadows and surrounded Diego and Greg and beat them over the heads with their rifle butts. They collapsed and were dragged off.

"Shit, now what?" said Ben.

"We gotta get them," Gino responded. "We can't leave them."

"You're crazy," said Ben." They're goners. Nothing we can do. Let's get outta here or we're all fucked."

They hesitated a moment and then they heard Greg screaming in agony. He and Diego had been revived and were being held in the middle of the street on a rise just up from where the others were hiding. A small searchlight illuminated the two of them. They had been stripped naked and a soldier holding a bayonet was digging it into Greg's genitals. One of the officers said, "Now you are girl, pig." Turning down the alley, the officer shouted, "American pigs! You shall all die tonight. Come. Come save your friends."

Ben, Gino and Phil were dumbstruck. Gino turned away and

could not look. In the distance, sirens sounded. A large contingent of Japanese troops was on its way. The clatter and crunch of tank treads on pavement echoed through the night.

"I don't give a shit, I'm gonna save them," said Phil standing up. A machine gun burst opened up from fifty feet away and hit him in the gut, opening it wide. He reached down as if to hold his intestines from emerging through the gaping wound. His face went blank. He was dead before he hit the ground. Ben tried to reach out to him, but Gino pulled him back. They crawled away and hid under a parked truck. Shrieks echoed in the alley. It was Diego screaming now in a deep guttural moan that chilled them even in their adrenalin-filled fear.

They bellied out from under the truck, stood and ran. They rounded a corner into a dark alley and froze, looking and listening for any sound the enemy might make. They could hear scurrying footsteps in the streets. "We can make it out of here. This way," said Gino pointing down the alley. He didn't see the tank that had stopped in the murky night a hundred fifty feet down the alley. The last thing either of them remembered was the peculiar blue flame emerging from the tank's canon.

With shots and explosions reverberating in the salty night air over the city, the "Queen Mary, Too" slipped its moorings and with over a hundred men, women and children on board made its way out of the harbor to safety in the south.

Fair Park (Dallas), Texas

At precisely nine o'clock, a caravan of more than twenty

trucks arrived at the main gate of the Bicentennial complex and came to a halt by the tall tower that marked the entrance of the park that annually hosted the Texas State Fair and the Cotton Bowl. German troops flanked the broad roadway, and had established barriers that allowed only official vehicles to pass.

Several troops inspected the vehicle's registration and travel orders and laconically waved the driver forward. The vehicle ground through the gears, picked up speed and headed toward the façade of the Cotton Bowl.

Carl, his face bruised and bleeding, sat huddled towards the back of the third truck, humming quietly. Where was Randy, he thought. Wonder if he got killed last night? Wonder if somehow he and the white folks got away? With him were some of the men who had been arrested the night before. Unlike his compatriots, Carl was manacled. His hands were shackled behind him and leg irons confined his feet to no more than about a foot's movement in any direction. A single German soldier sat leaning against the tailgate of the truck, his rifle at the ready, his watchful eyes scanning the black people in the truck.

As the truck came to a jolting stop once again, only the masses of bodies crammed against him stopped Carl from being pitched forward to the floor. Dozens of fearful eyes watched two German corporals unfasten the tailgate. The German soldier who had been their guard jumped to the ground, waving at the black men inside. Slowly, one by one, they clambered down to the ground. One of the guards roughly shoved the lead black man, guided him by the shoulders and then stopped him. The other followed suit and lined the prisoners into a file of two abreast.

Finally, only Carl was left in the truck. The two soldiers looked at the huge man, laughed, jumped onto the truck and dragged Carl to the tailgate where they unceremoniously rolled him to the edge. Carl tried to maneuver himself into position so that he could swing his legs over the edge. He was too late. The soldiers shoved him despite his weight. Carl fell, grunting from his diaphragm but emitting only a loud, incomprehensible gurgle as he hit the rough asphalt. The two soldiers had jumped down from the truck, still laughing and exchanging crude jokes about Carl's size. They pulled the large black man to his feet and prodded him with their rifle butts to the end of the two columns of nearly thirty men.

"Los, Forwärts, schnell!" they yelled and gestured with their hands, signaling the men to move along. Wordlessly the two men at the front understood and complied. The columns started to move. Bringing up the rear, Carl shuffled along by himself, the leg irons making it difficult for him to keep up with the rest of the group. He slowly trudged up the steps to the entrance of the Cotton Bowl, one step at a time. He saw hundreds of black faces standing in the morning sun. Some lines were strictly men; others were solely women and children. One woman was suckling an infant as she stood in line, her eyes fearfully looking about her, her arms cradled lovingly about the baby. Few had bags or other belongings with them. They clutched their meager possessions protectively.

Above the assemblage waved dozens of Nazi flags in the Texas breeze. Their red, white and black colors and the black swastika were alien to most of the people, many of whom had saved up an entire year to watch a Texas football game only once or twice in the past. Everywhere, uniformed SS men watched carefully as regular soldiers carried out the task of herding the men, women and children into the interior of the stadium. One line of about two hundred fifty white men, women and children stood out incongruously in the sea of black faces.

"Wonder what they done?" asked one of the men in the line.

"Don't know. But they ain't bein' treated no better'n us. Must be Jews," guessed another.

"Didn't know we had no Jews," said the first. "Look like reg'lar white folks to me."

After he managed to climb the stairs, Carl followed his fellow prisoners to the left, where makeshift signs directed them to the visitor's locker room. An old "Go Mustangs" sign posted on the wall had been partially removed and a poster with a portrait of Hitler looking prophetically into the future was glued over it. They followed the signs marked "Visitors" and soon reached the locker room. They were herded in groups of twenty. When at last he shuffled into the room, Carl could just see a group of naked black men disappearing into the shower room, casually supervised by only four Nazi guards.

A Nazi officer spoke to Carl's group. Amazingly, Carl could understand the man. He was speaking in English.

"You will immediately disrobe. You will take glasses and other things you may have, such as rings and chains or other jewelry, and set them next to your clothes. You will then follow a guard into the showers, where you will be cleaned. You will be issued uniforms once you are clean. Understood?"

Carl's hands and feet were still manacled and he looked about helplessly while the other men disrobed. His humming increased in both pitch and volume. Eventually, he caught the eye of one of the guards who shouted in German to the man who had spoken in English to the group. The Nazi spotted Carl and ambled over to him. He eyed the black giant with admiration, running his small baton up and down Carl's biceps.

"A shame, really. Such an excellent body! Such a cock you

must have, you black swine. We could make good use of you."

He commanded a few words to the guards. Immediately they came running across the locker room, brandishing their army knives. At the sight, Carl's humming increased threefold. In his mind, he prayed. "Lord Jesus, Lord Jesus, Lord Jesus! I'm sorry for whatever I ever did to displease you! Forgive me, Lord Jesus!"

The men did not kill him. Expertly, they held the giant, slit his shirts and pants and tore them off Carl's body. Within seconds, Carl stood stripped naked before them, his hands and feet still in handcuffs and leg irons. Carl tried in vain to cover his manhood as the guards shoved him roughly with the others into the shower room.

Believing that the showers would, indeed, be spraying them with welcome water after the sweat and dirt of last night's fight and two nights in jail, most of the men took positions under the showerheads jutting from the walls in the tiled room.

"First time I ever been in an 'All Whites Only' place," said one of the men jokingly.

"Don't seem no different than a "Negroes Only" one, 'ceptin' it's cleaner," answered another. Carl waited in silence for the welcome trickle of water he expected.

Seconds later, they heard a clicking sound as a lock was being turned. Seconds later yet, the showerheads gave a low hiss. Instead of water sprays offering the men welcome relief, white gas clouds formed at each head, deadly fumes instantly enveloping the heads of the men standing beneath them.

"What the ..." one tried to yell only to be choked as he tried to finish the phrase.

"Sweet Jesus!" cried another.

The pandemonium rose as a few men sank to their feet, while others tried to run toward the doors, only to collapse just feet from where they had been standing. Within a few seconds more, all were coughing and wheezing, their lungs instantly filled with the poisonous gas. A few of the men writhed on the floor made slippery by urine and feces which were involuntarily expelled in fear. Many, the lucky ones, quickly passed into the oblivion of unconsciousness and death. Others gasped or tried to hold their breath in a futile attempt at warding off the gas.

Carl was one of the last to remain standing. He tried in vain to hold his breath against the sweet smell that permeated the room. Suddenly, he was back home, running into his house. He was a boy again, only seven years old. It was lunchtime and Mama had baked a pan full of cornbread, the sweet smell filling the house and drifting out into the yard. Daisies by the door danced in the wind. "Come in, baby," his mother said. "Oh, Mama, I love you so. You's the best mama in the world." "And you the best son." She held him tightly in her arms and swayed to and fro. "Now, go to sleep, my baby, go to sleep. Mama's here and I will always love you and keep you safe." He felt himself becoming sleepy and leaned into his mother's bosom. Then his huge bulk fell to the tile floor in the Mustangs' shower room as his knees gave way. He blacked out and soon his humming ceased forever.

The journey of Carl's body to the incinerator was short. Ten or so young tough black prisoners carried the bodies out to the yard and loaded them into waiting garbage trucks. On the sides of the trucks it said, "Dallas Dept. of Sanitation." When the truck was full, it ambled slowly away over the deep ruts in the dirt road to the incinerators.

Carl and the others were dumped at the incinerator conveyor belt. Three prisoners lifted Carl's body from the truck. One of them was Carl's cousin, Ned.

"Oh my dear sweet Jesus," he shouted, hugging his cousin and crying. "I'se sorry, cuz, I's sorry...."

One of the two German guards came over and said, "What is the matter, swine. Load this shit into the incinerator now!" and he struck Ned in the side of the head with his rifle butt. Ned leaped up and tackled the guard who, off balance, fell to the ground with Ned on top of him. Ned sat on his chest and squeezed the guard's throat with a power he did not know he possessed. The guard kicked and squirmed and pushed Ned back with a solid punch to the face. They both jumped to their feet and stood looking at each other as the guard yelled out a cry for help. He tackled Ned and both of them in a death grip fell onto the conveyor belt which ceaselessly moved toward the incinerator door. The other black prisoners fled for safety behind the garbage truck.

Two German guards appeared, rifles in hand. They quickly saw what was happening and ran over to the belt. One stabbed Ned through to the spine with his bayonet forcing him off the belt. The other grabbed the guard by the boots and yanked on him; he fell to the floor, but it was too late. His head had been held inside the oven by Ned and his face was a blackened char. He screamed in agony and pulled his helmet off, the skin and hair of his scalp sticking to the helmet and pulling off like a wig. He writhed uncontrollably for a few seconds and died.

Other guards arrived and carried their fallen comrade off while the others rounded up the hiding prisoners and beat them with hand clubs.

In a matter of minutes, new prisoners were continuing the work of the old. They hurriedly tossed Carl into the cast iron maw of the burner with as many other bodies as could fit. Children were tossed in where there was space. The door was closed on its screeching hinges and the flames did their work with a scowling roar.

The moisture from his body made the long trip up the huge chimney and flew freely up into the Texas sky. Carl's ashes, and those of thousands more, were scattered on the fallow cotton field that lay north of the city. When he was a boy, he and his father and brothers would pass by on the way to church. His father often said, "God willin', some day I'm gonna own somma that there land and when I'm gone, you boys gonna own it."

New York City

The next morning, Lillian awoke with a compulsion she could not ignore. She knew she had to try and get inside Lucien's apartment, not only to be around his things and, there-fore, his spirit, but also to update him on everything. She was ignoring the fact that he did not try to contact her. She ration-alized for him. She would leave a note about where she and Susan had been. The museum had been closed. When she went there right after getting back, there was no one to ask. It was all a dead end and she needed to take matters into her own hands.

She dressed hurriedly, determined to fulfill what she con-sidered her obligation to the man she loved. She was miserable without having heard from him in so long and not even know-ing where he was.

Lucien's apartment was closer to the museum than hers was by about twelve blocks. She managed to catch a bus without having to wait longer than half an hour. New York hadn't changed much since she'd been gone, other than there were more boarded up storefronts and fewer pedestrians. The people that were bustling from one place to another seemed to be in a bigger hurry than usual and no one, no one she saw, looked as if he or she was content or self-assured. Fear owned New York City. People seemed to be waiting for something evil to happen.

Lillian walked up the steps of Lucien's brownstone and rang the buzzer to his apartment, but there was no answer. She shrugged and buzzed the superintendant's apartment.

"Yeah? Who is it?"

"Hi, uh, Miss West. . .I hate to bother you, but. . ."

"So, then why are you?"

"This is important. My. . .my brother, Lucien West, has been gone for a very long time. He asked me to get something for him so I. . .I need to get in his apartment so I can…"

"You must be crazy. Go away."

"Please! He's in the service and this is important. Really important."

There was silence. The buzzer opened the door.

Lillian stepped over the threshold and closed the door, smiling at the super waiting for her in the hall.

"I shouldn't be doin' this, ya know,"

"Thank you, so much, for letting me in."

"Look, he's a good guy. Pays his rent on time. Actually paid it all in advance. Not like some people I know," he said eyeing an elderly woman who walked by.

Lillian followed him up the stairs to the second floor then down the dark hall, to the apartment.

"This is it." He unlocked the door to Number 2 B and stood aside.

"O.K., lady. I guess it'll be O.K., seein' as you're his sister.

Lock it up on the way out."

"Thank you, oh, thank you, Mr...?"

"Not important. Just make sure you lock it. Got me?"

"Oh, yes. Of course."

He disappeared down the hall and Lillian stood inside Lucien's apartment, unable to move at first.

It was as if he were there and would appear at any moment. There was a fine layer of almost invisible dust on everything. The apartment was as organized and neat as Lucien himself had always been. She closed her eyes and detected the faint aroma of the after shave he wore that always made her want to make love to him. Not long after they met and he had told her the brand, she bought herself a small bottle of it and sprayed it on her pillow. Dean never noticed. He never noticed any of the little things she did, good or bad. Thinking of Dean and her marriage in Lucien's apartment made her feel dirty, somehow. Guilt was a terrible thing. Oddly, she thought, there was no sign anywhere of Lucien's wife, no feminine touches, nothing. Perhaps, she had wrongly assumed that as she still lived with Dean, he still lived with....she didn't even know her name.

She walked around the living room, running her fingers along the back of the club chair, with an unfinished crossword puzzle and a pencil waiting on the small adjacent table. The footstool was indented where the heels of his shoes liked to rest and the decorative tile coaster, a souvenir from a resort in Bavaria, awaited his cup of coffee or one of the ornate beer steins he collected. She touched each one of the colorful mugs, lined up precisely in order on one of the shelves of the walnut bookcase. Another small bookcase with glass doors held his collection of novels, poetry and history books many of them in German. His fluency in the German language was, no doubt, one of the many reasons Lucien had been selected for government work.

The wool area rug underfoot was woven of muted burgundy and forest green, and the fringe around its oval shape was a soft camel color. She stared at the rug for a few moments before she realized it was an intricate castle scene, with a nobleman on a handsome steed leaving for the hunt with his squire on a smaller horse alongside. There were some indecipherable words woven into the pattern, and she could make out only the words "von Wilhelm" at the end of a line of letters.

She kicked off her shoes and wiggled her toes in the plush cut pile of the carpet. She hugged herself, smugly content being in Lucien's private place.

She walked into his bedroom and was impressed again with the neatness of the man. Nothing was out of place. His bed was tightly made. His closet was completely in order. She stood in front of the perfectly aligned shirts and was enraptured with the thought of Lucien's arms around her and his hands on her body and her deep longing to see him again. She lifted a pale blue chambray long-sleeved shirt from the hanger and closed her eyes as she buried her face in it, inhaling his scent. She swayed backward with emotion for a moment, then caught herself, opening her eyes wide and stared at the shelf above the hanging clothes. Carefully replacing the blue shirt, she reached up and pulled down the old alligator suitcase with large buckles on the stiff straps holding it closed. Motes of dust danced in the sun's afternoon rays streaming in through the bedroom windows.

She carried the suitcase to the bed, sat next to it as if it were sacred and opened it. Inside was a collection of old photographs of unfamiliar people, although Lillian knew the young man in many of the pictures was Lucien. There were two older people, a couple, which she assumed were his parents, and a younger blonde girl, who looked so much like him she had to be a sister. A castle in the background of several of the group portraits was of the same configuration as the one depicted on the living room carpet. It took her several minutes to realize these were picture of Lucien's years studying in Berlin in the 1920s. He had told her often of his family there and how it had split into factions, one admiring the Nazis for bringing pride back to the German people after the humiliating surrender terms that ended World War I. The other, his parents and two uncles saw Hitler for what he was, a monster in the guise of a politician. There had been heated arguments between all of the various members of the family, brother against brother, son against father. Many of his uncles and aunts fled in the early thirties to South America. His parents took the children and the family fortune to New York. Lucien and his family were at first embarrassed, then appalled as news of German atrocities made their way to America. He was one of the first men to join the service. His knowledge of Germany, the language and the geography landed him in the OSS. His job at the museum, important as it was to protect the art treasures from the coming invasion, was simply a holding pattern until his real mission was accomplished. She was sure of that. He would be chosen for something important, heroic, even. What that would be, was not for Lillian to guess. She could only imagine the inner turmoil Lucien had to face fighting the country of his birth. But he knew, as many German-Americans did, that Hitler did not represent all Germans. Lucien knew from the bottom of his soul that Hitler had to be stopped at all costs. Lillian felt honored to know Lucien.

She replaced everything in the suitcase. She tidied the bed and went into the living room to get a piece of paper to write a note. She found paper and a pen in the middle drawer. She sat in his chair and noticed that there was a radio made of mahogany and arched at the top like a gothic window. She turned it on and sat for a moment, hoping to hear some fitting music. Instead, an announcer said something indistinct about President Roosevelt. She placed the pen down and listened. The president's patrician voice was unmistakable.

"My fellow Americans, one and all, whether in uniform or bearing arms as a civilian, those who remain at home and wait and those who have come to know only fear. God has seen fit to test our great nation and its resolve. We are engaged in a conflict the likes of which our country, one hundred and fifty years old, has never seen. We are besieged by foreign powers who know no limits, who respect no living thing and who harbor within their dark hearts hatred, cruelty and the ravenous desire for the destruction of not only our country, but the world as we know it. By fate or design, God, for reasons we cannot know, has placed upon me the burden to steer this nation through its most trying hour. I did not expect this task and did not want it. I merely want to do God's will, to serve the country I love, and love it I do, in all its many forms and shapes. Never before have we faced an enemy on our home territory, never has an enemy foot stepped on this sacred land and never has a foreign enemy unleashed the engines of war upon us in our very homes. This nation was and is the last and best hope of mankind; it was forged in the furnace of the old world and tempered with the far-seeing vision of men like Washington, Adams, Jefferson, and Lincoln. We owe it to their memory to keep this nation alive. We owe it to ourselves to keep this nation free and we owe it to posterity that this nation, indivisible, shall not perish from the Earth. As God Almighty is my witness, we will fight the enemy in the fields, we shall fight him in the hills, we shall fight him in the streets of our gleaming cities. Never on these shores shall an invader find surrender. Never on these shores shall an enemy make us bow our heads. Never on these shores shall we be deprived of our freedom. Never on these shores shall liberty die. Never on these shores shall the enemy find one of us standing who will not give his life for our just cause. May God help you aim straight. May He fill your heart with courage and hope. May He fill your soul with righteousness and ease your pain and doubt. May He never desert you or your family or friends when your need is greatest. And may He bless this country of ours, this United States of America, with honor and with victory."

The gravity of it all struck Lillian in the face like a tidal wave. The war was bigger than anything she could have imagined. None of her troubles or personal pain mattered anymore. She would dedicate herself to the cause. No sacrifice would be too large.

Tears blurred her vision as she began to cope with the possibility that was staring her in the face. Her life would never be the same. She might never see Lucien again and she so wanted to be by his side in their fight with the enemy. She wrote a short note, telling him where she could be found, telling him of her love and how she missed him. She propped it on his desk where he was most likely to find it. She looked around the apartment one more time and slipped out the door making sure it locked behind her.

When she got out to the street, night had fallen on the city. The streets were deserted. That was fine, she thought. The walk would do her good.

The End

COMING SOON

Never on These Shores, Volume II: Battle in the Heartland